The Cambridge Plot

By Suzette A. Hill

A Little Murder
The Venetian Venture
A Southwold Mystery
Shot in Southwold
The Cambridge Plot

—◆—

The Primrose Pursuit

The Cambridge Plot

SUZETTE A. HILL

Allison & Busby Limited
12 Fitzroy Mews
London W1T 6DW
allisonandbusby.com

First published in Great Britain by Allison & Busby in 2018.

A CIP catalogue record for this book is available from
the British Library.

First Edition

ISBN 978-0-7490-2288-4

Typeset in 11/15.5 pt Sabon by
Allison & Busby Ltd.

The paper used for this Allison & Busby publication
has been produced from trees that have been legally sourced
from well-managed and credibly certified forests.

Printed and bound by
CPI Group (UK) Ltd, Croydon, CR0 4YY

To Julian and Mary again
In gratitude for happy times

CHAPTER ONE

Rays of the early evening sun gave the usually sombre study a mellow hue, and to those seated around its gleaming mahogany table a spurious air of kindly warmth. The Plot and Monument Committee was gathered to discuss the final details of the college's bid to obtain from the municipal grasp a patch of land in which to honour one of its eminent and erstwhile members.

'So what are we going to call it,' enquired the bursar, 'the Bugger's Burial Ground?'

Dr Maycock, Senior Fellow, tittered. 'An inspired suggestion if I may say so – but a trifle too explicit, surely. What about Percy's Patch? A sort of ironic nod to Parker's Piece, and—'

'Huh,' interrupted John Smithers, 'from what I've heard, the old boy didn't appreciate irony. Besides, I doubt if the daughter would sanction "Percy" – far too diminutive for the noble parent. She takes his title very seriously and don't we know it!' Adopting a braying falsetto, he cried: '"*May* distinguished father, you know, *Sir Pahcival* Biggs-Brookby."'

The bursar grinned. 'Got her in one, Smithers. I didn't know you were such a mimic.'

Sir Richard Dick the college's newly elected Master, sighed. 'Yes, all very risible, I am sure, but this is hardly the spirit in which to approach our project. Sir Percival may not have been to everyone's taste, but his contribution to the university, and to this college in particular, is undeniable. I need hardly remind you that the honour we bestow is in rightful recognition of his services. As to our present purpose, the choice of name for the site is immaterial; we are here to discuss the finances of the acquisition and how much the benefactors can be persuaded to donate. But when we *do* come to discuss the question of nomenclature, I trust you may give the matter a rather more sober appraisal.' He paused, looking round at the table, before adding grimly, 'And that goes for the issue of the daughter too. Do not underestimate.'

He was about to continue, but the bursar interrupted. 'What issue? What has Gloria B-B to do with things? Admittedly, she does loom rather *large*' – he smirked – 'but I can't see why she should cast a shadow in this particular matter. Presumably she is pleased that distinguished Daddy is being thus honoured. So what's the issue? After all, it is hardly her—'

'But that is just it,' the Master replied wearily, 'it is precisely because she is so pleased that I am not getting a moment's peace. She is determined to involve herself personally with every aspect of the project, from the commissioning of the sculptor to the planting of the rhododendrons.'

'Rhododendrons?' Professor Turner exclaimed. 'Who's talking of rhododendrons? Odious plants, in my opinion, vulgar and overrated. Besides, they'll swamp the whole plot. We can't possibly have those.'

The Master closed his eyes. 'We may have to,' he said quietly. 'Apparently they were Sir Percival's favourite shrub and much beloved by the daughter too. I have already been bombarded by plant catalogues from Suttons and gather I am required to peruse them with her.'

'But you know nothing about horticulture,' Turner observed.

'I soon shall,' was the gloomy response.

'Well, whatever the damn plants, at least she can't dictate the choice of sculptor,' the bursar snorted.

'No, but she would like to,' the Master replied. 'She has a personal dislike of our man – something to do with his voice and gait apparently – and is convinced there are others just as suitable.'

'Absolute nonsense! We have already approached Winston Reid and he is more than willing: a sound fellow, reasonable rates and not too imaginative. Just the man for the job. He'll produce something solid and uncontroversial.' The bursar turned to his neighbour, a small man with pinched face and darting eyes. 'Wouldn't you agree, Aldous?'

There was a pause while Aldous Phipps, Emeritus Professor of Greek, reflected. He gave a dry cough. 'Oh yes, he would do that all right, but whether he will get the chance is another matter.'

'Oh, come now, it's in the bag,' the other protested. 'His terms are excellent and it's simply a matter of stamping the contract. A mere formality.'

Phipps sniffed. 'It may be in your bag, Bursar, but I rather suspect it may not be in Gloria Biggs-Brookby's.' He scrutinised the ceiling and then lowered his eyes to appraise his fingernails.

The Master frowned. 'It would be helpful if you could enlarge on that statement, Aldous. I am not sure if we entirely grasp the point.' He sighed, and added, 'Or at least I don't.'

With a gleam of relish the elderly Fellow leant forward and scanned their faces, then assured of the table's attention, said: 'I happen to have some information . . .'

When doesn't he? John Smithers wondered, and checked his watch. It was nearing the violet hour and she would protest if he were late again. 'What information?' he asked brusquely.

'To do with Monty Finglestone, the young sculptor that London is currently lionising. He has great appeal, or so I hear, and great talent. Quite à la mode, one gathers.'

'Doubtless there are many such *modish* artisans in London, but I can't see how he affects our project here in Cambridge,' the Master said dismissively.

'Ah, but that's just it,' Aldous Phipps retorted, 'at the moment he is not in London but – if I am not very much mistaken – here in Cambridge. I saw them together in a corner of The Eagle when I was there sipping my usual pear and brandy bitters – such a refreshing melange, I always find. You should try it.' (The Master winced.) 'Yes,' Phipps continued, 'Finglestone and Gloria Biggs-Brookby. She was playing her usual grande dame role and he was being all charm and oily attention. Naturally, I couldn't hear what was being said: it's this wretched contraption, never works when you want it to.' He tapped the device in his ear. 'But I can assure you they were talking very earnestly – very earnestly; and I *did* manage to catch one word. Oh yes, it resonated clear as a bell.' He paused. 'It was . . . *rhododendrons*.' Phipps shot a triumphant look at Professor Turner, beamed happily and leant back in his chair.

There was a bemused silence. And then the bursar groaned. 'Oh Lord, you don't think she's trying to nobble him re the statue, do you? The cost will be extortionate!'

Aldous Phipps beamed again, pleased with his little grenade. 'Exactly,' he murmured.

'It will *not* be extortionate because it is not going to happen,' the Master declared. 'I can assure you the college's choice of artist does not depend on the diktats of Sir Percival's daughter. We have selected our man and that's an end of it. And if you don't mind my saying, Aldous, you are spreading unnecessary alarm and despondency . . . that capricious deaf aid may have been playing you false. And in any case, how do you know it was this Finkelstein fellow?'

'Finglestone, actually. His photograph was in *The Times* only the other day. The young man's features bear a pleasing resemblance to Michelangelo's David; most engaging, really, virile yet seemly. Thus I cut it out to use as a bookmark for that nice volume of Euripides your wife so kindly presented me with.' Phipps smiled benignly.

'Sir Richard is right,' interjected Smithers. 'Are you sure the word was "rhododendrons"? Perhaps it was some other plant – like pansy, for instance.'

The benign smile vanished, and Phipps fixed him with

one of his blanker stares. He disliked John Smithers. 'I may be approaching decrepitude, Smithers, but I am still able to distinguish a rhododendron – both the plant and the word – from a pansy. You, of course, may not.' He sniffed and resumed inspection of his fingernails.

The Master cleared his throat, 'Yes, yes, gentlemen. That is quite enough about plants, or indeed other speculations. Let us return to the subject in hand: whether, as a means of hastening their turgid deliberations, we should revise our already substantial offer to the City Council; and if so, can we rely on the donors' additional generosity? Some mightn't be overly willing. But one or two, like Dame Margery and Cedric Dillworthy, are most keen and I suspect can be relied upon to comply – especially if it were hinted their names should occupy pole position on the plaque.' He smirked.

'Good idea. Nothing like a little subtle bribery to ease the purse strings,' observed Dr Maycock.

'Huh! Hardly subtle' – the bursar laughed – 'but if the benefactors will fund a higher bid to induce the City fathers to push the purchase, I'm all for it. Why the delay, anyway? We've been kept waiting far too long as it is.'

'It's Alderman Cuff – hates the whole idea,' Maycock explained. 'He is the one man holding out and feels the area should be retained as an exclusive spot for children – a sort of toddlers' Tiergarten, I gather. Anyway, he is dead against it and hence the delay.'

'Well, we can't allow the fanciful pieties of Alderman Cuff to obstruct us,' the Master snapped. 'He is pure redbrick, you know. Besides, there's obviously a hidden agenda: he has at least five offspring of his own and is doubtless looking for a handy dumping ground. No, it won't do. We must increase our offer and get them to complete the deal post-haste.'

The others nodded and began to talk animatedly about the figure for the new bid and whether the sponsors could be persuaded to cooperate . . . All except for John Smithers, who, having checked his watch again, saw that it was well past the appointed trysting hour and that the husband would soon be returned. Piqued by Aldous Phipps' earlier put-down he lapsed into gloomy silence brooding on his present position.

As the youngest Fellow in the college he did not always feel at one with his greying peers, impatient of what he saw as their complacent suavity, ostensible camaraderie and their collective penchant for port (Death by Vodka being his own preference). Neither did he share their settled domesticity. With the exception of one or two confirmed bachelors, such as Aldous Phipps, most were married and with children. While Smithers could not envisage himself becoming an ageing bachelor of the Phipps variety, neither was he currently seeking marital bliss . . . nor blight for that matter, agreeing with Cyril Connolly[1] that the pram in the hallway too often led to punctured dreams and muddled aspiration.

Smithers' aspirations were far from muddled. Clever and self-absorbed, he was also exceedingly ambitious and fully intended to scale the heights of scholarly distinction. But he also knew that such scaling was helped, or at least accelerated, by public involvement and integration with one's colleagues. Beavering obsessively over manuscripts in dark corners was all very well, but something else was needed: the stamp of social approval.

---

[1] See Cyril Connolly, *Enemies of Promise* (1938).

In this belief he had been supported by the Senior Fellow, noted not just for his academic triumphs but for his sure grasp of matters practical and worldly. After dinner one evening and in a mood of kindly altruism, Maycock had offered the younger man advice. 'It would help your career,' he had urged, 'to present an image of sobriety: dedication to the interests not just of your own research, but to those of the college. It would persuade the Master and those of influence that you are *sound*.' He must have seen Smithers' look of nervous recoil, for he went on, 'You see soundness isn't always such a bad thing; it can be, of course, and some never get beyond it, but more often than not it is *handy* – especially when you are trying to establish yourself quickly. You must be seen to be of use, to be contributing value beyond the solely academic.'

'Oh yes?' Smithers had asked warily. 'And so how can I be useful?'

'Oh, easily enough,' Maycock had replied airily, 'committee work. Committees count, Smithers. Take my advice: join one.'

And so, sulkily, cynically, Smithers had consented; and with a bit of squirming and a word from the Senior Tutor, he had found himself a member of the Plot and Monument Committee and apparently supportive of its commemorative aim. In fact, he had little interest in Sir Percival Biggs-Brookby (dead long before he had come up to Cambridge), and even less for the man chosen to sculpt his monument. Sir Richard had called Winston Reid's work 'solid' . . . yes, solidly dull in Smithers' view, and the chap himself puffed up with egotism and a contrived eccentricity. Still, this hardly mattered. If being on the committee would be to his own professional advantage, then so be it.

* * *

14

The shadows lengthened and the room grew stuffy; a desultory fly attempted hara-kiri on the windowpane. The bursar thumped the table to make some point or other, Sir Richard firmly asserted, Maycock meandered, Turner doodled daggers in his otherwise pristine notebook and Phipps twittered while others grew bored . . . and John Smithers lapsed into further melancholy. He brooded upon his mistress, the rather luscious wife of Trinity's assistant librarian – and in Smithers' view far too luscious for that whey-faced little adjutant who was surely born to be upstaged. He gave a mirthless grin. And then he scowled, recalling that the adjutant's wife had assured him that were he to postpone one more rendezvous he could go jump in the Cam and not in her bed.

Pondering this, it occurred to Smithers that the Luscious One was getting too big for her high boots; perhaps he should start looking elsewhere. He glanced across the table and caught sight of his face in the long mirror behind the Master's chair, and wondered whether he should grow a beard. Some women liked that, apparently . . .

On the whole, Dr Maycock reflected as he walked home to his house in Grange Road, things had not gone badly. The new Master had conducted the meeting with a decent competence, Phipps had been quelled (moderately), there continued a consensus in favour of Winston Reid and – even more satisfactory – annoyance had been voiced at the interference of Gloria Biggs-Brookby. In his view, such annoyance was entirely right and proper: the woman was a veritable pest and at all costs should be prevented from inserting her fat oar into college concerns. Just because she was the daughter of the man to be honoured did not make her eligible for consultation, or at least only in the most cursory way. After all, she didn't even hold a degree, let alone a Cambridge one; yet from the way she behaved you would think she was Erasmus himself!

Born three years before the death of William Gladstone, Dr Maycock took pride in having been an infant contemporary of the Grand Old Man; and as recognition of that fact, in adulthood he had espoused the liberal cause. However, although a liberal in politics, Maycock's instincts were innately conservative. With him old habits died hard. Maycock liked old habits – which was why he deemed it so necessary to preserve the college's autonomy and not let it yield to the outlandish dictates of interlopers like Gloria Biggs-Brookby. What mattered was not so much the choice of sculptor per se, but rather the confounding of Gloria's will. That was the essential issue.

The Senior Tutor scowled at a passing cat, who, taking not a blind bit of notice, sauntered across his path mewing blithely. Its passage almost caused him to trip; but resuming both balance and then good temper, he too sauntered on. After all, he mused, other than the Gloria issue, matters were progressing as they should and Richard Dick was coping quite adequately in his new position. He had no quarrel there.

His mind went back to the Magisterial Election held a few months previously. His own candidature had been defeated, but only just. Did he mind? No, not really. In fact, the more he thought about things it was probably just as well. It meant he had more time to devote to what would become his magnum opus: *The Unsheathed Dagger: Balkan Tribulations and the Ottoman Empire*. Most certainly the conduct and progress of the college was vital, but even more

16

vital was the integrity of academic research. The status of Master might have been gratifying (and deserved) but even more gratifying would be the applause of colleagues and the universal recognition of his years of scholarly contribution. Another laurel to be worn with modest pride!

And then, of course, there was his wife, dear Sally. From the outset she had been opposed to his getting the Mastership. 'I dread the very day,' she had said. 'Just think of all those extra wretched dinners and functions one would have to attend: being on show all the time and you being called hither and yon at a moment's notice! You're busy enough as it is, and with all those extra duties our lives simply wouldn't be our own. Besides,' she had added slyly, 'you are so much better as a covert wire-puller, calling the shots while lying doggo. That's your forte, my boy.'

Maycock smiled into the gathering dusk. It was true. He liked playing the *éminence grise*, the trusty second fiddle whose genial deference belied his actual power. As a youngster he had fought on the Somme, and in the last war served rather more safely as an acting major in a clerical capacity at a large desk. Perhaps it was there that he had won his spurs as the consummate wire-puller. He recalled once overhearing the words of a young subaltern whose leave he had managed to wangle against all odds: 'Oh yes, old Cockers will help. He's the best fixer in the business!'

The now even older Cockers stopped to light his pipe and brooded upon Sir Richard Dick: well intentioned, he reflected, but essentially weak. Yes, he would have to fix that all right. Dick couldn't be allowed to slacken. Currently the Master was totally against Gloria, but could that stand be sustained? Uncertain. Yes, it was surely his own bounden duty to see that the man didn't flag; to keep him fired up and not worn down by her insidious wiles. At all costs the woman must be thwarted. The college's honour was at stake!

Resolutely, he marched up the steps to his front door, poised for whisky and the emollient arms of his wife.

CHAPTER TWO

While shaving some mornings later, John Smithers decided that a beard was not the answer to a maiden's prayer – nor indeed the answer to the threats of Myrtle Miller to ditch him. He would stick to the chiselled features of earlier conquests. They had served him well in the past and would do so again.

He had just made that decision, when he was startled by the sound of the telephone. He scowled at the mirror. It was surely a bit early in the day to be called; he hadn't even had breakfast. Perhaps it was for Dr Leavis next door. His flat shared a party line with the doyen of Downing Street and occasionally wires got crossed.

He put down his shaving brush, went into the bedroom and picked up the receiver. 'Hello,' he said tentatively.

'*Hello*,' the caller breathed. 'And how are we this morning?'

'What?' Smithers snapped, wiping a wisp of foam from his cheek.

There was a chuckle. 'Well,' said the voice, 'having espied you last night in the back row of the Arts Cinema with *you know who*, I rather wondered how things had been progressing . . . That is to say, I trust weedy Wilfrid didn't turn up and spoil things for you both.' There was a sepulchral snigger, and then the line went dead.

For an instant Smithers' mind also died. But then with a lurch it rallied. 'Who the effing hell!' he cursed, glaring out of the window as if somehow the unknown caller might be seen loitering on the rooftop. One thing was for sure, it couldn't have been his neighbour F. R. Leavis, nor presumably any of the chap's colleagues. Leavis had once declared that he loathed the cinema; and besides, the formidable scholar was hardly known for his humour, either jovial or malign.

So who the hell was it? The librarian himself, Wilfrid Miller, cuckolded and crazed? It seemed unlikely – far too phlegmatic. In any case, would he have used the unflattering term 'weedy'? Not unless he had a skewed vein of self-mockery, and Smithers couldn't recall observing any of that in the moon-faced mole. Thus, who had it been, for pity's sake? Who had seen him and Myrtle canoodling in the back row and was daft enough to play silly beggars on the telephone?

Angrily, he finished his ablutions and then downed some black coffee. He was just pouring a second cup and deciding that it must have been some smart-arsed undergraduate, when a thought struck him. Was it his imagination or had the voice held a slight lisp? He frowned, going over the sounds of the words in his mind . . . *Espied, last, progressing* – yes that was it, the faintest lisp: ethpied, lathd, progrethed. He brooded upon those mild distortions, and as he did so he recalled something else, something to do with the actual timbre of the voice, a sort of crackly resonance, a kind of . . . Yes, by God, he had heard it before!

He shoved the coffee pot aside and wracked his memory; and then stared at the wall in disbelief as a name came into mind. Could it really have been him? Surely not; he must be mistaken. He gave an impatient laugh to dispel the thought – but the voice remained, jibing and insistent.

Smithers got up from the table and started to pace the room. It was not an exercise he was practised in, and in his agitation he tripped on a pile of books, sending them sprawling across the carpet. With a curse he bent to pick them up, but stopped halfway, diverted by the image of the caller that now danced before his eyes . . . Yes, he thought grimly, it was definitely him and he would damn well get the bastard!

Kicking the books aside, he strode back to the bedroom, leafed through the telephone directory and dialled the number.

It rang repeatedly. And with a sense of disappointment he was about to hang up, when a voice answered. 'Cambridge 85320,' the speaker intoned.

Smithers tensed, and then in cold fury said: 'Oh yes, thank you, I've got your number all right – and in answer to your earlier crass enquiry I am perfectly well, thank you: well enough to blow you to buggery if you ever try that on me again. So just watch it. I mean what I say.'

Snapping out the threat, Smithers felt fully in control

and pleased at the sound of his words. That would settle the bugger's hash all right! Yes, he thought, attack was definitely the best line of defence.

He was about to replace the receiver, but was checked by a roar of laughter. 'My dear chap,' the other said, 'how brutal you sound! Just like my old nanny. There's nothing to worry about, I assure you. Merely my little joke. And besides, lovely though she is, if I am not mistaken, I rather think you may have a more intriguing fish to fry – and perhaps just a *teeny* bit more dangerous?' He gave a light laugh, before adding, 'But fear not, your romantic tomfoolery is entirely safe with me. I never divulge . . . or at least, very rarely.'

There was a click, followed by silence. Smithers screwed up his eyes and sunk on to the bed.

Elsewhere in Cambridge another telephone call was causing less consternation.

'Oh, Monty dear,' crooned Gloria Biggs-Brookby, 'how good of you to ring. As a matter of fact I was just about to do that myself and suggest that you come up to Cambridge again and stay chez moi for a couple of days. This time I can show you around, and you can assess the site and get the feel of the place . . . What? Am I being premature? Who? Oh, you mean Alderman Cuff. My dear, weakening by the hour. He'll soon give in – I've bribed his children with cinema tickets and his wife with a seat on the board of the WI. You see, the college will get that plot of land all right. *And*, once Sir Richard learns of my intervention on their behalf he is bound to climb down.' Gloria smoothed her hair and chortled, before adding, 'I mean, I know Sir Richard is a fearful stick-in-the mud, but

I am working on him, and just you see – before long the rabbit will come lolloping out of the hat! It's just a matter of patience, really.' She gave another hearty chuckle, which was followed by a silence as Monty Finglestone evidently had further questions.

'Oh no,' she assured him, 'don't worry about the others. I think you will find them sufficiently malleable. After all, where there is a will little Gloria generally finds her way! And as to your fee – I shouldn't worry about that. The only tricky one is Mostyn Williams, the bursar, a tight-fisted fellow. But the essential people are the donors. A few are coming up here shortly, so I shall have the chance to massage their egos and sing your praises.' She gave another snort of confident mirth; and then more seriously, said, 'Be assured, Monty, Daddy would be thrilled with my choice and I just *know* you will do him justice. Come soon and we'll make plans!'

Unlike John Smithers, Gloria was pleased with her telephone conversation; and once it was over – and far from collapsing on the bed – she hurried off to Fitzbillies to renew her manipulative energies over a small, sweet coffee and a large Chelsea bun.

CHAPTER THREE

'I intend buying a plot of land in Cambridge,' Professor Cedric Dillworthy announced.

His friend Felix Smythe, absorbed in stitching a floral tapestry, looked up startled. 'Why on earth should you want to do that?' he asked. 'You have a perfectly good garden here in London.'

'Ah, but this is to be a Garden of Remembrance.'

Felix put aside his tapestry and stared at his friend. 'What an extraordinary idea. Remembering what?'

'My old tutor, Sir Percival Biggs-Brookby. The college is going to erect a small statue to his memory and plans to acquire a patch of derelict ground bordering the south wall to accommodate it. A group of' – he broke off, giving a discreet cough – '*suitable* alumni has been approached to bear the cost. Naturally, I said I would.'

'But you never liked the man, or so you've always said. I recall the words "bumptious" and "unhinged" being mentioned; and at some point the term "monumental prig" was applied – or at least I *think* the word was prig.' Felix giggled.

Cedric regarded him coldly. 'Just because one may have made a few negative observations does not mean one has overlooked his invaluable contribution to archaeological scholarship. And his book on Cappadocian topography is a minor classic.'

'Hmm. But if I'm not mistaken, I seem to remember you also saying that in your opinion he was an unmitigated humbug and charl—'

'I am sure I said no such thing,' Cedric exclaimed angrily. 'You exaggerate as usual.'

'If you say so.' Felix shrugged and with a sniff resumed his stitching. For a time silence reigned. But then unable to contain puzzled curiosity, Felix enquired: 'So are you the only one selected to fund this plot, or are other "suitable" alumni involved? I mean to say, it sounds a bit expensive to me. I trust it won't inhibit your travel plans. It would be unfortunate should you have to replace Bologna with Bognor; or indeed forgo our scheduled cocktails with Mr Somerset M. at his villa on Cap Ferrat this summer.'

His friend gave a wintry smile. 'I can assure you that Bognor is not on the agenda; and as for our distinguished host, the arrangement remains. We shall most certainly be among his honoured guests. And in answer to your query: no, Felix, I am not the only one involved. My old colleague Basil Leason has also graciously accepted sponsorship, as has Dame Margery Collis, the Girton girl we all quite liked . . . Oh, and Hinchcliffe too – can't recall his first name, never saw him much. There are various others as well. Anyway, once the ground is cleared and the statue installed, our names as benefactors will be inscribed on a discreet plaque beside the gate.' Cedric gave a light laugh and added, 'Apparently there are plans for a grand inaugural ceremony with the press and so forth. Interviews, you know, and all that sort of absurdity – even television cameras, I hear.'

The light slowly dawned on Felix as the motive for the professor's interest became clear. However, not wishing to muddy already slightly choppy waters, he merely said: 'How jolly. Now we shall both have our plaques: me with my Royal Warrant over the shopfront and you with your name up in lights in a Cambridge garden. Most fitting.'

Cedric agreed that it was indeed fitting, but reminded Felix a little stiffly that the statue project was a dignified public tribute and not a Broadway show.

'Oh, absolutely, dear boy,' agreed Felix, 'a mere *façon de parler* . . . Now, let us toast the plot and its imminent incumbent – and, of course, the munificent benefactors.' Discarding the tapestry, he bustled from the room to retrieve the ice bucket from the kitchen.

Left alone, Cedric reflected on his friend. Really, delightful though Felix could be, there were times when it was difficult to sift jest from seriousness, and this was one of them. He pursed his lips.

The professor's connection with Cambridge, both as an undergraduate and later as a visiting lecturer, had been a source of modest pride; and it was pleasant to think that somewhere among its features and monuments his own name might be preserved for permanent display . . . even if it was to be linked with the insufferable Biggs-Brookby.

Ah well, he mused resignedly, one couldn't have everything and doubtless there were some who admired the man.

He turned his mind to Felix's Royal Warrant graciously granted by the Queen Mother the previous year. Polished daily, it shone out like a beacon above the entrance to his friend's flower shop: *Smythe's Bountiful Blooms*. Not a speck of Sloane Street dust was allowed to besmirch that crown of honour! Cedric smiled. Was it the proprietor's avowed love of corgis (Felix hated them) that had finally tipped the balance and secured him the coveted accolade? Perhaps. And if so, then Felix and he shared the tacit recognition that occasionally one type of pride had to be traded for another. It was the way of the world.

On that philosophical note the professor greeted the returning ice-bearer with a lavish smile and the offer to mix the cocktails. But just as he was perfecting these, the telephone rang from the hall and, signalling his friend to complete the process, he went to answer it.

'Who was that?' Felix asked when he returned. 'Anyone I know?'

Cedric nodded. 'Oh yes, you know her. It was Rosy Gilchrist.'

'Really? Whatever does she want? I trust it's nothing involving the Southwold shindig. The last thing I want is to be reminded of that dreadful experience!'

'It wasn't all dreadful,' replied Cedric mildly, 'you must admit that some of it was quite nice.'

'Oh, I suppose you mean me being savaged by that marsh creature and all those other dire events.'

'Come now, you know very well that the creature never touched you.'

Felix tossed his head. 'Not for want of trying, I can tell you!'

Cedric was about to murmur that he had been told a number of times, but was pre-empted by Felix repeating his question about Rosy.

'As a matter of fact she wanted my advice. A bit of a coincidence, really: it was to do with Cambridge.'

'Oh yes? And what is Rosy Gilchrist's interest in Cambridge?'

'She was up there; years after me, of course. She read history at Newnham. Don't you remember her telling us? Anyway, apparently she is planning to go there for some sort of reunion next month and wants to know whether it would be best to drive or take the train. She hasn't been back since she left so is a bit vague about travel arrangements, and wonders if it would be sensible to motor. I recommended the train; the drive can be tedious. But as she would have to endure the rigours of King's Cross – not the most salubrious of areas – I suggested that first class might be advisable: a blessed relief after that dreary concourse and dismal waiting room.'

'Hmm. Did she ask after me?'

'No.'

'Typical!'

Later that evening Cedric revealed that as a prelude to the statue's completion it had been suggested by the Plot and Monument Committee that the prospective donors be invited to view the proposed site and to learn more about the project. It would be an opportunity for such alumni to meet informally prior to the grand ceremony scheduled a few months hence. He suggested that his friend might like to join him on the trip.

Felix frowned, pondering. 'Er, well,' he began hesitantly, 'it *could* be rather tricky—'

'Well, naturally, you don't have to come,' Cedric said mildly, 'but I just thought it would make quite a pleasant little outing for the two of us. After all, I don't think you've actually visited Cambridge before, have you? I could show you around – give you an insider's eye-view, as it were. In fact, we might stay up there for a bit and perhaps go over to Grantchester, or motor out to Ely and visit the cathedral.'

'Oh, indeed,' Felix replied, 'but it all depends on the dear Queen Mother. It's in the wind that she is about to give one of her little soirées, and naturally *were* I to be on the guest list I couldn't possibly refuse, could I?' He succeeded in looking both apologetic and smug.

'Well she might want you to do the flowers, I suppose,' Cedric agreed, 'but as to being on the actual guest list, I think that if that were the case you would have heard by now, don't you? Clarence House is rather punctilious in such matters – something to do with the corgis' preferences, one gathers. *Are* you one of their chosen?'

'Not that I am aware,' Felix said tightly.

With practised tact Cedric pursued his suggestion. And after some speculation about the date of the royal soirée, the perversity of the fastidious corgis, and Cedric's assurances that in any case it was bound to be a rather stolid affair, Felix was persuaded to accompany the professor to Cambridge.

'I mean to say,' Cedric had said encouragingly, 'you were *such* a success at the Warrant Holders' Reception, so there is bound to be a royal invitation later in the season. Meantime, you can enjoy the cloistered harmonies of Cambridge with me.' He smiled and patted his friend's thin shoulder.

* * *

In her Baker Street flat, Rosy Gilchrist replaced the receiver and pondered. First class was all very well for the likes of Professor Dillworthy, but wasn't it a trifle extravagant? She frowned, wavering . . . And then, recalling her recent pay rise from the British Museum and reminding herself that the Cambridge jaunt would allow relief from the hectoring claims of Dr Stanley, her volatile boss, she decided to blow the cost and take Cedric's advice. After all, the reunion with old university chums promised to be a special occasion, so why shouldn't she push the boat out and do the thing in style?

She grinned, thinking that the last time she had been en route to 'eastern parts', specifically Suffolk, it had been in the company of Lady Fawcett[2] – a charming but maddening co-traveller whose incessant chatter and wild gesticulations had nearly brought the car off the road. Well, this time she would be alone, unfazed by the Fawcett presence and sitting at ease in a first-class carriage. What could be nicer?

Memories of that previous journey also brought to mind the extraordinary state of affairs that had awaited them at their destination. The Southwold business, now happily resolved, had engulfed the two women plus their companions Cedric and Felix in a clutch of truly grisly incidents. At least she wouldn't be faced with that sort of thing this time . . . How lovely to spend a few days amidst the civilities of Cambridge (so different from London's roar), boating on the calm waters of the Cam (as opposed to the mercurial tides of the North Sea) and being merry among lost friends from the class of '49.

Rosy had gone up to Newnham soon after the war, having done her stint in the ATS manning searchlights and

[2] See *A Southwold Mystery*

30

maintaining guns near Dover. After the hectic camaraderie and stringent discipline of service life (plus, of course, its constant dangers), post-war Cambridge had seemed another world, and Rosy had immersed herself in it with pleasure and wonder. Yes, it would be good to be back there: to retrace old haunts and renew old friendships – or at least catch up with once familiar colleagues. Settling in her chair, she lit a cigarette and savoured the prospect.

Alas, too often plans and prospects are intruded upon by other people. And in Rosy's case one of those people was her boss, Dr Stanley. Naturally, she had squared her absence with him well in advance, but later that week he had called her into his office and enquired (rather politely for him) whether she would care to modify her arrangements.

Guardedly, she had asked in what way exactly.

'Oh, the best way,' he had replied airily, 'be assured of that, Rosy.'

Rosy was far from assured and probed deeper.

He explained that once she had finished 'hob-bobbing' with her girlfriends at the 'doubtless *scintillating* reunion' she should take the opportunity to stay on longer and absorb the atmosphere of the Fitzwilliam Museum.

'Oh yes, and why would I want to do that?' she had asked.

The reply had been swift and characteristically curt: 'Because your boss requires it.'

Whoops! Silly blunder. Rosy hastily composed her features into a look of rapt attention.

In response, Stanley's own features assumed an expression of furtive guile. 'You see, Rosy,' he said, leaning forward and lowering his voice, 'I want you to be my mole.'

'Your *what*!'

'Well, perhaps not a mole, exactly, but – how shall I put it? – a sort of covert observer, a discreet agent ready to report back the moment you get any significant intelligence. It would be most helpful.' Stanley leered.

Rosy stared at him, literally open-mouthed. Over the course of time she had become inured to her superior's whims and oddities, but this really took the biscuit. What the hell was he talking about? She cleared her throat. 'I'm sorry, I am not quite sure that I—'

'Understand? Oh, it's easy enough. During the last year I have noticed one or two snide references appearing in the press – specifically the *liberal* press – to the effect that the British Museum has become stuck in its ways, is too complacent and immured in its own renown. We are, I gather, clamped to the bosom of the nineteenth century and lack the "pizazz" – whatever that's supposed to mean – required by its twentieth-century visitors. Indeed, one critic had the brass neck to suggest that in originality and artistic verve we were being rapidly outgunned by Oxford's Ashmolean – and, if you please, by the Fitzwilliam!' Dr Stanley paused to let the awful accusation sink in.

'How frightful,' Rosy replied mechanically. 'But I still don't quite see what my role is . . . I mean, what exactly is this "significant intelligence" that you want me to bring back, and how do I get it?'

'You get it by keeping your eyes and ears open. And as to what it is – I tell you, Rosy, it could be total dross or dynamite. I have it on good authority that the Fitzwilliam's trustees have recently approached Peregrine Purblow to give them his *enlightened* views on how the museum should revamp its image to appeal to a younger, and apparently more discerning, clientele. To

32

my mind, that is an oxymoron. Nevertheless, that is what the trustees are intent on doing. And daft as their idea sounds, I consider that it is the British Museum's cultural duty to learn what is being proposed. As you know, Purblow is a self-aggrandising bastard' – Rosy did not know, never having heard of him – 'but it doesn't hurt to be abreast of things: forewarned et cetera. Personally, in my role as a senior executive in our venerable institution, I do not propose being upstaged by the Fitzwilliam, let alone by that smart-arsed pundit Purblow. He appears on television, you know.'

Rosy took the final remark to be the ultimate cut and contrived to look suitably shocked.

'So what do you want me to do? Loiter slyly among the columns of the Fitzwilliam with notebook poised and wearing a fedora?'

He looked at her coldly. 'Certainly not. I expect you to make a thorough reconnaissance of the place, noting how the exhibits are displayed, what kind of labelling is used and the quality of the lighting effects. I also want you to sign up for Purblow's two lectures on "Art and the Modern Public", and – most importantly – ingratiate yourself with their chief curator, a Mrs Sally Maycock, wife of one of the university's worthies, and find out what she has in mind for the future. For example, it's rumoured that someone has the bright idea of mounting an exhibition of the Old Bailey's recent Chatterley trial – sketches and photographs of the barristers and chief witnesses etc. I gather such a project is intended to impress those not normally familiar with the interior of museums.' Stanley's voice took on a sardonic note.

'Huh!' he continued, 'the novel was tame enough, so why

pictures of the trial should entice a philistine public I cannot imagine. A far better bet would be to do a mock-up of the Brides in the Bath murders, or John Christie and Rillington Place. Now they could be a crowd-puller! In fact, if it transpires that the Fitz really is going to do the Chatterley thing, then I think the British Museum might well counter it with a Christie recreation, gas tubes, ropes and all. We could even get the Madame Tussauds' lot to lend a hand. So what do you think of that, Rosy?'

'Wonderful,' she replied woodenly.

CHAPTER FOUR

Cedric had been right: negotiating King's Cross had not been particularly jolly, the buffet being closed and the platform draughty. Rosy was glad that she had taken his advice and opted for first class. She settled back comfortably in the padded seat, and watched as the grey and muddled vista of London's eastern suburbia meandered past the window: Finsbury Park, Potters Bar, Welwyn . . . names etched in her mind, but places never visited.

Gradually, the train gathered speed and open spaces began to appear: random indeterminate tracts of wasteland, half-hearted cast-offs from the city. Uninspired, Rosy turned to her book, a biography of Disraeli. Yet despite her liking for the subject, this too failed to capture her interest. That afternoon the wiles of Dizzy were eclipsed by the wiles of her boss, and she put the book aside. Was she really going to have to spend part of her time in Cambridge playing at being a fifth columnist? The idea was absurd! And how was she going to 'ingratiate' herself with the curator, the Maycock lady? After all, they might not like each other. Rosy sighed irritably. She was getting a little tired of the missions imposed upon her by the imperious Stanley!

But then she brightened. Still, if such a mission meant she could extend her leave and thus have longer to relive the past and enjoy the present, why complain? She started to envisage how she might spend the extra time (other than skulking within the portals of the Fitzwilliam). A number of possibilities came to mind. And then turning to gaze out of the window again, she noticed how the landscape had slipped into proper countryside, open and green, sprinkled with farms and cows, hedges and willow-herb. She glimpsed more names, Baldock, Royston . . . ah, at last they were getting nearer and London was far behind.

Far too early she started to gather her things, eager to arrive yet a little nervous as to what she might find. Supposing there would be an anticlimax. Supposing that after London, Cambridge seemed flat and parochial. Supposing her college contemporaries had grown staid and dull. And what about herself: how would they view her? Ah well, these were things she would soon discover . . .

The train was punctual and Rosy alighted at the instantly familiar station – mercifully unscathed by the axe-wielding Dr Beeching. She picked up her case, smiled at the ticket collector and, declining a porter's offer, made her way out to the cab rank.

As she trundled along in the taxi, taking in all the old familiar landmarks, she noticed two men walking slowly along the pavement. They were talking animatedly, the taller waving his left hand as if to make a point, the shorter nodding in seeming agreement. There was something familiar about the former's manner, as also about his companion's short, spiky hair and thin shoulders. They looked a little like . . . Oh no, surely it couldn't be? Not here, suddenly in the middle of Cambridge. Ridiculous! But as Rosy turned, straining her neck to get a better view, she realised that it most certainly was . . . Yes, Cedric Dillworthy and Felix Smythe. *Oh really*, she thought indignantly, *Cedric might have said they were planning a visit when I phoned asking him about travel arrangements – but oh no, not a word.* Fairly typical, of course, the professor rarely disclosed anything unless you took a hammer and chisel!

The last time she had seen the two of them was in Felix's chic sitting room above the flower shop, imbibing cocktails and reminiscing theatrically about their earlier imbroglio on the Suffolk coast. Rosy had been part of that imbroglio and was only too glad to be free of its memory and, for a time at any rate, from the company of her two colleagues-in-arms. ('Comrades' was too intimate a term; 'reluctant accomplices' might be more apt.) What on earth were they doing here – and oh dear, was there a danger of meeting them?

She leant back against the seat, a little bemused by the term that had entered her head: why 'danger'? she pondered. After all, they were a perfectly decent pair – civilised and mannerly; and fate having conspired to engage the three of them in rather alarming circumstances, she certainly knew them well enough. Hmm . . . well *enough*, but not enough for intimacy or real friendship. For some reason such closeness had never been established. It wasn't that she disliked them (a view which as far as she was aware was reciprocated), but neither did she feel any special joy at the prospect of encountering them here. She saw them enough in London. But Cambridge was a place removed, a world of her past, and she did not want it suddenly invaded by Cedric and Felix.

Rosy gave a rueful smile, remembering her mother's words of long ago: 'Oh really, Rosy dear, don't be so picky! You know you quite like Alison and her little sister – why on earth don't you want them at your birthday party?' There had been no answer except a mulish pout.

As the taxi slowed and the familiar shapes of her old stamping ground came into sight, the spectres of Cedric and Felix were instantly banished. Absurd to think she might meet them, and besides what if she did? Would it really matter? She scanned the gracious facade of her old college, nervously engrossed by the prospect that awaited her. Yet somehow, gazing up at those large white sash windows and solid Queen Anne gables stark against the blue sky, she felt reassured: the same harmonies, the same elegant proportions, the same *stability*. Yes, things would be all right.

Momentarily she paused in front of the archway to the porter's lodge – an imposing feature added only in her last year, yet now wreathed in foliage and seeming to have been there forever. Irrationally she felt a sense of welcome, and gripping the handle of her case stepped forward. So . . . back again, she thought.

Yes, indeed, she was back again; and from what she could make out little had changed. Sitting that evening in the Senior Common Room she surveyed her past contemporaries, and with a few exceptions recognised them all. Older, smarter and perhaps more assured and worldly, they were essentially the same bunch with whom she had spent three years of her life studying, disputing, confiding, growing – and perhaps most importantly having fun. Like herself some had been in the forces during the war, one or two had worked at Bletchley or Medmenham, while others had done vital civilian work. They and Rosy had been the 'old ones', the war veterans; but there had been a younger group too, youngsters fresh up from school amazed by their new freedoms and eager for adventure and 'real life'.

And now, despite certain differences in age, background and experience, here they were again varied in their achievements and domestic status; and yet surprisingly cohesive and all intent on getting the best out of the next few days: gossiping, reminiscing, forging new friendships and renewing the old.

To her regret, three of Rosy's closest chums were absent abroad, either with working husbands or in their own right. But there were several old faces that she was delighted to see – Betty Withers, now a flourishing psychiatrist attached to one of London's medical schools, and the mop-headed, gap-toothed Mary Bradshaw, once a literature student and now herself busy instructing callow first years in the exploits of Beowulf and the cerebral intensities of John Donne.

Mary had brought a guest with her, an older woman: tall, elegant and in her fifties whom she introduced as Dame Margery Collis ('Frightfully high-powered in education,' Betty Withers had whispered) and whose name Rosy vaguely recalled from references in *The Times*.

'Afraid I am a total interloper,' the woman laughingly confided to Rosy. 'I'm a "Girton gal", nothing to do with Newnham at all. I am up here to attend a meeting of benefactors at my late brother's college, St Cecil's. They are hoping to erect a statue to one of its past luminaries, a rather eccentric Middle East archaeologist. Not my field at all, but I owe a lot to Cambridge so I'm happy to contribute. Besides, I know the Dicks slightly. His wife and I share the same London club, the University Women's, and I get the distinct impression that Sir Richard is rather expecting me to cough up. He has only recently been appointed Master, so I suppose one ought to rally round.' She laughed, and then added, 'But apart from that business, I am also scheduled to give a short course of talks over at Girton. Apparently their guest wing is currently experiencing some horrendous problem with the plumbing and so they thoughtfully asked if I would like to be accommodated elsewhere. As you can imagine, I didn't exactly dither! Still, I shall only be here a couple of days or so. Luckily, a friend is lending me her flat and it's an arrangement that suits me better. Nice though collegiate life is, at my age one rather relishes one's independence.'

Her allusion to the brother's alma mater rang a bell with Rosy. Hadn't that been Cedric's old college? A benefactors' meeting, the woman had said. Could that be the reason for Cedric and Felix being in Cambridge? Cedric's sphere was Cappadocia, its history and topography, so quite possibly he had known the scholar in question.

'You don't happen to have come across a Professor Dillworthy, do you?' she enquired casually.

'What, old Dilly? Certainly I have – or at least I used to. We were up together years ago, and he knew my brother, so we would meet from time to time. He was quite nice in a muted sort of way.'

Rosy recognised the description and confirmed that little had changed.

'So, I take it you know him well,' the other said.

'Oh, not well,' Rosy told her hastily, 'but I see him in London on and off – receptions, concerts, that sort of thing . . .' (She spoke vaguely, deeming it imprudent to mention those times when she, Cedric and Felix had been reluctantly embroiled in situations more than a little bizarre.)

'He married a botanist schoolteacher,' Dame Margery continued thoughtfully. 'At the time I remember our thinking it rather a peculiar move, and I gather it wasn't a success – disaster, in fact. Is he attached now?'

Attached? Rosy hesitated slightly, before saying that she didn't think Cedric was really the marrying type – 'Too independent,' she said lightly.

'I don't blame him. It's a condition that can be fearfully cramping; for a woman at any rate. Fortunately one has been spared.' She spoke with crisp conviction.

It was a conviction Rosy did not entirely share, and for a moment she thought of her pilot fiancé shot down over Germany in '45 . . . *My God, I would give my right arm to be married to him now!*

They were joined by others babbling fresh greetings and introductions, and her companion was whisked away to mingle with another group.

As they trooped into dinner, Betty Withers plucked Rosy by the sleeve, and further to her earlier aside explained that Dame Margery was one of those 'fearfully competent' women who actually had the temerity (and ability) to sit on educational committees and advise the government. 'One hears the ministers stand in total awe of her. It must be the long legs and regal bearing – plus that immaculate manicure!' She chuckled, looking ruefully at her own sturdy calves and bitten nails.

Alone in her room that night, Rosy reviewed her first day. It had been, she decided, a distinct success. How easily everyone had got on, and what worthy and fascinating things many were doing. And by all accounts even those alumni remaining 'merely' housewives seemed to have produced offspring of spectacular oddity or achievement! She smiled, recalling some of their anecdotes. Yes, it had been an excellent start to the reunion and she knew she would enjoy the scheduled events. Even Dr Stanley's sternly prescribed task to vet the Fitzwilliam now seemed less of a chore than originally felt.

She took up her book and once more immersed herself in the dedicated manoeuvres of Benjamin Disraeli; and then with lids beginning to droop, flicked off the light and fell into deep sleep.

CHAPTER FIVE

Being able to introduce Felix to his old college gave Cedric enormous pleasure. And immediately after their arrival he took him on a brief tour, relating well-worn anecdotes and pointing with pride to those features of particular historical interest or aesthetic appeal. Felix was duly impressed, especially by the college's gracious grounds with the arcaded rose arbour and the luxuriant, scented acacia clambering waywardly beneath the window of his room.

Less impressive was the room itself: neither luxuriant nor scented, and indeed to Felix (never having experienced the austerities of a boarding school) distinctly spartan. *Ah well*, he thought, stoically eyeing the narrow bed, *perhaps it will do me good . . .* though in what way he was not exactly clear.

However, he thought brightly, there were doubtless

charming prospects in store – leisurely boating on the Cam, meandering in the Botanic Garden, poring over the porcelain at the Fitzwilliam – and not least, enjoying the company of the discerning and erudite . . . Actually, Felix was not so sure about the erudite: would the conversations prove uncomfortably rarefied? Would he flounder beneath the 'wit' of academia? He frowned and considered.

No, of course he wouldn't. Why, attired in his new dinner jacket and explaining the finer facets of the Himalayan lily and its integration within a floral pillar he could hold his own with anybody. Besides, if at a real loss he could always talk amusingly about the piquant charm of those beastly royal corgis. Oh yes, undoubtedly his Cambridge sojourn was bound to be a success!

Bolstered by such thoughts, Felix opened the gaunt wardrobe and looked vainly for enough hooks on which to hang his suits.

In his room on the same staircase, Cedric was also unpacking and thinking. Over the years he had frequently returned to his old college and the pleasure never palled. Whatever the season – mistily autumnal, gusty in spring or, as at present, bathed warmly in summer sunshine – Cambridge was ever welcoming: its ancient stones and secret corners exuding an air of unchanging benignity. And this time, by bringing Felix with him the pleasure would be surely doubled. How gratifying to be able to introduce his friend to the university's history and architecture – and indeed to the company of old cronies and colleagues. Cedric smiled at the prospect. And unlike Felix he was perfectly satisfied with the somewhat basic amenities of his allocated room (although perhaps befitting his alumnal status, its proportions were a little more capacious than that of his guest's – something the guest had been quick to note).

The wardrobe being perfectly adequate for his needs, he quickly hung up his suits and made ready for the evening. And then spruced and eager, he opened the door and made his way a few steps down to Felix's quarters below.

'We are invited to the Combination Room for preprandial drinks,' Cedric explained as they walked across Middle Court. 'With luck, there should be one or two of my old associates there who I know will be delighted to meet you – although a word of warning, you may have to endure the prosings of ancient Phipps. Oh, and by the way, as honoured guests we shall be seated at High Table.'

'Ah, well, that's nice,' Felix replied vaguely, unsure about Phipps and even less about the high table.

However, as things turned out Felix felt moderately at ease in his new surroundings – the Combination Room being a smaller, plainer and more intimate version of the drawing room of the Athenaeum, an institution that on rare occasions he had been privileged to visit.

Neither did he feel ruffled by the reception party: the Senior Tutor Dr Maycock and Mostyn Williams, the bursar. Both chaps seemed easy, amiable and surprisingly free with the sherry. As predicted, 'ancient Phipps' appeared – not exactly amiable, but who nevertheless granted him a wintry smile and a word of welcome. 'Hmm,' he had remarked, 'I don't suppose you will find Cambridge like Camberwell, but I daresay you will get used to us.'

Camberwell? Felix had bristled. Why bloody Camberwell? He had started to explain that his home ground was Knightsbridge – Sloane Street to be exact –

but his words were lost in a plethora of genial jokes and pleasantries as others joined them.

Somebody turned to Cedric and made a reference to a Lord Bantry, apparently an undergraduate of years previously.

Cedric looked slightly perplexed. 'Lord Bantry, who's he? I don't think I recall—'

'You might well ask,' Aldous Phipps interrupted acidly, 'a bit of a *rara avis*, or so he used to be. In theory he had the effrontery to be reading Greek under my supervision; in practice he was never here – always on the river or out with hounds.' Phipps gave a derisive snort. 'Mind you, everything was Greek to him except larking on the Cam or hunting foxes. Useless! Do you know, he actually kept two hulking great hounds in his room, or at least he did until one of them bit the staircase scout. There was a tremendous ballyhoo and he was sent down; and a good job too, in my opinion – he couldn't construe for toffee.' Phipps looked indignant.

'And yet he is one of the benefactors?'

'Oh yes, indeed,' the bursar broke in. 'He insists that he nurses a masochistic nostalgia for the place . . . And along with that nostalgia there goes a good bit of dosh.' He grinned. 'Not only has he pledged to support our plot purchase, but better still he has hinted that he wants to endow a scholarship fund for the lame and indigent. So what do you think of that?'

'Very commendable,' Cedric said, slightly puzzled. 'But, er, why the lame?'

'He limps,' said Phipps, 'always did. On one of our rare encounters he told me that he had to have his right stirrup specially shortened. *I* told him that if he didn't submit his

46

Greek prose punctually that his time in Cambridge would be shortened too . . . Fortunately the hounds saw to that anyway.'

At that moment they were joined by John Smithers and Professor Turner. 'Was that Bantry I saw just now?' the latter asked. The others nodded, and Turner laughed: 'Well we had better keep him well away from glorious Gloria, they can't stand each other!' He turned to the bursar. 'Do you remember when they had that fearful row a couple of years ago and she called him a posturing playboy?'

'Hmm. A bit past playing now, I should think,' the other observed, 'and he's certainly never postured; doesn't need to. He says and does what he means – which is why the endowment is a safe bet. Still, we don't want any hitches. I must try to be my charming best.'

'Difficult,' Aldous Phipps was heard to mutter as he moved away.

Felix, who up to now had been silently hovering, was intrigued by Turner's allusion to the row between Bantry and Gloria, and asked what it had been about.

Turner shrugged. 'Could have been anything. Rumour has it that years ago they had a little walk-out, a sort of experimental dalliance that went spectacularly sour. Wasn't it Congreve who wrote, "Heaven has no rage like love to hatred turned"? Perhaps that had something to do with it.'

Felix wasn't sure who Congreve was, but nodded all the same, recognising the condition.

'Well, let's hope they don't start scrapping now,' the bursar said impatiently. 'Negotiations with the City Council are at a very delicate stage and the last thing we need is fisticuffs among the sponsors. The Master will get ratty, and I shall get the flak and the fall-out. It's that Gloria –

she stirs up everything. Always has. Mind you, Bantry isn't exactly the essence of tact. He once asked Phipps if he had fought in the second Afghan War under General Roberts.'

'Really?' Smithers chuckled. 'I bet that didn't go down too well.'

'Actually,' Turner said, 'I am told that Phipps was quite restrained, merely informing his student that since hostilities had ceased five years before his birth, alas he had been denied that honour. I bet his mind was otherwise engaged, else the response would have been more toxic.'

'Well, let us just hope the three of 'em don't cut up rough while the benefactors are here. If they start sniping at one another it won't look good,' the bursar said irritably. 'The last thing we want is to unsettle our esteemed sponsors!'

'Oh, I think you will find the sponsors have pretty thick skins,' Cedric said smoothly, 'I am sure we shall be absolutely fine.'

The other laughed. 'Yes, I'm sure you are right. Deep pessimism is my forte. Always has been. Now, gentlemen, let us dine. I believe there's some rather fine hock awaiting us.' He ushered them towards the oak-raftered dining hall.

Here amid candlelight and gleaming silver, and to the muted accompaniment of postgraduate voices (term over, and most younger students gone down), they ate well and convivially.

Seated between two old colleagues and talking academic shop, Cedric was in his element. At the further end of the table Felix was less in his element, but was nevertheless mildly enjoying himself. The man on his right was George Rawlings, one of the sponsors, and who although opinionated and garrulous was quite amusing. On his left was the elderly Professor Phipps, largely concerned with the contents of his plate, but who on occasions would make an observation of startling indiscretion. Plucking Felix's arm, he nodded towards John Smithers.

'Not my type,' he murmured, 'but sharp as a needle. Oh yes, that young man will go far – providing, of course, the ladies don't do for him first. Always a hazard with that sort. He would be wise to be careful.' He gave a sepulchral chuckle. And after a pause and a swirl of his hock goblet, he asked, 'And so what exactly is your metier, may I ask?'

Felix started to explain modestly that he was one of London's foremost florists, but before he was able to get on to the subject of his royal patron, Phipps remarked that he must then doubtless know a daffodil from a tulip and that not many people did. 'Take that fellow Winston Reid, the one we are all supposed to support for this sculpturing job, he hasn't a clue about gardens – or indeed much else, in my opinion.' The professor gave a disdainful sniff.

Felix was slightly at a loss. 'Well, I suppose he can make a statue,' he suggested vaguely.

'Oh yes, he can do that all right. But he is not exactly one of life's *enhancers* – or at least I shouldn't have thought so.' Phipps took a small sip of his wine and gave an appreciative nod.

'Er, isn't he very nice?' Felix asked.

'"Nice"? Now there's an interesting term,' the old man mused. 'I shall have to give thought to that; it's not a concept I often dwell upon. It has a sort of anodyne ambiguity, wouldn't you say?' He fixed Felix with a quizzical gaze.

But fortunately, before Felix could formulate an answer, George Rawlings requested that he pass the water jug and then demanded to know what kind of flowers his wife should select for their daughter's wedding. 'They tell me you're the expert, so let's have it from the horse's mouth!' he trumpeted.

The horse duly obliged, recommending pink roses and bunches of 'nice' delphiniums.

Later, as they mingled over port and coffee, Felix felt a light tap on his shoulder. He turned, and slightly to his surprise was confronted by the earnest face of Aldous Phipps. 'You know, since our earlier conversation I have been cogitating upon your use of the epithet "nice". I can only assume you intended it to mean "mannerly" – in which case, given the *subject* of your query, I should say not at all.'

Delivered of this observation and giving a pinched smile, Phipps drifted away to cadge an Abdulla cigarette from Rawlings . . . 'Reminds me of my Cairo days,' the reedy voice enthused. 'Ah, the pleasures of gilded youth!'

Cairo? Youth? Felix was amused. It was difficult to associate Phipps with either image! There was a hollow laugh from behind, and he looked round sensing one similarly amused. Emboldened by a slight surfeit of wine, Felix asked his new companion in what latter-day pleasures the old man indulged.

'Oh, that's an easy one,' John Smithers replied sourly, 'putting the knife in, mainly.'

Back in his room that night Cedric felt pleased (and slightly relieved). Dinner had been most agreeable, and it was clear that once over his initial diffidence, Felix had enjoyed himself. This boded well for their time in Cambridge, and he was sure that his guest would be equally diverted by the engagement the following evening: an informal soirée held at the Master's Lodge to welcome the prospective benefactors and to give them the opportunity to meet the new incumbent. Cedric had encountered Sir Richard Dick only a couple of times in the past, but from what he recalled he had seemed an able enough chap and one who in his new status would doubtless be an asset to the college.

He fell asleep quickly, soothed by the prospect of a most civilised sojourn.

CHAPTER SIX

After a day of congenial diversion, the two visitors were faced with the pleasant prospect of the Master's drinks party. In his own time as an undergraduate Cedric had never had reason to enter the Lodge, in those days a rather grim-looking building – a feature shared by its then incumbent.

Now, however, with its timbers painted a neutral cream rather than the fuscous grey of his memory, and the dense ivy on the once grimy stonework replaced by a mass of climbing roses, it exuded an air of seemly welcome. Indeed, on that particular evening such welcome was enhanced by the sight of the front door propped wide open by a basket of leather-bound tomes (rejects awaiting the dustman?), presumably a sign to the prospective donors that their arrival would be met with grateful warmth.

Sounds of muted laughter could be heard from within and, once in the hallway, Cedric and Felix were greeted by an attractive woman in her forties, whom they took to be their hostess, Lady Dick, the Master's wife. Introductions were made, small talk exchanged, and they were ushered into a large, mellow drawing room where, Felix was glad to see, copious drinks and canapés were briskly circulating.

Also circulating and clearly enjoying themselves were the other guests – men mostly, but with a sprinkling of women. One in particular caught Felix's eye. She was tall and fine-boned, with sleekly bobbed, silvery pale hair. Her jacket of blue shot-silk was rather dashing and she wore it well. Felix was taken with this and wondered if he too might suit such a garment. Doubtless Cedric would disapprove . . . Still, it was certainly rather chic. Perhaps, in the course of the evening, he could find out where she had obtained it. Harrods? Or perhaps tailor-made?

'Who is that woman?' he asked.

'What?' Cedric looked over to where she was standing, talking to their host. He was about to say, 'I've no idea,' but stopped short. 'Good Lord,' he exclaimed, 'it's Dame Margery – well, she's certainly looking good! We haven't met for years. That must be remedied!' He set off across the room.

'Ask her about the jacket . . .' Felix began, but was unheard.

'It *is* rather snazzy, isn't it, Felix?' a familiar voice said in his ear, 'but too pale for your colouring.' He turned, to be met by the smiling face of Rosy Gilchrist.

He was surprised; he had learnt from Cedric that she was in Cambridge, but had not expected to see her here at the sponsors' reception.

He sniffed. 'Some of us prefer subtlety,' he remarked, appraising her scarlet skirt and matching shoes. 'Anyway, what on earth are you doing here? I thought you were attending a reunion at that women's college. Don't tell me that you just happen to be one of the sponsors for this Biggs-Brookby statue as well. I shouldn't have thought that was at all your style.'

'No more than yours,' Rosy retorted; and then, grinning, said, 'Actually, like you I'm just here for the beer – riding in on the coat-tails of the cognoscenti, as it were.'

Had Felix not been intent on procuring a glass of champagne for himself and some rather enticing cocktail bits, he might have taken umbrage. As it was, he merely asked to whose coat-tail she was attached.

'Your lady in the blue jacket, Dame Margery Collis. She is staying temporarily at Newnham and we got talking. Apparently she is a friend of the Dicks – hence her being dragooned into contributing to this monument business. When I mentioned that I knew one of the other intending donors, i.e. our Cedric, she invited me to come along as her guest. I gather that Anthea Dick had been worried that there would be a dearth of women and wanted to even things up . . . So, here I am.'

'Hmm, so I see.' Felix frowned and glanced at her glass. 'You're lucky to have that,' he observed, 'some of us haven't even had our first sip. A chap could die of thirst – I'm beginning to think that waiter is deliberately avoiding me. I know that sort, they get so bumptious.' Excusing himself quickly, he slid away in dedicated pursuit.

He was replaced at her side by a small, elderly man with white hair and somewhat perilously perched spectacles. 'I admire the skirt,' he remarked. 'A bold touch, if I may say so. Makes one stand out from the crowd, which is why I always ensure my Popsie wears a red coat – in the winter months, at any rate. She looks rather dashing.' He beamed.

Rosy regarded the diminutive figure, taking in the wispy hair, sharp eyes and wizened cheeks. 'I see,' she said warily. 'And, er . . . does your, uhm, popsie like doing that, standing out from the crowd?'

'Oh *yes*,' Aldous Phipps replied with enthusiasm, 'she loves it. She's such a little show-off – but then, of course, that sort all are. Little tarts, really.' Rosy blinked.

'Do you have one?' he asked conversationally. 'Or perhaps you prefer cats – difficult creatures in my view, you can never quite get their measure. Whereas my Popsie is as open as the day is fair! They are like that you know, Norfolks.'

Rosy smiled in some relief, and explained that unfortunately, due to the constraints of her job, she had neither dog nor cat.

The old man deemed that a pity. And then, leaning towards her and in a conspiratorial tone, added, 'Mind you, not everyone is suited to domestic pets. For example, take our nominee sculptor, Winston Reid; he used to keep a cat for a while, but it took offence and walked out. Yes, went to live two streets down and never looked back. Frankly, if I were a cat, I'd have done the same. The man can turn out a competent bronze, all right, but he is not the brightest of fellows. The cat probably got bored. Reid and I used to play Scrabble occasionally. He wasn't especially good and I invariably beat him.' Phipps gave a satisfied sniff.

Then he muttered something else, which sounded a little like: 'Nor is he especially pleasant,' but the words were difficult to catch as he had turned away, distracted by a commotion at the door. A large woman in a ballooning blouse was berating a waiter who had evidently dropped his tray. '*Not* very clever,' a hectoring voice declared. 'You *must* have seen me standing here. Pull your socks up, Michael!'

Aldous Phipps closed his eyes and gave a groan of displeasure. 'It's Gloria,' he murmured, 'one must take evasive action.' He lowered his head, and without further utterance moved with surprising speed to a far corner.

Rosy couldn't help noticing that Anthea Dick, standing a few yards away, was looking distinctly put out – presumably piqued at the officious authority shown by Biggs-Brookby's daughter. She sympathised. After all, if it was your party, did you want some raucous woman thrusting herself forward and cursing the staff like that?

However, practised in such upsets, Lady Dick was quick to soothe both flustered waiter and tiresome guest – the latter achieved at Rosy's expense. Deftly, she took the new arrival's arm, and propelling her towards where Rosy was standing, made hasty introductions.

'Miss Gilchrist is a big friend of one of our project's sponsors,' she explained with some exaggeration, 'and was up at Cambridge after the war. But do you know this is the very first time she has been back. We must give her a really warm welcome!' Smiling and with manoeuvre accomplished, she wafted away to talk to John Smithers, leaving the two women eyeing each other politely. (Or at least Rosy looked polite, Gloria mildly bellicose.)

'Ah,' the latter brayed, grasping Rosy's hand with assertive grip, 'I've heard a bit about you from Betty Withers. You were up with her after the war reading history at Newnham, I gather, and are now at the British Museum under the frightful Stanley.'

For a moment Rosy was flummoxed, not sure whether to be offended by the term 'under' or 'frightful'. Neither seemed entirely accurate, but since the latter was the more disparaging she chose that.

'Well, he's not all that bad,' she said stoutly, 'quite nice, really; but yes, he can get a bit ratty.' (A bit? The B-B woman was right. He could be dreadful! But she certainly wasn't going to admit that to an outsider, least of all to this woman. Not for the first time Rosy felt herself being defensive of her formidable boss.)

'Oh well.' Gloria sighed. 'I suppose it takes all sorts, but personally from what I've heard I certainly wouldn't choose to work with him.'

Nor he you, Rosy thought acidly, eyeing the woman's florid cheeks and truculent expression. She took a sustaining sip of her champagne.

In turn the other supped her gin and tonic, and proceeded to interrogate Rosy about her work at the British Museum and what precisely were her duties. (Precisely? Rosy wondered. Nothing was especially precise except ministering to Stanley's whims and calming the troubled waters that he had invariably stirred.) Her interrogator then enquired who her tutors had been as an undergraduate. At the mention of one name, the older woman drew in her breath: 'Good Lord, do you mean Prissy Prendergast? Not one of Cambridge's more inspiring scholars, or so my friends tell me.'

'Actually, she was fascinating,' Rosy replied, wondering who on earth Gloria's friends could be.

Unperturbed by Rosy's coolness – or oblivious – Gloria

started to rattle on about her eminent father and the current proposals for his memorial. 'It's not before time,' she said tartly, 'at least Richard Dick has got that right.' She cast a disapproving look to where the Master was chatting with Dr Maycock. 'He is typical of that brand of academic,' she said darkly, 'set in his ways, stubborn as a mule and with a mind closed to artistic invention.'

'Goodness,' Rosy exclaimed, 'that's quite an indictment.' She gave a light laugh. 'Do you mean it?'

'Indeed I do,' the other replied grimly, 'and that goes for most of the others on that Plot and Monument Committee. Conventional and undiscerning, that's what! They are determined to commission that dreary Winston Reid – not the most savoury of people, and given his alcohol intake I am surprised he can even see the bronze, let alone sculpt it. My choice is a *much* brighter spark. You may have heard of him: Monty Finglestone, a young man of excellent promise, charming manners and keen ambition. That's who Daddy would approve, someone fresh and dynamic. Now he *would* do him justice. Yes, I can tell you, Miss Gilchrist, Finglestone is the one for the job – and if I have anything to do with it, he'll get it!' With a gesture of resolute purpose she downed the dregs of her gin in one fell gulp.

Rosy smiled compliantly, while at the same time casting a hasty eye around the room for means of escape. However, Gloria was approaching full throttle. 'Of course,' she went on, 'the worst of the bunch is that Senior Tutor Maycock. I can't think why, but Dick seems peculiarly impressed by him. Pah! In my view, a windy fuddy-duddy, stuck in the past and a blot on the present. Should have been put out to grass years ago!'

The last two observations were delivered far from sotto

voce and, somewhat embarrassed, Rosy glanced round hoping the comments had not reached the ears of their subject. Judging from the sharp flush that had appeared on Maycock's cheeks she suspected they probably had.

Racking her brains for a means of retreat, she was just about to make polite excuses, when Gloria's lowering features brightened. 'My dear,' she whispered, gripping Rosy's arm, 'Anthea said you were a friend of Professor Dillworthy, one of the major sponsors. Perhaps you could say something in Finglestone's favour, persuade him of the young man's talents. The more sponsors are interested the better his chances with the committee. Would you do that?'

At last Rosy had her escape route. 'Oh, but it would be *much* better coming from you. Look, he's over there by the window. I am sure he would welcome your views.' (Rosy was far from sure, but spoke with firm conviction.)

'Ah, so that's him, is it? Yes, indeed, I'll nobble him myself.' With jaw firmly set she started to make a beeline for the unsuspecting target, while Rosy finished her drink in peace, amused at the prospect of Cedric being 'nobbled'. Gloria would have a tough task on her hands.

'I like your red shoes,' a voice suddenly said in her ear, 'very fetching.' She looked up to be confronted by the bluff face of one whom she later discovered to be Lord Bantry. But before she could acknowledge the compliment, he muttered, 'I should watch that one if I were you: off her rocker and nasty with it. Oh yes, take my word. *Dangerous.*' He put a finger to the side of his nose, winked and moved on.

Slightly taken aback, Rosy scanned the room seeking the safe harbour of one without axe or bias. Her glance fell on Dame Margery in conversation with another guest who looked reassuringly normal. In some relief she made her way towards them.

By the window, and unaware of what was looming from the Gloria direction, Cedric was chatting about undergraduate days with his old friend Basil Leason.

'Yes, there *are* changes, of course,' Leason was saying, 'but not too radical, and in my view mainly for the better.'

Cedric agreed, but remarked that one thing was constant: the Cambridge weather. 'It's always pretty blustery, especially in the outskirts. Doesn't E. M. Forster say something about the east wind blowing forever and the mist never lifting off the mud?'

'Yes, I think he does. But if memory serves me right, in the same essay he also makes a woeful reference to governesses.'

'*Governesses?* You mean in Cambridge?'

'Yes. He talks of them lugubriously holding court in its suburbs . . . a terrifying picture, don't you think?' They laughed.

'Fortunately we were spared that spectacle,' Cedric said, 'or at least I was! Ah yes, good old Forster: so gently mordant, if that's not too contradictory.'

The other agreed. And leaving the subject of mists and governesses, they turned to survey the room and their fellow guests. Cedric was just about to make an approving comment about Dame Margery – her charm and cool competence – when they were joined by Felix. He had clearly managed to requisition a good ration of champagne and his normally sallow cheeks were looking quite pink. 'So who's that geezer over there?' he asked, nodding towards the slightly stooped figure of Geoffrey Hinchcliffe. 'Is he among your old cronies or is he one of the college bods?'

'I wouldn't say a crony, exactly,' Cedric replied, 'but yes, he was here when I was . . . You remember him, don't you, Basil? I think he was on your staircase. Perfectly innocuous.'

The other nodded. 'Perfectly.'

'So what was he studying?' Felix asked. 'He looks like a bank manager.'

The two colleagues exchanged quizzical glances and shrugged. 'Not sure,' Cedric mused, and then smiled: 'For all one knows it could have been astrology! Anyway, it was something like that – intangible and other-worldly, theology perhaps; although Eastern philosophy was popular at the time, maybe that was it.' He paused and added, 'But actually, I have an idea he had a relation who was a bishop – so yes, perhaps it was theology. We never really saw much of him, but when he did emerge he was always perfectly polite – genial, in a sober sort of way.'

'Hmm. There's no change there,' Basil Leason remarked, watching Hinchcliffe toying with a modest sherry and nodding dutifully at whatever it was Aldous Phipps was expounding.

'Well, he's not like his namesake – or almost his namesake – that's for certain,' Felix observed.

'What?'

'Heathcliff in *Wuthering Heights*.'

'But you've never read *Wuthering Heights*,' Cedric protested.

'No, but I've seen the film with Olivier in the role – that's all that's needed.' Felix leered happily.

He also stepped backwards; and in so doing his foot

became entangled with another's – or rather compressed by a heavy shoe. Felix emitted a squeak of pain.

'So sorry,' said Gloria Biggs-Brookby impatiently, 'but I really *must* speak with Professor Dillworthy, it is most essential!'

CHAPTER SEVEN

Following the strenuous evening at the Master's Lodge, the next day Felix felt a mite fragile and had elected to skip breakfast. However, he had assured Cedric, he would be perfectly fit by midday, and to assuage pangs of hunger could manage to meet him at Fitzbillies. Cedric had taken him there on their first afternoon and he had a hankering to return.

And so as predicted, later that morning he had indeed succeeded in reaching Trumpington Street, eager for gossip, strong coffee and rich pastries. Thus, on entering the cafe he was none too pleased to find his friend absent. 'He was supposed to have bagged that corner table,' he grumbled to himself, glaring at its current occupants.

He settled for a suitable alternative and consulted the menu, his eye running down a particularly lush list of cream buns . . . Hmm, if he were to sample one of those, perhaps he should line his stomach with a Welsh rarebit first? They did look rather good! He cogitated, expecting to see Cedric arrive at any moment. The latter's failure to do so prompted his decision: 'I'll have a *buck* rarebit to begin with,' he told the waitress, 'an egg on top blends so exquisitely with the cheese, don't you think?' He beamed. The girl nodded cheerfully and scurried off. Given Cedric's lateness he felt fully justified in starting before him.

Five minutes later Cedric appeared. 'Well, you took your time,' Felix protested, 'I have been here for ages.' (An assertion not entirely accurate.)

'I was talking to George Rawlings,' Cedric explained. 'He's not a happy man; distinctly windy.'

'Really? What has Rawlings got to be windy about? From what I saw of him last night at dinner he seems the soul of complacency.'

'Yes, that is his normal condition, but not at the moment. He is worried that the press will get on to Sir Percival's proclivities and stir up trouble. It could jeopardise the whole project and alienate the benefactors, or some of them at any rate.'

Felix was intrigued. '*Proclivities*? You never mentioned those before. What sort?'

'Oh, the usual kind,' Cedric replied carelessly.

'Boys?'

'No, or at least not often. It was girls: tarts mainly, masses of them; fed his ego and his appetites. In fact' – he paused, giving a sly smile – 'it is quietly rumoured that the bumptious daughter is what might be termed a blunder, i.e. not the product of the pristine wife, but the offspring of an itinerant female acrobat. Personally, I rather doubt that – the lady's physique is not exactly consonant with the litheness of a circus artiste, itinerant or otherwise.'

Felix nodded, visualising the girth and lumbering gait of the person in question. 'No,' he agreed, wincing at the memory of a heavy foot being planted on his polished shoe, 'not the most agile of ladies, I agree. Still, it's a good story.'

'Not for our purposes it isn't,' replied Cedric. 'Rawlings is right. In such circumstances prurient gossip can only damage our cause. The less said about such things the better.'

Not sharing an affinity with the 'cause', Felix pursued the matter. 'But did you know of these "proclivities" when you were his student?' he asked.

'Certainly not. I kept my distance; a most obnoxious chap.'

'And yet you want to be associated with his monument and its surrounding garden?'

His friend gave an impatient sigh. 'As I have already *told* you, tribute is not to be confused with taste. Biggs-Brookby did much for Cambridge and our college, and I for one would like this marked in appropriate fashion.' He sniffed and added, 'Now, since you have chosen to begin without me, it would be courteous if you were to procure a waitress and order me some coffee and toast – with jam.'

Felix smiled inwardly, and with the prominent plaque of distinguished benefactors in mind, rose to go to the counter. 'The professor over there has an insatiable craving for toast and jam,' he said to the girl. And winked.

Returning to the table he gave Cedric a fulsome account of his conversation with Lord Bantry, whom he had cornered while the other was being hectored by Gloria. 'The noble lord and I got on extremely well,' he said airily. 'I considered him most civil, very nice, in fact. He likes flowers.'

'Oh, bound to be nice, then,' Cedric agreed, and smiled. 'And so, have you invited him to your shop?'

Felix replied that the chance had not arisen, while also crisply reminding his friend that what he owned was not so much a shop as a floral emporium.

Duly corrected, Cedric busied himself with his toast and coffee. And then to offset the solecism, he said, 'But in the course of your pleasant conversation, I don't suppose he said anything about the Biggs-Brookby woman, did he? I mean, wasn't it Turner who said they were daggers drawn?'

'Well, now you mention it, yes, he did; and it wasn't a compliment, either,' Felix replied with some relish. 'I noticed him glancing over to Gloria a couple of times while she was talking to you, and then he apologised for being distracted and muttered something to the effect that it would be better for all of us if certain people were dropped off this planet . . . I assumed he wasn't referring to you.' Felix broke off and spluttered into his napkin.

'Let us hope not . . . But do you think he was being serious or simply making a passing jest?'

'Well, I've never seen a jester look quite as grim as that. I can tell you, the noble lord was not amused.'

'That being the case, Finglestone will have lost Bantry's vote should it ever get that far. If he can't stand her, he's hardly likely to favour her candidate.'

'I suppose not. So how did she fare with you? By the look of things, she was going hell for leather.'

'I listened attentively to what she told me of the young man's qualities, nodded, smiled and was my usual amiable self.'

'Huh! Which means she achieved nothing.'

'Precisely – although she may think she did.'

They strolled back to the city centre with Cedric once more assuming his role as guide and mentor.

En route through Peas Hill, Felix had been particularly struck by the ancient and ochre charm of St Edward's Church, tucked away in its 'secret' square. He had not realised that it was a subject so dear to Cedric's heart. In fact, there was little that the professor did not know about its history and architecture – or was not eager to impart. He spoke at length and untiringly. And appreciative though he was, Felix began to feel one could have too much of a good thing.

'I shall have to come back tomorrow and absorb it all quietly,' he murmured. 'As a matter of fact I am still feeling a *teeny* bit fatigued after last night's revels. I think perhaps I shall take a seat in Great St Mary's and be soothed by the organ practice. Not sure if I shall be up to the hurly-burly of the Combination Room this evening, but once you have finished there we might amble over to The Eagle for a late snack and snifter. Anyway I'll see you later and we can discuss plans.'

Cedric was a trifle surprised, not so much by his friend's fatigue (a not unusual condition) as by his partiality for the organ – an instrument, which in all their years of friendship, Felix had never once mentioned. He smelt a rat. *Mad keen to buy some new shirts, I'll be bound!*

* * *

They agreed to meet back at Cedric's room in the early evening. And thus leaving Felix to his music and deciding to skip lunch, Cedric continued on his way back to the college debating his afternoon's programme: a session in the library, he decided, and then a little snooze. What could be better? As he entered the Market Place a station taxi trundled towards him. It slowed further to negotiate a cyclist, and as it did so he caught a glimpse of its occupants. Unmistakeable . . . or at least Gloria Biggs-Brookby was. Her companion was unknown, but from what she had gabbled at the party, he could hazard a guess. A young man, with 'strong, handsome features and remarkably curly dark hair' (yes, those had been the gushing words) sat next to her, the focus of her smiling attention . . . Presumably it was the idolised Finglestone come to stay.

Some hours later and quietly ensconced in his room, it was now Cedric's turn to consult his watch. Where was Felix? Dawdling as usual, he presumed. What had kept him – some slick undergraduate who had stopped to enquire the time and whose enquiry had been answered in fulsome detail? Or (most likely) seduction by an Ede & Ravenscroft tailor's dummy equipped with the latest slit cuffs and thin lapels . . . Ah well, doubtless the dear boy would turn up in his own good time. And in the meanwhile, he could begin the pleasure of rereading Orwell's *Coming Up for Air*. Cedric removed the book from his briefcase and settled comfortably.

He had just finished its opening sentence about the new false teeth, when without a knock, the door was flung open and his friend stood on the threshold, wide-eyed and dishevelled.

'I say,' he cried, 'you'll never guess!'

'Oh really?' Cedric remarked, setting his book aside, 'what won't I guess?'

'*Well*,' Felix began explosively, 'it's been simply *frightful*. I can't tell you what I've been through!'

CHAPTER EIGHT

It was early evening, and given the warm weather the Combination Room was surprisingly full. This, of course, may have had something to do with the bursar's birthday, and in celebration of that fact he had generously ordered some rather fine Montrachet to be sampled and applauded by colleagues. He had also invited a few of the monument sponsors to share in the tasting. However, of this group a notable absentee was Professor Dillworthy.

'Not like him to forget,' murmured Basil Leason to Dame Margery, his guest for the evening. 'Very punctilious is Cedric; and from what I recall he used to be rather keen on the white burgundies.'

The latter smiled and observed that tastes changed, and that perhaps he had been detained by that chic florist person. 'Quite an amusing little chap, and from what

I could make out rather taken by that blue jacket I was wearing last night. He kept casting sideways looks. I think they are sharing the same staircase, so he may have got waylaid. Anyway, I am sure he'll turn up.'

She was perfectly right, for two minutes later the door opened and Cedric stood on the threshold.

'I apologise for my lateness,' he announced to no one in particular, 'but there has been a fatal accident.'

Conversation ceased as people looked up with startled interest. 'Oh dear, anyone we know?' Hinchcliffe enquired mildly.

'In a manner of speaking, yes.' Cedric paused, and then added, 'It's the sculptor.'

There was a shocked silence as they stared at Cedric.

'Hell,' muttered the birthday boy, 'that's torn it.'

The air was rent by a yelp from Aldous Phipps' Norfolk terrier, followed by his master's thin voice. 'I should have thought that rather depends . . .' he murmured.

'Depends? What do you mean, Aldous?' the bursar snapped.

'On which sculptor, of course. You may recall that there are now two candidates – theoretically, at any rate. And based on the popular principle that the good die young, my money's on Finglestone. He is here in Cambridge staying with Gloria.'

'In which case you would lose your money,' Cedric said. 'It is Winston Reid, and he has fallen down his staircase sustaining lethal injuries. His neck is broken and a smashed whisky glass was found close by.'

There was a collective gasp, a sound that generated more yaps from the dog.

'Shut up!' Smithers snapped, attracting a glare from its master.

71

The bursar was the first to comment: 'As I feared,' he groaned. 'And with no one else in the running, that London fellow is bound to put his price up even further.'

Geoffrey Hinchcliffe cleared his throat. 'If you don't mind my saying, I don't think that is *quite* the attitude, do you? Before considering the practical consequences, perhaps we should say a quick prayer for the poor chap.' He put his hands together.

Shocked by the news and discomfited by Hinchcliffe's words, the others duly bowed their heads.

Then with prayer over and heads lifted, there erupted a babble of voices.

'Where did you hear that, then?' Dr Maycock demanded of Cedric.

'And who found him – not you, presumably?' chimed Leason.

'When did it happen?' another voice cried.

'Has the Master been informed?' someone else asked.

Cedric turned to the last speaker. 'He doesn't need to be,' he replied. 'It was he who found him – about an hour ago. He had gone to discuss a small matter concerning the statue – something to do with the positioning of the subject's doctoral hood, I believe. He arrived at Reid's house at five-thirty as arranged, and the door being open went in. The body lay immediately in front of him at the foot of the stairs. Rather a nasty shock, I should think. According to my friend Felix Smythe, he was white to the gills.'

'Felix Smythe?' asked Dame Margery. 'Whatever was he doing there?'

'He happened to be taking an evening stroll and had stopped to admire the roses,' Cedric explained. 'I gather they cascade over the garden wall. Felix was unfamiliar with the type, and noticing that the front door was open decided to make bold enquiry of the owner. He walked up the path, and on reaching the threshold was confronted by the Master's back stooped over the body.'

'So what happened?'

'Sir Richard directed that Felix stay with the body while he went to telephone the police; however, my friend is a little sensitive in such matters and said that he had no intention of staying alone with the deceased, but would undertake to do the telephoning. Fortunately there is a phone box close to the house.'

'But there's a phone in the hall. Why didn't they use that?' Maycock asked.

'I gather it was out of order – had been for days, apparently . . . typical of the Post Office engineers, always diverted by another job.'

'Yes, yes, but are you sure he is *dead*?' Hinchcliffe interrupted, clearly agitated. 'Perhaps Sir Richard and your friend misread the signs – I gather it is not always easy to tell. Who knows, the poor man may have been spared and at this very moment is being resuscitated by our splendid medical staff.'

'You mean having the hooch pumped out of him?' Smithers gave a caustic laugh.

'*No*, Dr Smithers, I do not mean that. It is just possible that—'

'He is perfectly dead,' Cedric assured them. 'It has all been officially verified, and Felix is now resting.'

'So what has Felix Smythe got to rest about?' enquired Aldous Phipps, stroking the now quietened terrier.

'He had a brief glimpse of the body and has been questioned by the police – all rather harrowing.'

'A bit harrowing for old Reid too, I should imagine,' observed Basil Leason quietly.

'Appalling,' Hinchcliffe agreed. 'But I fear drink was always his thing – used to get a bit wobbly of an evening, or so one hears. Presumably he overstepped the mark – literally – and fell headlong.'

'But why was the front door open?' Dame Margery asked.

'Probably expecting someone,' Smithers suggested. 'The Master, one assumes. Or perhaps he was one of those who wilt at the first sign of heat; it's amazing how hysterical people become when faced with a ray of sunshine.'

'Ah well, doubtless Sir Richard will make an official announcement shortly,' Hinchcliffe remarked. 'Meanwhile, I am going to the chapel to say a word for the departed. Anyone coming with me?' He scanned the room hopefully, his eye falling on Cedric.

The latter intimated he must bolster his flagging friend . . . but privately was glad to note that in spite of the hesitant looks, Hinchcliffe had elicited two volunteers. Thus, relieved of sober duty Cedric quit the room to return to Felix and a sustaining Gin and French.

Walking across Main Court, Cedric saw that he was not the only person to have eluded Hinchcliffe and the madding throng. Strolling ahead of him was John Smithers, hands in pockets and whistling jauntily.

Cedric disliked whistling. He also had an irrational dislike of brown plimsolls, especially when worn with a grey suit. Smithers was clad in both. Thus irritated by sound and sight, and having no wish to speak, Cedric slowed his pace hoping that Smithers might branch off towards the library. This the young man did, but not before ceasing the whistling and breaking into a baritone rendition of 'John Brown's Body'. Cedric was startled. Such a display seemed inappropriate in the cloistered surroundings . . . and indeed, given the news they had just received, far from tasteful.

He shrugged. *Perhaps I am getting old*, he thought, *crabby and critical. If I'm not careful I shall become another Aldous Phipps.* He winced and quickened his step to the beckoning refreshment.

As he passed the Master's Lodge he saw the drawing-room window brightly lit and curtains open. Standing prominently in the bay were Sir Richard and Lady Dick, and behind them more obscurely two other figures he did not recognise. They seemed in deep conversation, the Master gesturing dramatically.

As well he might, Cedric thought as he hurried past. After all, no one liked to be faced with a dead body sprawled at their feet when paying a social call. And in this particular case the death held ramifications far beyond the merely personal. With Reid dead, members of the Plot and Monument Committee would need to review their choices; and from what he could make out the field was small. Conventional Edwardian-style statues were losing favour in artistic circles, and those still practising the form far from the first rank – crude derivative hacks, for the most part. In this respect Winston Reid had been rare: blending convention with genuine ability; the result would have been moderately decent. However, with the change of circumstances – and assuming they would discount the third rate – the selectors might now perforce settle on the novelty of the vaunted (if expensive) Finglestone.

Cedric frowned, considering his own position. Should that happen, was he ready to contribute further finances to the project? He pondered. A moot question: whether to see his name up in lights in a Cambridge garden (as dear Felix had so elegantly put it) or to invest more lavishly in savouring the delights of the French Riviera and other such pleasures. On the whole, life being short, he preferred the latter.

Still pondering the problem, he entered the now darkened Middle Court and made his way to his 'own' staircase. Here a thought struck him, and with grim amusement he visualised the reaction of Gloria Biggs-Brookby: veiled triumph, no doubt. Or not so veiled . . . perhaps at this very moment she and her house guest were toasting Lady Luck. With the scene vividly in mind, he mounted the stairs to minister to his fragile friend.

'Ah,' cried Felix, looking far from fragile, 'I was wondering how long you would be. Here, take this. I am one ahead of you.' He thrust a glass of the palest dry martini into Cedric's hand, and the two settled down to review 'events'.

CHAPTER NINE

Events were also being reviewed in the Master's Lodge. The two figures talking with Sir Richard and Lady Dick, as recently glimpsed by Cedric, were in fact interviewing policemen pursuing the earlier enquiries held in the front hall of the dead man's house.

The sergeant called to the discovery was again present, but the young constable had been replaced by Inspector Ted Tilson, currently not enjoying the dry sherry thrust upon him by Lady Dick. The Master's wife had been out when they arrived, but on return and learning of the disturbing event had been quick to adopt the role of gracious hostess. In fact, kindly though she had been, Tilson would have preferred a cup of tea – or anything really rather than this acrid dose of vinegar. He glanced at the sergeant who had assumed his coffin-like teetotal face and declined the offer. Just occasionally Hopkins' moral obstinacy had its benefits, while his own lighter touch calculated to soften the wary (or so he felt), could sometimes backfire.

Casually, he placed the barely touched sherry on a console table, nudging it behind a photograph, and with sympathetic expression listened to what Sir Richard was saying.

'I mean it was such a shock, Inspector,' the Master protested. 'As I told your sergeant at the time, the door was wide open. And when I entered, what was the first thing I saw? Reid collapsed at the bottom of the stairs! At first I assumed he had just tripped and couldn't get up, so I went to give him a hand. "Oh, you're in a poor way, Reid," I said. "Here, let me help you." And then, of course, I saw my mistake and that the man was dead. It was frightful; he was all twisted and absolutely saturated in whisky. My God, I can smell it now! And then—'

At that moment the Master broke off, distracted by a sudden moan from his wife. Anthea had sat down on the sofa, a hand over her face. 'Do I really need to listen to these details?' she murmured. 'I'm afraid I am not terribly good at this; in fact, I feel a bit faint. Does anyone mind if I go and lie down?'

'Of course not, Lady Dick,' Tilson said gallantly. 'It's not as if you are a material witness, it's only your husband's account we need. You are like my wife – she can't abide dead bodies either. You just run along now and rest.' He beamed a paternal smile, inwardly relieved. No more sherry, thank God.

He turned back to Dick. 'Very sensitive, the ladies. Now sir, you were saying . . .'

* * *

78

Half an hour later as they walked back through the centre of Cambridge to the police station in St Andrew's Street, Sergeant Hopkins made the observation that he could do with a good cup of tea and hoped that young Spriggs hadn't forgotten to order more sugar.

Tilson agreed. 'Yes, I'd have asked the lady myself, except she seemed keen on pushing the sherry. Besides, it's bound to have been that lapsang thingamy or whatever they call it. Probably worse than the sherry.' They strolled on, reflecting upon the strange preferences of Cambridge academics.

Then with the anomaly shelved, they returned to the sculptor's death. 'Pretty clear cut, I should say,' Hopkins remarked, 'what you might call self-evident: old, tight as a tick, lost his footing, bashed his head and went out like a light.' He glanced at Tilson for confirmation.

'Well, providing the laboratory chaps are happy, I should say you are right. Sir Richard Dick's account seemed genuine enough. Plausible, at any rate. Mind you,' Tilson added, 'for all his concern, I couldn't help sensing there was something else on his mind. It was as if it wasn't so much Reid's *death* that was disturbing him, so much as his loss.'

Hopkins gave his superior a puzzled look. 'You've got me there, I'm afraid. What's the difference?'

The inspector grinned. 'Oh, it's very subtle, Hopkins, a fine nuance – a nuance that has clearly escaped you.'

'Oh yes? Can't wait to hear.'

'Well, obviously the chap was ruffled by the physical shock of finding him like that and the sheer unexpectedness of him being dead. But I got the impression that he wasn't just shocked but *bothered*. Almost as if by Reid dying something had gone amiss, that something important had been lost beyond the man himself.'

'You mean that he had had a function that could no longer be used?'

Tilson regarded Hopkins in some surprise. 'Yes, yes, I think that's exactly what I do mean. Clever of you to spot it too.'

'Oh, I didn't spot anything,' Hopkins replied airily, 'but I can tell you what the function was. Winston Reid was the bloke who Sir Richard Dick was going to hire to do the statue of the Biggs-Brookby fellow. The thing is going to be erected on that bit of scrubland the university is after. My aunt knows Alderman Cuff's wife and says she's always rambling on about it. With Reid dead there are two consequences: a) they won't have a sculptor for their project, and b) it will make it more difficult for the college to get its hands on that patch of land. Less justification, you see.'

Inspector Tilson frowned, slightly put out by his sergeant's insider knowledge, and for once feeling upstaged. 'Ah,' he said impassively, 'yes, of course; that would be it.' Then after a brief silence a thought struck him. 'And so you see, Hopkins,' he continued firmly, 'with that being the case, and despite his being seen bending over the body, I think we can safely exclude Sir Richard from any further enquiries. After all, the man would hardly want to dispose of the linchpin to all his plans. A somewhat retrograde step, I should say!' He gave a hearty laugh. 'Oh yes, I think you're right: accidental death – that'll be the coroner's verdict.'

They nodded in mutual agreement. And as they neared the police station Tilson said, 'So with luck that's one more case we can tick off the list . . . Now, what about that cup of tea you were chuntering on about? Once we get the green light from the forensics the thing can be wound up, and the only thing left will be to write the report for the chief inspector. You'll like doing that.'

The grapevine having already twirled into action, the next morning Rosy too was discussing the sculptor's death – not on the streets of Cambridge, but upon the sedate lawns of Newnham College.

It was a beautiful day, and a few of the circle had taken the opportunity to sit out by the sunken garden and admire the herbaceous borders . . . Except that it wasn't really the summer flora that was claiming their attention, but rather the recent news.

'Oh yes, I've had it from the horse's mouth,' Betty Withers confided, 'the Biggs-Brookby woman herself. She was racing along King's Parade – well, pounding briskly, I suppose – and nearly knocked me over. I was just steadying myself, when she gripped my arm and cried: "Frightful, frightful! He's fallen down the stairs!" When I asked if she meant her cat, she called me a fool and said it was the sculptor Winston Reid. "How is he?" I said. "He isn't," she said. "He's *dead*." Apparently she had just heard the news from Trinity's porter who had got it from someone else. I was about to ask for details, but she pushed me aside declaring it was all a terrible shock and rushed on.'

Betty paused reflectively, before adding, 'Actually, now I come to think of it, she sounded not so much shocked as excited – but then some people are like that: they get a morbid rush of adrenalin whenever a sudden death is announced.'

Rosy nodded in deference to Betty's psychiatric expertise, but privately suspected that it might not have been death in general that had caused Gloria's excitement, rather the death of this particular victim. She recalled some of the woman's words at the Master's soirée: 'He's such a boring old codger and has been around for far too long; and given his alcohol intake I'm surprised he can see the bronze! What Daddy needs is someone dynamic, like young Finglestone. Now he *would* do him justice!' What else had she said? Something about it being time Reid packed up his toolkit and took a long holiday . . . In which case, Rosy reflected, he had certainly given himself the trip of a lifetime. She flinched, embarrassed by her own flippancy – but at least the thought had been silent. Instead she asked if he had left a wife.

Betty shrugged. 'There was never one in evidence, not that that means anything. Spouses are not always apparent: take Mr Rochester's, for instance – though whether Reid had an attic, I couldn't say. But a studio would do, I suppose.' She gave a faint smile and added, 'But seriously, I think he did live alone – in fact, I seem to remember someone saying he considered wives inimical to the Muse.'

'The converse might also be true,' Rosy remarked lightly. 'But at least that's one less grief. What bad luck to be snuffed out like that at sixty-five or so. It's a bit soon.'

'"Death hath ten thousand doors,"' quoted Mary Bradshaw darkly, adding, 'and moments too . . . all the more reason to *carpe diem*. Let's have a drink, it's not too early.'

They decided that was an excellent idea and, gathering their things, set off for a walk into the city centre and The Eagle.

* * *

Reid's death was also the chief topic in the Combination Room of the older college, where Cedric and Basil Leason were enjoying the company of Professor Turner and Vernon Carter, one of the younger dons.

'Well, of course, he was always clumsy,' Professor Turner said, 'and for a sculptor surprisingly cack-handed, though oddly enough that didn't seem to affect his actual work. Still, I bet that's what contributed to his fall – probably missed the banister.'

'What made him miss the banister,' Carter interrupted, 'was not lack of dexterity, merely a surfeit of drink. There was a lot of that going on recently. He was growing very peculiar too.'

'Peculiar? In what way?' Leason asked.

'He would take irrational dislikes to people.'

'Oh, that's nothing.' Cedric laughed. 'I gather from Rosy Gilchrist that her boss at the British Museum is like that much of the time, particularly if he has spent a gruelling time with the trustees. He says that a good spate of vitriol soothes his nerves – that and a shot of brandy.'

'Perhaps, but I doubt if he follows them about.'

Cedric blinked. 'Follows them about? Er, no, I don't think so. Whatever do you mean?'

'It was something Reid had developed recently. Odd, really: lurking in doorways at night – a bit like Orson Welles in *The Third Man* – and then suddenly emerging to give his quarry a gracious smile and broad wink. If that had been all, it would hardly have mattered, but it was when he started to pad along behind you that things got a bit unnerving.' Carter turned to Turner: 'Do you remember when he tried it on with Gloria Biggs-Brookby?'

'Do I not! He had picked the wrong one there,' the

latter laughed. 'She had been at some meeting at King's, and as it was a mild night she had decided to walk back to her house in Madingley Road instead of cadging a lift. Reid emerged from the shadows, executed a deep bow and suggested that he escort her back home. Being Gloria, she declined his invitation, saying that she was perfectly capable of making her own way and that, besides, she was in no mood for social chit-chat. It was the sort of rebuff that would have made most people scuttle away. But not Reid. I gather that he stuck to her like a leech, pacing himself at about ten yards behind. After a bit Gloria stopped in her tracks and rounded on him. According to my cousin, who had witnessed the whole incident from the other side of the road, she bellowed out that in her opinion he was short of multiple screws, his sculpting as dead as the dodo and he would get the college job over her dead body. She concluded by calling him a lisping bastard, if you please!'

'Did he lisp?' Cedric asked.

'What? Oh yes, a bit, I think. Anyway, apparently that was too much for Reid, who wisely slunk back into the shadows from whence he had come.'

There was general laughter. 'Poor old boy,' Leason said, 'lost his marbles, his teeth and his footing!'

'Ah, but perhaps Gloria bumped him off,' said Carter with relish, 'piqued at being pestered and determined to oust him in favour of Finglestone.'

'That sounds a bit excessive, even for Gloria,' Turner remarked. 'Mind you,' he smiled, 'Aldous Phipps has been dropping dark hints that he was murdered, though I don't think he has anyone particular in mind – though knowing Phipps, he's bound to pin it on somebody before too long.'

'Huh! Wishful thinking,' Carter exclaimed. 'Aldous Phipps has murder on the brain – it's all those Greek tragedies he reads, those and the Mickey Spillane thrillers. They fuel that waspish imagination.'

CHAPTER TEN

'So with the sculptor dead, what's the college going to do?' Felix asked Cedric. 'I wonder if they'll scrap the whole thing; at least that should save you all a bit of money. I bet the others are already making plans on how to spend their windfall.' He grinned.

Cedric did not grin. After remarking that Felix had a singularly mercenary mind, he explained that the essential thing was the procurement of the plot itself, and that even without a statue it could doubtless be put to some good use.

'Hmm. Pity about the plaque, though.'

'What do you mean?'

'Well, without a statue, presumably there won't be a list of benefactors displayed.'

'That doesn't necessarily follow,' Cedric replied rather stiffly. 'Besides, having had the dubious pleasure of being canvassed by Gloria B-B about this Finglestone character as an alternative to Reid, it is quite obvious that she certainly won't let the thing rest. In fact, Reid's death can only be a spur: you'll see, she'll be sticking to the Master like a leech.'

Felix pulled a face. 'Poor Master.'

'Exactly. Anyway, doubtless we shall hear something shortly. Meanwhile, I propose that today I give you a conducted tour of a couple of the other colleges. Pembroke is particularly fine and so is St John's. But my own favourite is—'

'As a matter of fact I am rather busy,' Felix explained. 'I am going off to buy a hat. These things can't be done in a hurry.'

Cedric groaned. 'I trust it won't be another panama; it caused enough trouble last time.' He closed his eyes, recalling their Suffolk sojourn.

'It will not be a panama,' Felix said stiffly. 'It will be—'

'A tasselled mortar board?'

'Oh, very funny, I'm sure.'

'Sorry – I just thought academia might be taking a grip on you.'

Felix ignored the comment and confided that he had a hankering for a homburg. 'Now that I am approaching forty-eight and a personal friend of the Queen Mother, I think a little *gravitas* might be in order, don't you? Sir Anthony always used to look very elegant in his.'

While acknowledging the matter of age, Cedric was less sure about the royal friendship, although admittedly Her Majesty was very appreciative of Felix's flower arranging. However, out loud he said: 'Oh, indeed. But, of course, you don't *quite* have Anthony Eden's height; I wonder if perhaps—'

Felix sniffed. 'It is bearing, not height, that counts.'

The matter was clearly closed, and Felix departed to do his shopping.

Left to his own devices, Cedric decided to take a stroll along the Cam. As an undergraduate he had never been a punter, still less an oarsman, but he had always liked the sight of the meandering river with its trees and waterfowl, the elegance of the Backs and the sense of rural peace amid ancient stones. Thus, whenever he visited his alma mater he made a point of retracing the amblings of his youth.

He had pocketed a copy of Trollope, hoping to find a convenient spot where he could enjoy the genteel joustings of Archdeacon Grantly and his bishop. But the hope was not fulfilled, for the first suitable bench was occupied; and as he made to pass, a reedy voice hailed him.

'Ah, Professor Dillworthy, if I am not mistaken. Revisiting old haunts, I presume.' Aldous Phipps' spiky hand beckoned him over. 'Bide awhile and tell me your news.'

Having already recounted his recent travels and the success of his Cappadocia book during their encounter at the Master's soirée, Cedric was at a slight loss. What more did the old fellow want to hear? Presumably he had forgotten their earlier talk.

He sat down next to Phipps and, clearing his throat, tried to think of a new theme. He slid his hand into his jacket pocket. 'I bought a fresh edition of this the other day,' he said brightly. 'They have just produced the whole series in a sort of condensed form – same size print, but smaller pages. Rather smart and so handy for carrying.'

Phipps glanced at the copy of *Barchester Towers* in Cedric's hand. 'Ah yes, Trollope,' he said, 'very droll.

Personally, I prefer Mickey Spillane – although they *tell* me that the Marquis de Sade is as good as any . . .' His voice faded as he watched a swooping heron.

Cedric was a trifle startled, not sure how serious he was being. 'Oh well,' he observed vaguely, 'tastes differ, of course.'

'Ah, *taste*,' Phipps snorted, 'a waning commodity if you ask me – or it certainly is in Cambridge. I can't tell you how boorish some of our young dons are, worse than the undergraduates!' He frowned.

Clearly as a topic of conversation *Barchester* wasn't going to work. Cedric put the book aside and tried another tack. 'It's, uhm, tragic about Winston Reid,' he ventured. 'I mean, apart from anything else what a waste of a good craftsman. Death by misadventure one hears – a drop too much of the hard stuff, apparently. And from what my friend noticed, those stairs are terribly steep.' He sighed. 'Easily done, I fear.'

Unlike the matter of taste, this elicited nothing. Phipps was unresponsive, his eye still seemingly drawn by the heron. Cedric was just wondering what else he should say to oil the wheels, when with a dry cough the elderly Fellow remarked: 'A drop too much of the hard stuff, you say. What sort of "hard stuff", may I enquire?'

'What sort? . . . Well, er, whisky. That's what was reported. A smashed glass was found next to him.'

'Oh *yes*, but what type? That's what I should like to know.' Phipps turned and regarded Cedric intently.

The latter was bemused and mildly irritated. Why should he be quizzed with such pedantry? 'Well, I really don't know,' he replied. 'One of the usual brands, presumably – Bell's, Johnnie Walker or some such.'

'Hmm.' Phipps continued to stare silently at the river,

while Cedric considered how he could politely take his leave.

'So, he had been drinking Scotch, had he?' Phipps murmured eventually.

'*Yes*,' said Cedric trying to keep the impatience from his voice, 'the press report mentioned a half-empty bottle of Scotch uncorked on his drinks cabinet. The missing half he had partly imbibed and partly spilt on his shirtfront.'

'I find that hard to believe,' the other replied. He paused, and then added: 'In my experience, Reid couldn't abide the stuff. I once made the mistake of taking him a rather expensive bottle of Talisker. He had somehow contrived to beat me at Scrabble and I thought the novelty should be celebrated. Alas, he was far from grateful, quite rude in fact – the artist in him, I suppose.' Phipps looked distinctly peeved at the memory, before adding: 'You see *his* tipple was Irish whiskey, not Scotch at all. He had a fetish of not drinking the stuff and made a great to-do about the superiority of the Hibernian – what you might call a case of Jock bad, Paddy good!' He gave a croaking laugh, pleased at his little quip.

Cedric shrugged and said something about people not always keeping to their principles. 'Perhaps he had run out – a matter of necessity: any spirit in a storm, as it were.'

His companion shook his head. 'I doubt it. Winston Reid was not a good adaptor, too rigid – a trait reflected in his sculpting, some would say. No, if he couldn't get his Jameson's or Bushmills he would have opted for port. His mind wasn't of the most flexible, hence my many victories at Scrabble.' Phipps gave a thin smile. He seemed about to continue, but stalled, his attention caught by a passing punt. 'What extraordinary behaviour,' he exclaimed, 'and who are they waving at? Not to us, surely?'

Cedric followed the direction of his gaze to where a punt was eddying in choppy circles, and from where there wafted faint hoots of laughter. The figure standing seemed to have an uncertain grip both of his pole and his balance, while his seated companion – crouched, really – continued waving wildly.

'It looks as if they're making for the bank,' Cedric remarked.

'A forlorn hope,' said Phipps dryly, 'it is bound to tip. It's the visitors, they get so excited. Haven't a clue how to handle things . . . Ah well, it's time we were off.' He got up. 'Now come along, Popsie.'

In a flash the punt and its manoeuvres vanished from Cedric's mind. He stared in consternation at Aldous Phipps . . . and then felt a pang of grateful relief as the latter stooped and dragged from under the seat the concealed Norfolk. 'She's an idle little thing,' the owner grumbled. 'Goes fast to sleep the moment I sit down. Any other dog would want to lark about.'

Bidding goodbye to Cedric, he gave the creature a gentle prod with his toecap, and the pair trotted off across the meadow. Picking up his book, Cedric was also poised to leave (diversion quite enough for one morning), but happened to glance back at the river. The punt was still there, both occupants now gesturing frantically towards the landing stage some yards further downstream. 'Oh really.' He sighed. 'I should have known!'

With an exasperated scowl he waved an acknowledgement to Felix and Rosy, and then made his way to where they were pointing.

'I thought you were after a homburg,' he enquired brusquely of Felix as he met them off the quay. 'Where is it? Dropped in the Cam, no doubt, when you were arsing about.'

'Not arsing, but drowning,' Felix giggled, giving the poet a mental bow. 'And as for the hat, clearly Cambridge doesn't run to homburgs; they're insufficiently Fabian, I daresay. I'll wait till we get back to London: Lock's are bound to stock dozens.'

'I am amazed at my powers of persuasion.' Rosy laughed. 'I bumped into Felix in Petty Cury and cajoled him into coming on the river. It was fairly all right till we saw you, Cedric, and then everything suddenly went wrong; we seemed to lose our bearings.'

'Yes, he can have that effect,' Felix remarked. And turning to his friend enquired who he had been with.

Cedric explained that his companion had been the elderly Professor Phipps and that he had spent the last half-hour in stilted conversation with the old boy when he would rather have been on his own. 'One is rather fatigued and could do with sustenance,' he announced.

They retired to The Anchor in Silver Street and ordered the essentials.

'So what had Professor Phipps got to say?' Rosy asked Cedric as they sat round a table in the window. 'Ticking you off about your lack of Greek? He was certainly doing that with me when we met at Sir Richard's party. I felt as if I was eighteen again.'

'Unlike you, Rosy Gilchrist, I have quite a substantial grasp of Greek, so I escaped that particular assault. But since you ask, I did undergo a rather peculiar interrogation. It revolved around Winston Reid's preferred style of whisky. He seemed obsessed by it.'

'Who did?' Felix asked. 'You mean Reid?'

'In one way, yes – or so I gathered. But it was Phipps I actually meant. He had a bee in his bonnet about Reid's preference for the Irish type. He seemed to think this held some interest, but I can't for the life of me see what.' Cedric proceeded to recount the gist of what Phipps had been saying.

When he had finished Felix winked at Rosy, remarking that elderly professors could be like that. 'Oh yes,' he said firmly, 'it's a well-known fact: they develop a sort of tunnel vision and get hung up on small details. It generally shows itself around seventy – in which case our friend here has another ten years.'

'Eleven, if you don't mind,' said Cedric dryly. 'Meanwhile, to sustain my fading faculties, I shall require a large brandy. Perhaps you would be so good as to . . .'

On her way back to Newnham, Rosy reviewed her morning and the session on the river with Felix. It had been pleasant enough, but hardly peaceful. She recalled that her earlier experiences of punting on the Cam had verged on the idyllic – gliding gently on languid waters and lazily soothed by silence and a dappled sun . . . Briefly she indulged the reverie and then smiled wryly, knowing that time lends enchantment and nostalgia beguiles. Besides, what her current trip may have lacked in sensuous languor it had certainly gained in perilous gaiety: a sort of hydro dodgems ride!

As she walked on, images of that ride brought her mind back to Cedric sitting close to the bank with Aldous Phipps. How odd for the old man to have gabbled on about Reid and his tastes in alcohol. Had it simply been idle reminiscence, or had he been making some point, which Cedric, eager to be left alone, had failed to grasp?

She reflected. So what exactly had Cedric been telling

them? That Phipps had been insistent about Winston Reid's penchant for Irish whiskey and his distaste for Scotch? Yes, it had been something like that. Still, if that were the case, was it of interest? Hardly. She was about to dismiss the matter when she stopped abruptly, causing the person behind to sidestep smartly.

Rosy hesitated mid-pavement . . . If Aldous Phipps was right about Reid's habits, wasn't it indeed strange that the press reports had all alluded to that bottle of Scotch on his drinks cabinet? They had made a great drama of his being soaked in the stuff when found spreadeagled at the base of the stairs . . . Yes, surely it did seem pretty odd for him to have been slurping the one when he had so preferred the other. Evidently Aldous Phipps had thought so.

She walked on briskly, unimpressed by her own reasoning. Why should it be so odd? After all, few people were entirely consistent in their behaviour, most being subject to whim or mood; her wayward boss Dr Stanley being a case in point! Perhaps poor Reid had had an inexplicable urge to renege, to turn quisling and retest his responses to the long-spurned Johnnie Walker. If so, there had certainly been a response all right! Poor chap, what a way to go: pickled in whisky, a missed step, headlong fall – and crash, out he went. Still, she mused, there were certainly worse and more protracted ends, but the sheer shock must have been appalling.

Rosy winced and turned her mind to pleasanter things: her forthcoming reconnaissance of the Fitzwilliam and its fabulous collections. One could certainly be charged with more onerous missions. Her mind went back to her undergraduate days and the pleasurable hours she had spent in the building, gawping at the paintings and gathering material for her dissertation.

It had been a haven of peace and visual delight. Surely to goodness they weren't really going to revamp it into some sort of theme park: slick, glitzy and 'relevant' to popular taste, as Dr Stanley had darkly predicted?

And what about that Lady Chatterley exhibition he had mentioned? Entertaining in its own way no doubt, but a bit of wasted space at the Fitzwilliam, surely. And if indeed it was scheduled, what other contemporary legal cases might they have in store for the 'questing' public? Perhaps Eastbourne's Bodkin Adams enquiry would be next. Doubtless they could slip it in between the mediaeval manuscripts and the Dutch paintings, with flattering portraits of the doctor and less flattering ones of his elderly patients. And what about a waxwork mock-up of the Ruth Ellis trial – a veritable showstopper. Rosy grinned. *Oh honestly*, she thought, *my mind. It's becoming wild and lurid just like Dr Stanley's!*

But then more seriously she thought about the television pundit Peregrine Purblow, whose lectures she had been instructed to attend. To put it mildly, Stanley had been scathing, but with luck the chap might be interesting with some valuable ideas. She certainly hoped so. After all, who wanted to sit through hours of claptrap?

Still, Rosy decided, it was time she started to think seriously about her task. The museum was closed the next day, but after that she really would push on with things. Knowing her boss, he would probably expect a meticulous list of her findings. Perhaps she should buy a special notebook for the purpose (on expenses, naturally) and mark it *Urgent: Top Secret*.

CHAPTER ELEVEN

As planned, a couple of days later Rosy set out on her mission with notebook purchased (unlabelled) and pencil poised. She mounted the museum's steps and walked through the doors a little apprehensively, fearful it might already have undergone some mighty transformation.

Oh, of course it hadn't. It was exactly as it had always been: elegant, august, seductively gracious. She paused in the great hallway, absorbing the hushed stillness and sense of history. Yes, since she had last been there time had stood still . . . and a good thing too!

Automatically, she began to stroll around – not inspecting but revelling, the notebook staying firmly tucked within her handbag. At that relatively early hour few visitors were about and she could revisit her favourite areas, wandering freely without distraction. The first port of call was the collection of Turner watercolours, followed by the bronzes, and then those intriguing clocks, and then . . .

Rosy checked her watch. Past midday and she hadn't even begun her enquiry! It was time for critical assessments, she told herself sternly – and promptly sat down on a nearby bench. The hours went quickly when you were enjoying yourself, but so did physical stamina. She felt quite worn out. She could also do with a cup of coffee and a fortifying sandwich. Wasn't there a cafe of sorts? She had an idea it had been on the first floor – or had it been the basement? An attendant was bound to know.

She was about to move, when someone sat down beside her and gave a faint cough. 'Standing is often more tiring than walking, wouldn't you say, Miss Gilchrist?'

Rosy looked up, startled, and was confronted by a pale face, vaguely familiar.

'You may recall we exchanged a few words at the Master's party the other evening,' Geoffrey Hinchcliffe said politely, proffering his hand. 'Or at least I recall; you, of course, may not,' he added, smiling apologetically.

Rosy recalled the exchange perfectly well – although they hadn't said much, having been interrupted by the Master's wife who had whisked him off to be introduced to Gloria. Clearly he had survived the ordeal. Or perhaps for him it had been a pleasure? She rather doubted this: he did not strike her as being especially robust.

'Of course I remember you,' she said firmly, 'you were telling me about your passion for Schubert.'

'I wouldn't say passion, exactly,' he murmured, 'but I do find his music most soothing – the lieder, I mean. Such exquisite melodies. And when sung by that young Dieskau, or indeed a tenor such as Pears, it is a veritable treat . . .' He gazed pensively into the distance as if hearing their voices.

Rosy was about to make some observation on the same theme, but before she had the chance, he said, 'That is one of the things so gratifying about being in Cambridge and that makes one want to stay. Wherever you go there is *euphony*: musical harmonies in college, hall and church. Naturally, London has its venues, but they are more widespread and less intimate. Whereas here . . . well, the place is a true balm to the soul!'

Rosy saw his point, although perhaps not quite sharing his evident rapture.

'It is a lovely city,' she agreed, 'and as you say, has so much to offer. I think we have all enjoyed coming back here – which makes it so sad that things have been a bit overshadowed by that poor Mr Reid's death. A shock for everyone, but I imagine especially for those of you involved in the sculpture project.'

Hinchcliffe nodded. 'Yes, we were on the point of celebrating his commission. It was quite a blow. And I doubt if that Monty Finglestone would have stood much of a chance had he still been here – although one or two people seem to favour him. As it is things are hanging in limbo, for the moment at any rate. It's conceivable that the whole project will be cancelled, but I rather doubt it. I think the powers that be will want to press on.'

'So where does that leave the sponsors? Presumably they'll go home and await developments.'

'Most will. But one or two, such as Lord Bantry, and I think George Rawlings, live locally so will have their ear to the ground. And I gather Dame Margery has some lecturing commitment at Girton.'

'Yes, she has. And you?'

'Ah, I am one of the stayers,' Hinchcliffe said with a smile. 'One doesn't often get up to Cambridge and it is a wonderful chance to have an intensive dose of the music. Although, as a matter of fact I have a rather less indulgent reason for staying on: I am writing a little monograph on East Anglian saints for our local church society, and as a Cambridge alumnus both Trinity and Emmanuel have kindly allowed me access to their libraries. So *that's* where I shall be beavering for the next fortnight. It will provide me with much pleasure – and no doubt relief for my dear sister. She keeps house for the two of us in London, and when I am away I suspect she makes wild whoopee!'

Hinchcliffe laughed. As did Rosy. Yes, it was difficult to envisage the mild and decorous Hinchcliffe having a riotous sister.

After a few more pleasantries and with the thought of coffee having been replaced by the thought of a stronger libation, Rosy stood up and made her excuses to leave. Hinchcliffe also rose and, shaking her hand, said he hoped they would meet again. 'With you being a friend of my old colleague Professor Dillworthy, I trust we shall.' He gave a diffident smile.

Rosy walked down the museum steps debating where to have lunch. She was torn between The Eagle and the Free Press; both were congenial. She liked the latter's intimacy, but the other was nearer, and it had nooks and corners where one could read a book or wrestle with a crossword undisturbed. In fact, she bought a copy of *The Times* for just that purpose, and entering The Eagle ordered a thick ham sandwich, pickled onions and a half-pint of bitter. She found an alcove table, and after turning to the newspaper's inside page to scan the day's headlines, settled down to pore over clues.

Alas, the clues proved particularly fiendish, but it was pleasant nevertheless seated quietly sipping her drink amidst the low hum of others' conversation . . . what her busy mother would have called 'disgracefully restful'. Rosy gave a wry smile, being suddenly reminded of the sound of that voice long stilled by the Blitz, and for a moment she was pensive . . . And then inwardly she shrugged. Ah well, such hauntings were inevitable – the loved and the dead, they never really left you. It was a blessing. Briskly, and as her mother might have done, she shook off the past and applied herself to the present practicalities of sandwich and puzzle.

Engrossed in the latter, she was at first unaware of the two men who had seated themselves in the adjacent alcove. But their voices, though subdued, did eventually reach her. She glanced up and recognised the broad features of Lord Bantry: the man who at the Master's soirée had gallantly applauded her shoes and most ungallantly mocked the tiresome Gloria. His companion was Dr Maycock, the recipient of Gloria's own scathing mockery. Judging from the aroma wafting in her direction, they were tucking into one of The Eagle's famously robust casseroles. She returned to the conundrums.

Concentration was broken by a sudden rumble of laughter from Lord Bantry and the scraping of a match as he lit a cheroot. But then in a far from jovial tone could be heard Maycock's voice: 'I am glad you think it's so funny; personally I think it's a crying disgrace. Reid may have been an unsavoury blighter, but at least he was *ours*: our choice. As it is, we are now expected to appoint some callow unknown at the behest of a total outsider. Talk about the power of the barbarian. It's insufferable!'

(Rosy, who had been vainly seeking inspiration from the airmen's hieroglyphics on the ceiling, lowered her head and duly wrote in the word BARBARIC and thus completed the puzzle's left-hand corner. If she kept her ears pricked, perhaps more solutions might come her way!)

'You are right. Although I believe Finglestone is quite well regarded by some in London; and as for Gloria, I suppose it *could* be argued that being our subject's offspring, she isn't exactly an outsider – though she is certainly barbarous.' There was the sound of a faint chuckle from Bantry.

'She is an outsider to the college, let alone its executive.' Maycock snapped. 'You'll see, we shall have the WI putting its oar in next! Frankly, Arthur, you seem to be taking a very calm view of things. I thought you couldn't stand the woman.'

There was a silence. And then Rosy heard the other say in a tone now empty of humour. 'I can't. And I agree: the interference is intolerable. And what's more, if she can impose her will in this issue, where will it end?'

'And I'll tell you something,' the other said, 'rumour has it that she is now angling to have a corner in the library specially dedicated to her father's books and manuscripts.'

'What, the public library?'

'No. *Ours.*'

There followed a silence sufficiently long enough for Rosy to complete another clue. CONSTERNATION, she inserted.

'Outrageous!' Maycock finally exploded. 'That man's stuff can be shelved piecemeal like anyone else's. She has no right to—'

'Perhaps not a right, but that woman is unscrupulous. It wouldn't surprise me if she doesn't try to nobble Cuff and get him to climb down over the plot purchase. If she does that, she will have a lever on us and the Master will think he owes her one.'

'Ridiculous,' Maycock growled. 'That woman must be blocked.' His usually bluff tone had taken on a hard edge. 'Dick tries his best, of course, but there's a weakness there, you know, and when push comes to shove he'll yield.'

'Then we must ensure that it doesn't reach that point, mustn't we?' Bantry replied quietly.

He said something else, but the words were lost in a small commotion as someone stumbled past the tables manoeuvring a massive Great Dane, and Maycock's response was largely lost except for a final snippet: '. . . ah well, put like that, but, yes, there are always ways and means – and accidents, of course. Take Reid, for example!' This time it was he who laughed, and with a scraping of chairs they got up to go.

Rosy watched as they made their way towards the door. At that moment the Great Dane, quietly recumbent at its owner's feet, chose to give a loud woof. Bantry glanced round, smiled at the dog, and then saw Rosy. He stopped and retraced his slightly limping footsteps.

'Ah, Little Red Shoes, if I'm not mistaken. What a charming coincidence. Had we known you were just behind us we would have invited you to our table – though I fear that listening to our ramblings mightn't have been the most uplifting experience.' He looked at her intently and then down at the half-finished crossword. 'As it is, I trust our voices didn't disturb the Muse; these wooden screens aren't exactly sound barriers, are they?'

Rosy smiled politely, gently seething at being addressed as Little Red Shoes, and shook her head. 'Oh no, the Muse has been most dutiful for once,' she lied, 'deaf to the world!'

'Delighted to hear that,' he said smoothly. He nodded towards Maycock hovering by the door: 'Always impatient, that one. I must be off – can't keep the good doctor waiting. Enjoy your stay.' He gave a mock salute and turned to join his companion.

After they had gone, Rosy put *The Times* aside and stared at the Great Dane. *Really, these chaps don't half enjoy putting the knife in,* she mused. *Old Gloria had better watch it!* But then reflecting on her own encounter with the lady she guessed the woman could weather most things, including caustic attacks from irate scholars. And thinking of the latter, she wondered if she should telephone her boss with a report on the Fitzwilliam – except, of course, she had so far gleaned nothing, not having made any attempt. Ah well, one couldn't be assertive and organised all the time. She would return the next day – or the day after – full of busy enquiry, and as Stanley had directed pick the brains of the curator. Meanwhile, the sunshine beckoned. She would take a leisurely stroll down to Clare Bridge, loll on the balustrade and watch the ducks and punters . . .

Outside in Bene't Street, Rosy's mind returned briefly to her recent neighbours. She grimaced: Little Red Shoes indeed!

CHAPTER TWELVE

Dr John Smithers was a worried man. Very worried. They were right, he brooded: one should never run two horses at the same time; there was bound to be trouble. And in this case double trouble, if the newer horse happened to be the Master's wife.

It was horribly ironic. After that abortive exchange on the telephone, Reid's death had seemed a godsend, and he had savoured the prospect of continuing the Anthea thing free from anxiety and with renewed vigour. Of course, there was still the hovering shadow of Sir Richard, but with Reid dead that was far less of a threat – although, if anything, the shadow had added a certain frisson to matters. (His mouth twitched with wry satisfaction.) But *now* with this latest business anything could go wrong, and how! When Anthea Dick had made her overture to him a couple of months back he had been surprised and amused; flattered, of course, and then intrigued. Curiosity: that had done it – a notorious goad in such matters.

Smithers smiled ruefully, trusting that he had no feline traits, and then stared disconsolately out of the window cursing his luck. He heaved a sigh. Yes, recently things had been proceeding nicely, *very* nicely . . . and then, out of the blue, this absurdity. What a fool she had been! She had brought the whole thing on herself. But why confide in him, for heaven's sake? The less he knew about it the better. After all, that's what *spouses* were for, wasn't it? To bear the brunt of their partner's stupidity. It was hardly the lover's role.

He scowled and admitted that in this particular case unburdening herself to Sir Richard would hardly have been wise – a divulgence inviting all manner of awkward questions. Still, that didn't mean she should have used himself as an alternative confidant; an alternative that potentially could land him in the sodding soup. The last thing he wanted was to become involved, however loosely, in a matter of that kind – far too close for comfort! Well, as his grandmother used to say: that would learn him! Perhaps he ought to become a monk: pursuing his scholarly researches in restful solitude far from the temptation of women, the snares of the world and other people's blunders.

Smithers ground out his cigarette and lit another, seeing its smoke wafting lazily from some refectory fire on Mount Athos. For a few seconds the reverie absorbed him. And then the chapel bell in the Main Court boomed, and with a jolt he was returned to the present and bloody Anthea.

Meanwhile – specifically in the bathroom of the Master's Lodge – bloody Anthea was also cursing her luck and dreaming of being elsewhere. She stretched a toe to turn on the hot tap and stroked a willowy arm with the flannel. She wouldn't mind *where* elsewhere, except not here in Cambridge amid all these tedious problems . . . although actually, it had to said, most problems were dealt with easily enough. But not this one. Certainly not this one! She closed her eyes, and for the umpteenth time thought of John Smithers and mildly hated him.

Useless. He had been utterly useless. Having a lover was all very fine and exciting, but one did rather expect an *ally* when times got tough, somebody to listen sympathetically and reassure one that all would be well . . . But what had he said when she told him about it? 'Ah well, sweetie, better keep your trap shut. I don't advise telling Tom, Dick and Harry.' And that was all. That was all damn all! Anyone would think she had merely announced she was going to be forty-nine next birthday. Instead of, instead of which . . . Oh Christ, she had been such a fool!

Anthea groaned and opened her eyes to glare at the ceiling. And then shutting them again, she put out a hand to grasp the brandy glass on the chair next to the bath. Predictably, she knocked it into the water, and watched as its contents trickled over her half-submerged breasts. 'Such a fool,' she murmured.

Sir Richard Dick struggled with his black tie, vainly attempting to screw it into the semblance of a bow. He could have done with Anthea's deft fingers, but where the hell was she? She had gone for her bath ages ago. High time she was out: they were due at the Senate House in twenty minutes, and it would take her a good ten minutes to apply her make-up, let alone titivate the hair.

He scowled into the mirror, annoyed with the tie and annoyed with Winston Reid. A sound sculptor all right, but privately hardly reliable. It was just typical of the man to have been toping so heavily at that early hour. And then, instead of sitting quietly with a black coffee, toying muzzily with the crossword while awaiting his guest, he had to roam around the landing and trip down the stairs. Yes, very bad luck and all that – but what of his poor horrified visitor? Finding him like that had been a terrible shock, and the later insistent probing from the police too embarrassing for words. They seemed to think that he knew something about it! The whole thing had been exceedingly disagreeable – and not helped by that friend of Cedric Dillworthy who had suddenly turned up out of the blue. At first he had assumed the fellow might be some support. Like hell! The little chap had taken one look at the body, declared that it was as 'cold as a kipper' and that he felt sick and needed fresh air.

It had been bad enough finding Reid's corpse in that way and having to deal with all the police palaver, but what of the ramifications affecting the project? Apart from poisonous Gloria and the tedious Cuff, things had been going moderately well. With a blend of tact and brute force their objections could surely have been squashed . . . But now there would have to be a totally fresh approach.

Would Finglestone fit the bill? Possibly – *provided* he was compliant to their requirements. The man was young and fashionable and would doubtless have ideas of his own, which might not accord with those of the conservative benefactors. What was needed was something of the kind Reid could have knocked up: sober yet elegant – not some fantastic variant of a Henry

Moore and whose human likeness nobody recognised. And what about the cost, dammit? It was bound to be absurdly inflated. Still, if the chap were cooperative it might be worth it. They would have to consider . . . Sir Richard frowned and gave another tug to his tie; and then suddenly grinned broadly. Perhaps they could offer him an honorary fellowship as an enticement to halve his fee. A *monumental* discount one might say!

Buoyed by that happy thought, he turned his attention to the immediate present. 'Do come on, Anthea!' he yelled at the adjoining bathroom. 'Hurry up or we'll be late. You know how the vice chancellor gets ratty.'

His wife emerged, pink-cheeked and hair in rollers. She glanced at him and then at the clock. 'It's ten minutes fast,' she observed, 'I keep telling you. And what on earth have you done to your tie? It looks like something out of a Charlie Chaplin film.'

CHAPTER THIRTEEN

Anthea Dick sat on a secluded seat in the Botanic Garden. It was the same seat where she had sat a week ago taking refuge from her recent shock. Then her mind had been in turmoil; now it was in sullen despair.

She had returned there in the hope that the garden's spacious tranquillity might inspire some solution, or at least relief. So far it had yielded nothing – not one iota of comfort, let alone a *way out*. So much for Marvell's 'green thought in a green shade', she thought bitterly, casting an eye at the looping spray of the distant fountain. Being here and contemplating the problem was no better than being in bed contemplating the ceiling and listening to Richard's snoring as he lay relaxed and oblivious beside her.

Relaxed and oblivious . . . long might he stay that way! She shut her eyes, wincing at the consequences were he to find out. Or indeed were anyone to find out. This last thought plunged her into further gloom for, of course, somebody *did* know: John Smithers. And she like the fool she was had told him! At the time, fearful and panic-stricken, it had been the instinctive thing to do. But now, despite his apparent indifference, she wished to hell she had said nothing. 'Always keep your own counsel,' her mother had once whispered in a moment of rare camaraderie. Oh yes, doubtless good advice . . . But then Mummy hadn't thrown anyone down the stairs; or at least, been next to them when they fell.

Normally assured and self-possessed, Anthea had not cried for years, but at that moment something seemed to snap inside, and to her consternation she found herself suddenly wracked with hard primitive sobs. Sobs of the kind that a child emits when fallen from a tree or bereft of its favourite toy: shocked and uncontrolled. Thus, with manicured hands pressed to her neatly coiffed temples and with heaving shoulders, the Master's wife rocked backwards and forwards on the public bench appalled by her plight.

Gradually in the midst of such misery – and to her embarrassment – Anthea sensed a presence beside her.

Someone cleared their throat. 'I say,' a tentative voice asked, 'would you like a handkerchief?'

Feeling an abject fool, she peered at the presence through half-closed fingers. Seated at the other end of the bench was the slight figure of a man, thin-faced and with short, spiky hair. He wore a look of mild enquiry and held a pristine white handkerchief, neatly folded.

She suppressed a gulp, took a deep breath and, with hands lowered to reveal ravaged features, nodded silently.

He passed the handkerchief and she dabbed her eyes, sniffed and smoothed her hair. 'I am so sorry,' she said stiffly, 'you have caught me at a bad moment. Ridiculous. I do apologise.'

'Oh, don't worry,' Felix replied, 'one has to let go occasionally, it's only natural. And as you can see, there's no one around.' He gestured at the empty lawns.

'Just as well,' she replied nasally, and blew her nose.

Following a brief and slightly awkward silence, Felix leant forward and said confidingly, 'Generally speaking, it's other people.'

'What?'

'Other people – they mess things up. Don't you find?'

Anthea hesitated, and then she agreed that indeed it was often the case.

'And in your case?'

She looked at him sharply. 'My case has nothing to do with anything.'

'Oh no, of course not,' Felix said hastily; and then to repair the damage, added quickly, 'If you don't mind my saying, that nail polish is most fetching – such a delicate shade of pink. So many colours these days are absurdly garish, wouldn't you agree?'

She was taken aback and spread her fingers, rather pleased; and then closed them abruptly. He didn't mean a word he was saying!

Catching her frown of scepticism, Felix pursued the matter. 'However,' he observed, 'a paler jacket would require a brighter shade, otherwise the nails would lose their impact. Subtlety is one thing, bland is quite another.'

She regarded him suspiciously. 'You seem to know a lot about colour. Are you an artist or something?'

'You could say so,' Felix replied modestly. 'I have the honour of organising the flowers for Her Majesty the Queen Mother. She is very particular, you know, and *so* discerning.' He beamed.

Anthea was a trifle startled, and then experienced a flash of recognition . . . wasn't this the little chap she had seen in tow to Professor Dillworthy the other night, the one that had virtually had a seizure when galumphing Gloria had trod on his toe? The slightly prissy tones overlying the merest South London twang struck a chord.

'Were you at our college reception the other evening?' she enquired.

Felix beamed again. 'Yes, indeed, Lady Dick, and how delightful it was – although I fear we didn't have a chance to talk.'

No, she thought, there had been others there of greater account. Out loud she said: 'Well, I am sorry you have caught me in this frightful state now. It hardly gives a good impression.' She gave a forced laugh.

'In my experience,' Felix declared, 'good impressions are frequently false.' He paused, and then added: 'Take that underfootman at Clarence House, for example – an absolute basket in my opinion, and yet to look at him you would think he was God's gift. God's gift, the little basket!' Felix spoke with a spurt of furious pique, obviously lost in some past drama utterly removed from the tranquillity of the Botanic Garden, or indeed from the presence of his companion.

The companion was both shocked and amused, and what a moment ago had been a forced laugh was suddenly replaced by a splutter of genuine mirth. What an extraordinary little man! The laughter flooded out of her – and then inexplicably, and to her horror, turned to tears again.

Although initially rather stung by her mirth, Felix once more felt sympathetic. Thus banishing the memory of the bastard footman, he said diffidently, 'Uhm, would you like to tell me about it?'

She shook her head. 'It would be no good and, besides, it would be dangerous – I've messed things up enough as it is.'

Dangerous? Messed things up – what things? Felix was intrigued.

'Oh,' he replied easily, 'I am never dangerous. In fact, my friend Cedric says I am the absolute soul of light and innocence.' He smiled disingenuously, and for some reason the claim's patent falsity had a disarming effect upon Anthea.

'All right,' she heard herself saying dully, yet with an odd sense of relief, 'I'll tell you.'

'All ears,' Felix said brightly and winked.

And so he got the whole story.

On a whim she had gone to Winston Reid's house to have it out with him.

'Have what out?' Felix had asked.

The fact that late one evening the sculptor had seen her and John Smithers having a crafty embrace in the precinct of the Round Church, Anthea explained, and that the man had been pestering her ever since.

Sir Richard had been away in London, and she and Smithers had taken the opportunity to snatch a few precious hours together. On their way back to his flat he had pulled her into the shadows of the little church, and as a prelude to things to come they had started to kiss passionately. It had been a foolish action, of course, utterly adolescent, but – Anthea had shrugged – in the heat of the moment caution takes a back seat. (Felix had agreed. 'Oh, all the time,' he murmured.)

They had been too absorbed to have noticed the watcher, and it was only later that Reid began his approaches – approaches that she had concealed from Smithers for fear of his getting cold feet and perhaps dropping her. She explained that Reid's attentions had not been sexual, nor it appeared of a crude blackmailing nature. Just maddeningly irksome. He had seemed to take a perverse pleasure in constantly reminding her of what he had witnessed – sly innuendos, knowing smirks, covert references. And then one day she had received a note delivered unobtrusively to the porter's lodge (Jenkins being in the back room brewing tea). There had been no signature, but it was obvious who it had come from. This time the allusions were more explicit, and one line had really riled her: *How fitting that a comely matron such as yourself should have a dashing young beau!* 'Oily bilge!' Anthea had exclaimed angrily to Felix. (The latter had agreed, though privately suspecting the crucial goad to have been less its style than the contrast of 'matron' and 'young'.)

Thus, although containing no hint of blackmail, the note had been the last straw, and on impulse Anthea had driven to Reid's house to confront the idiot and demand that he stop such nonsense. She couldn't make out what he was playing at, but whatever it was she had had enough.

Luckily, or unluckily as it turned out, Reid was at home and had invited her upstairs to his sitting room. Here she made her position clear, informing him that she disliked his attitude and that he must cease the 'persecution' and behave like a reasonable adult. Her demands had cut no ice. Quite the opposite, in fact: he had been coolly patronising. And while freely acknowledging he had seen the couple embracing, had accused her of exaggeration and hysterical paranoia. 'When ladies reach a certain age,' he had chuckled smugly, 'they get all manner of funny ideas.'

She had been appalled by the effrontery, and was just gathering her wits to make an acid retort, when he had stood up; and announcing that he was expecting an important visitor ('your distinguished husband, no less'), had briskly ushered her on to the landing. Here he had made some unctuous pleasantry and, gripping her elbow, had nudged her firmly to the top of the stairs. 'I fear they are rather steep. Be careful,' he had murmured. They were his last words.

Incensed by the sickening patronage and curt dismissal, his visitor had impatiently shaken free from his hand. He had taken an involuntary step backwards, stumbled slightly . . . and the next moment was hurtling headlong to the bottom.

Anthea ceased her narrative and for a moment gazed unseeingly at Felix, and then, white-faced, closed her eyes. 'It was ghastly,' she breathed, 'quite ghastly. I can hear the sound of that awful clock even now.'

Felix could believe it – the woman standing transfixed at the top of the staircase, the heap of limbs sprawled lifelessly at the bottom. The afternoon's awesome silence broken only by the relentless ticking of the hall clock . . . He shuddered, imagining the scene only too well.

'So what did you do?' he asked faintly.

'Nothing at first. I literally could not move. It was like one of those nightmares where you are totally paralysed and however much you try you can't stir an inch. Do you know what I mean?'

'Oh yes,' he answered with feeling. 'Sometimes I dream of being chased and pinioned by corgis. Terrifying!'

She gave him a puzzled look. And then gazing into the distance, she said conversationally: 'Do you remember that Marx brothers film where Groucho falls headlong down the stairs, and when sprawled at the bottom tells the onlookers to forget the glass of water and to just force brandy down his throat?'

It was Felix's turn to look puzzled, but he nodded vaguely.

'Well, it was a bit like that . . . except that Groucho got up, Reid never did. And for some reason, standing there I found that episode playing in my mind. Absurd, really. In the film the line about the brandy had been so funny – though I certainly wasn't laughing then! I was trying to think what on earth to do. I knew he was dead and I was terrified I should be accused; and somehow the thought of the brandy gave me an idea. On my way to Reid's house I had stopped to buy a bottle of whisky at the off-licence – Richard had complained we were short. I'd meant to put the thing in the car boot, but had been so concerned with the prospect of confronting Reid that I had forgotten it was still in my shopping bag.'

Felix said nothing, recalling Aldous Phipps' obsession about the Scotch and guessing what might be coming next.

Andrea sighed and then shrugged. '*Anyway*, I knew Winston Reid had a reputation for drinking over the odds. And so that's what I did: uncorked the bottle, poured some down his throat and over his shirt, fetched a glass from the drinks cabinet, smashed it on the banister and left the remains of the bottle upstairs with the other drinks in the sitting room . . . I was barely aware of what I was doing; it was like being in a dream or a trance.'

'But in this dreamlike trance, did you wipe your

116

fingerprints from the bottle and glass?' Felix enquired sternly.

Andrea gave a bitter laugh. 'Oh yes, I've read enough detective novels to remember to do that. And I even managed to press his own fingers on to the bottle.' She winced. 'It was horrible. But stupidly I left the door wide open when I ran out. Still, it didn't seem to matter. I gather it was thought he had deliberately left it like that.'

'Apparently,' Felix said dryly, recalling the open door and the sight of Sir Richard's posterior as he bent over the corpse. 'So what did you do then?' he asked curiously. 'Return to the Lodge?'

'Oh no, I was in blind panic and just wanted to get as far away as possible. So I came here, to this very bench, and sat for ages. I knew that by the time I returned Reid would have been found, if not by Richard then doubtless by somebody else. But at least by staying away I should miss the brunt of the uproar and so could arrive on the scene looking appropriately bemused and shocked.' Andrea gave a twisted smile: 'The only snag was that I arrived minus the whisky Richard had asked me to get. Given the circumstances he had a particular need that evening and was none too pleased when I returned empty-handed. We had to resort to sherry.'

'Frightful,' Felix observed.

He was just beginning to collect his thoughts, wondering what on earth he should say to the woman, when she turned on him fiercely and said in tones both accusing and anguished: 'Oh well, so now you know! And I suppose you will run helter-skelter to the police and tell them too, tell them the whole godawful tale!' She was gripping her handbag tightly, her voice harsh and strained, and for a moment Felix feared she would collapse in tears again. But the eyes remained dry and the look of anguish was replaced by one of drooping resignation.

'Look here,' he said awkwardly, 'what exactly would I have to tell them? That Reid's death was not an accident? That evidence had come to light suggesting his fall was deliberately engineered? But it wasn't, was it? You may have messed about with the whisky and played silly beggars with the tumbler, but the fact remains that the thing was an accident: he tripped by mistake, just as the authorities assumed. You have told me certain details of which they are ignorant, but those details do not alter the verdict. Death by misadventure – that is exactly what it was. No, Lady Dick, I have no reason to speak to the police.' Felix folded his hands firmly in his lap and gazed intently at a group of azaleas.

There was a long silence while she reflected on his words. And then she said quietly, 'It is very decent of you to say that, Mr Smythe, but perhaps, after all, *I* should report it to the authorities, make a clean breast of things. One gathers that "tampering with the evidence" or "interfering with the course of justice" is a serious offence. Perhaps you think that I ought to bite on the bullet and take the con . . .' Her voice trailed off.

'Not unless you have a fetish for confession, I don't,' Felix answered mildly. 'From what you have described I cannot see that the course of *justice* has been remotely hampered. As said, his death was an accident; you were in no way to blame. And as to the additional "embellishments" – well, unless they had materially affected the outcome I cannot see that they are of significance.' He returned his gaze to the azaleas, feeling distinctly uncomfortable. He was dying to spend a penny.

Anthea regarded him with grateful surprise. (How much more comforting than bloody John Smithers!) 'Even so—' she began tentatively.

'Listen,' Felix interrupted quickly, 'any such confession would open a can of worms, you must surely realise that. There would be an awful scandal, your husband would look a fool, the affair with your friend would be made public, you would be humiliated and possibly land in the divorce court, and the whole statue project and its link with the college would doubtless be tarnished and lose kudos . . . Is that what you want?'

'No!' she cried. 'That's just it, I don't!'

'Well then, take my advice: do not cross dodgy bridges whether arrived at or not.'

Felix wasn't quite sure of his metaphors for his bladder was taking precedence over thought. Besides, he was also desperate for a triple dry martini: he had spent an exhausting hour.

Thus he stood up to take his leave, assured her that by remaining quiet things were bound to be all right, and with a languid wave strolled off as casually as he could towards a clump of friendly trees.

CHAPTER FOURTEEN

'Where on earth have you been?' Cedric expostulated as Felix walked through the door. 'I have been waiting here for ages utterly parched!' He removed his spectacles and waved them irritably.

'Huh,' Felix replied, 'not half as parched as me. I have spent a most taxing afternoon.'

'But you only went out to look at some flowers in the Botanic Garden. Don't tell me you fell in the fountain or something?'

'No,' replied Felix, tight-lipped, 'I was being charming to a lady in distress. It required both tact and patience, and I am now rather fatigued.'

'You were exercising tact and patience? Oh, I can just imagine that,' observed Cedric acidly. He hesitated, before adding, 'Anyway, what lady? You don't know any except Angela Fawcett and the Queen Mother.'

'Nonsense, I know several, *including* Lady Dick, the Master's wife.'

'Well, hardly that – you only saw her the other night at the reception. A mere passing encounter.'

'I can tell you,' Felix retorted testily, 'that this afternoon's encounter was far from passing, and I should now like a large—'

'You have been with *her*?' Cedric asked, suddenly intrigued.

Felix nodded. 'I have indeed.'

'But why?'

'I was giving moral support and useful counsel,' the latter replied primly.

Cedric stared in wonder. '*You* were? But whatever about?'

Felix sighed and said that were he to be offered a strong drink he might be prepared to divulge – although in principle his lips were sealed.

'But not with me, they aren't,' Cedric reminded him. 'As you know, dear boy, I am famed for my silence. Nothing shall pass beyond these four walls.' He slid quickly over to the chest serving as a drinks cabinet, while his friend stretched out a wilting hand.

After Felix had finished his account and his second dry martini Cedric regarded him speculatively.

'Very dramatic,' he observed, 'but how do you know she wasn't making the whole thing up – the part about the accident, I mean? If the Smithers liaison were ever revealed she would have a lot to lose. Admittedly, it all sounds quite plausible – Reid stepping back and then tripping – but I can envisage another scenario: one where she clutches him with all her force and then with a knee in the back hoofs him down into the hall. The lady stands "immobilised" at the top of the staircase, not out of shock, but because she is holding her breath in the hope that the blighter has broken his neck.' Cedric lit a cigarette, while despite the two martinis Felix gave sober consideration.

Eventually he said, 'Had you been there as *I* was, you may have gained a very different impression; after all, it's not just words in themselves that persuade, but also the manner of their delivery. Admittedly, a mite tiresome, but on the whole her manner struck me as being entirely genuine.'

'Oh, you mean like Sir Laurence Olivier's? Yes, there's rarely a dry eye in the house. Dear Larry, such a fine actor!'

The corners of Felix's mouth went down and he said distantly, 'Obviously, you are in one of your contrary moods so we shall just have to agree to differ.' He smoothed his hair and picked up a magazine.

'*Alternatively*,' murmured Cedric, bending forward with a gleam of relish, 'we could open a book on it: twenty to one on?'

'Twenty-five,' was the quick response.

'Good, that's settled, then,' Cedric declared briskly. 'Now, I suggest you return to your quarters and get ready lickety-split. We are meeting Rosy Gilchrist for supper in half an hour.'

'What for?'

'I gather she has some news to relay.'

Felix pulled a face. 'It had better be good. I've had rather a lot of that for one day . . . whatever its accuracy.' He winked and left the room.

Left briefly on his own, Cedric mulled over Felix's tale. She might have been telling the truth, of course; although

122

equally, as he had suggested, it could have been an elaborate fiction to veil something more sinister. Certainly Felix had insisted the tears were real enough – but then presumably if one had recently hurled someone to their death one might indeed be a little shaky. (His older brother had once recounted an incident in the Great War when he had shot his first sniper. He had been right on target, and with a mixture of shock and pride had seen the man curl up and fall flat on the ground like a cleanly slain pheasant. Yet the initial triumph had turned to sudden tears and he been hard-pressed to conceal his distress. Subsequently, he had told Cedric, he became inured to such moments.)

However, even if one assumed the woman's account to have been genuine, she was clearly in a tight spot. As Felix had warned her, a candid confession to the police could lead to embarrassing consequences both publicly and privately. There would be a lot of explaining to do – not only to the police for impeding or misleading their investigation, but also presumably to her husband as to why she had been in Reid's house in the first place – a query surely requiring more subterfuge. And, naturally, were the press to get hold of the story (a fair likelihood) the publicity could be damaging both to the Dicks personally and perhaps temporarily even to the college itself – the matter inviting attention of the kind not normally sought. Cedric could just see the headlines:

COLLEGE MASTER'S WIFE REVEALS HER PRESENCE AT
SCULPTOR'S DEATH PLUNGE

Lady Dick, attractive wife of Sir Richard, has recently admitted to visiting Winston Reid on the afternoon

of his death to 'discuss an entirely private matter'.
Apparently during the course of that discussion
something happened to cause the sculptor to lose
his balance – with fatal consequences. When asked
what might have caused such loss of balance Lady
Dick snapped that she had no idea – an assertion this
newspaper finds hard to credit. Et cetera, et cetera . . .

Cedric was warming to his little fantasy. However, such
speculation was cut short by Felix returning spruced and
ready for the evening's sortie.

'Very smart,' Cedric observed, eyeing the new bow tie and
nodding his approval.

Felix smiled modestly. But smile changed to indignant
frown when Cedric added, 'You know, it occurs to me that
whether Lady Dick was telling the truth or not, she was
taking an absurd risk in telling you about it all.'

Felix bridled. 'What can you mean? I am the soul of
discretion – as Her Majesty well knows! You don't get a
Royal Warrant for being—'

'Oh, absolutely, dear boy,' Cedric said soothingly, '*I*
know that, but does Lady Dick? I expect that by now
she is having disturbing second thoughts – especially
as she has blabbed about John Smithers – and is very
possibly convinced that you are about to blackmail her
to kingdom come.'

'What nonsense. Do I *look* like a blackmailer?'

Cedric cleared his throat. 'Well . . .' he murmured.

When they arrived at the restaurant they were slightly
surprised not to find Rosy already there. She was generally

a sharp timekeeper. They took their bearings, selected a corner table and asked the waiter for menus.

'You know,' Cedric said conversationally, 'it must have been awful for Anthea Dick seeing all that blood. A pretty gory business, I should think: kneeling down and dowsing him in the whisky. Presumably she was able to wash off the stains when she got home and before playing the shocked innocent to her husband.'

'Hmm, I suppose so,' Felix agreed vaguely, absorbed in the more pressing matter of the menu.

'But didn't she mention it?'

'Mention what?'

'The *blood*. It can't have been easy keeping it off her hands and cuffs when pouring the Scotch down the poor blighter's throat.'

'Look,' Felix protested, 'I was about to choose the jugged hare "bathed in rich burgundy and its own juice". In the light of your words, I shall now have to opt for the Dover sole.' He pouted, and then added, 'Anyway, from what I recall she never mentioned the blood – just said his limbs were all twisted and his neck looked peculiar.'

'But you saw it?'

'Yes, yes, I glimpsed it, of course. There wasn't much, and it was hardly something one wished to gawp at. I was more concerned with getting away and going to the telephone box. Now if you don't mind . . . Ah, here comes Rosy Gilchrist with her vital news; at last we can order the drinks!' Felix waved to her and adjusted his features to an ingratiating smile.

Rosy's news was that they had been invited to attend an evening of English madrigals at Westminster College.

The event was part of Newnham's entertainment programme and although several of her fellow alumni would be attending, Westminster's music society was worried about numbers. Surprisingly there had been fewer responses than expected; and this was an embarrassment as a distinguished exponent of the genre was coming especially from London to give an introductory lecture. There had been a hasty rallying call and guests had been urged to spread the word and to bring friends.

'So that is exactly what I am doing,' Rosy said, 'spreading the word, and in a moment of rash optimism I put your names on the list. But, of course, you don't have to come if you don't want to,' she added hastily, noting Felix's expression.

Cedric considered. 'Well we might—' he began.

Felix, who had been about to summon the waiter to take their order, stopped in mid-wave. 'But I don't like madrigals,' he said.

'Nonsense, you've never heard one,' admonished Cedric. 'I have.'

'Oh yes? When?'

Felix deliberated for some moments, and then said vaguely, 'Oh, years before we met.'

'In which case,' Rosy cut in, 'perhaps you should try again. It is amazing how one's tastes can change. Who knows, you may become quite hooked.' She smiled sweetly, before adding, 'I have it on good authority that the place will be awash with champagne.'

Knowing Westminster to be a theological foundation of Presbyterian bent, Cedric rather doubted this, but kept a discreet silence.

Rosy urged her cause. 'Betty Withers tells me the speaker is first class and very witty, and the Westminster singers excellent. It might all be totally splendid.' She gave an encouraging laugh and poured more wine into Felix's glass.

CHAPTER FIFTEEN

They were assembled for luncheon: Aldous Phipps; Mostyn Williams, the bursar; and, rather morosely, John Smithers, still pondering his predicament and the fallibility of other people. Apart from the occasional commonplace, little was being said, each absorbed in his own thoughts or the newspaper.

Suddenly, the door was flung open. 'Sound the bells. Bring out the banners!' Professor Turner cried on the threshold. 'Hosannah!'

They looked at him with mild curiosity. 'Oh Lord, you haven't converted to something, have you?' the bursar remarked. 'We really can't have that sort of thing.'

'No, not me, but someone else has,' Turner said gleefully. 'Cuff has capitulated. He has withdrawn his objection and is ready to sell the plot. We can go ahead and put the damned thing up!'

'Provided we have a sculptor,' murmured Aldous Phipps. 'You may recall that our current man is permanently indisposed.'

'Well, we'll just have to settle for the other chap. The sooner it's done the better; the whole thing has dragged on long enough and there are more pressing matters to attend to.'

'Not for dear Gloria, there aren't,' John Smithers reminded him, 'she'll be wetting herself with glee.'

Aldous Phipps winced. 'Kindly control your tongue, Smithers. That is not the sort of image to be confronted with at this time of day – or indeed at any time.' He scowled at his pale sherry and pushed it aside.

Smithers grinned, and addressing Turner asked him if he had seen the rhododendrons currently displaying in the Botanic Garden. 'They have a new species, I note, a particularly virulent puce and apparently a rampant grower. It'll suit Gloria down to the ground.'

This time it was Turner who scowled.

'What made Cuff throw in the sponge, I wonder?' the bursar mused.

Professor Turner's scowl momentarily subsided and was replaced instead by a malevolent leer. 'I can tell you that straightaway: it was the old girl herself. Gloria wore him down and bribed his wife and kids. They took the bribes and continued her good work, i.e. nagged him to kingdom come until he caved in. I gather that his exact words to the council were: "That's it – I've had it up to effing here! And that effing college can do what it effing likes. Stuff the plot!"'

'Holy Moses!' Smithers exclaimed. 'And what was the council's reaction?'

'They cheered. Next thing they had signed on the dotted

line and sent off a demand for our immediate payment. Short odds, Bursar, it'll be on your desk tomorrow.'

There was a stunned silence, broken by Aldous Phipps' spindly voice: 'Rather arresting terminology, albeit a touch repetitive. I wonder how Plato would have put it . . .'

With lunch over, Professor Phipps shuffled off to feed his Norfolk terrier. The others returned to the Combination Room for coffee and Turner for a small brandy. He pulled a face. 'There's a trustees' meeting this afternoon,' he said, 'I need to be braced.'

They were joined by Vernon Carter accompanied by Cedric and Felix as his guests.

'Mr Smythe and I had a sighting of Monty Finglestone earlier on,' he announced. 'He was in the University Arms with Miss Biggs-Brookby en route back to London. They were having what looked like a farewell lunch.'

'So what were they doing – plotting his return as anointed sculptor?' Smithers asked.

'They were guzzling crab and Chablis,' Felix replied. 'Copiously.' He sounded peeved, and Cedric remembered that crab was one of his own favourites.

'Could you hear what they were saying?' he asked.

'They weren't saying anything, just gazing. Or at least she was. Sort of devouring his face – that is, when she wasn't devouring the crab.'

The bursar gave a snort of mirth.

'Hmm,' Smithers mused, 'the prospect of having one's face devoured by Gloria Biggs-Brookby is not a happy one. How was Finglestone coping?'

'Nervously, I should say. He kept downing the wine and casting oblique eyes at the waitress.'

'Ah well.' Cedric sighed. 'We have to suffer for our pleasures – or in his case, for our commissions. What do you think, Dr Smithers, does he stand a chance now that Reid is no longer with us?'

'Frankly, I am not that bothered. The essential point is the college has at last secured the plot itself: what they do with it is almost immaterial. I mean, they could shove a statue of the Queen Mother in it if they wanted – or one of her racehorses.'

There was general laughter. And then Turner said in mild reproof, 'I don't think that's *quite* the spirit, do you? After all, done well, the monument will surely be an asset. We may lack the grandeur of King's or the obvious beauty of Pembroke, but we do have a select elegance of our own. A good piece of sculpture will surely lend additional distinction.' He turned to Cedric: 'And to answer your question seriously, Professor, I should say the appointment is highly likely. I mean, I know the Master was dead against him when Reid was alive, but that was because things were going moderately well and that with a bit of luck, i.e. Cuff being won over, the whole thing could have been wrapped up and rubber-stamped. Gloria's sudden intrusion with a fresh name was tiresome and disruptive. Richard Dick is not keen on his apple carts being overturned. He never was. And now with his fresh status he is even less keen. The purchase of more land and its particular purpose will put a jaunty feather in the new cap, and I guess he was damned if he was going to have that chance delayed by Gloria messing things up. However, now with Reid's demise *and* with Cuff giving in—'

'But rather a *small* plot of land for the college to acquire,' Felix remarked. 'I mean, it is hardly going to add much to its acreage. The kudos will be minimal, surely?'

'Yes. But in a way that's what would have been so frustrating.' Turner smiled. 'After all, the project is a sort of qualifying test: if the new Master can't get that right, what can he? Circumstances alter cases; and I bet that with Reid dead and now Cuff gone, he will want to press on quickly and produce a solid achievement. And if that means paying out more, then so be it . . . Besides, as Phipps has been saying, I gather that the chap is starting to make his mark – and not just in the capital. Rumour has it that the *other place* is already putting out feelers for him.'

Felix looked blank. 'What other place?' he asked.

'Oxford,' Cedric whispered.

'So you see,' Turner continued, 'that's even more of a reason for the Master to grab him. If Finglestone really is good, then we may as well be the first seat of learning to display his work.'

'Unless the rhododendrons obscure it,' Felix tittered.

Professor Turner's smile was replaced by a scowl. 'I can assure you, Mr Smythe, contrary to what you may have heard, there will be no rhododendrons. That's one thing the daughter won't screw out of us. Sir Richard and she will have to reach an accommodation: Daddy on the plinth; plant catalogues in the fire!' He folded his arms and stared defiantly at his empty glass.

The conversation switched to other matters, but before they broke up returned once more to the project.

'So, assuming Finglestone does get the green light, where is he going to do his work – in his London studio or here in Cambridge? Aren't there some units near Jesus Green that are let out for that sort of thing? I know a couple of artists who use them. In fact, I think Reid used to have one there before he converted his garden shed.' Smithers looked enquiringly at the bursar.

The other agreed that it would probably be the case. 'But I tell you one thing, he won't be lodging with Miss Biggs-Brookby. Oh no! Sir Richard won't stand for that. If we are the paymasters, then we shall settle him in one of the university's rooms.' He turned to Cedric. 'There's one empty on your staircase, he can probably go there. The less that lady intrudes on things the better. She has already shoved her nose in far enough. Any more and our dear friend Maycock is liable to get the vapours and never recover!'

'Oh, heaven forbid,' said Smithers piously.

'Well,' Cedric declared, as he and Felix ambled back across Little Court and into town, 'at least the chief hurdle is down. With that alderman throwing in the sponge, they can get on with the statue itself. The sooner the better, in my view.'

'So you think Sir Richard will definitely go for Finglestone?'

'Bound to. The Reid business blew things apart, but from what I've seen of Sir Richard he'll pick up the pieces and push ahead. Turner was right: with Cuff caved in the college has both the means and the man. There's no point in delay. You'll see, Master Finglestone will be taking up residence before you can say knife.' Cedric laughed: 'In fact, what's the betting the bursar isn't composing a telegram this very minute.'

'Well that will certainly please Gloria B-B all right. Judging from the oozing flattery in the hotel she thinks he's God's gift.'

'So what is he like? I only had the briefest glimpse when I saw them in the taxi the other day.'

Felix gave an indifferent shrug. 'Tall, muscular . . . I daresay he can wield a chisel well enough. Handsome, if you like that sort of thing. I don't especially: too big, too obvious.'

'You mean he lacks a certain – how should one put it – suave subtlety?'

'Exactly.' Felix beamed at his friend.

They continued in silence, Cedric dwelling upon the benefactors' plaque scheduled for display at the plot's entrance. He wondered whether that too would be part of the sculptor's brief. He rather hoped so – after all, they didn't want some paltry piece of pasteboard cobbled up by the local ironmonger! That would be most incongruous. The thing should have a lasting solidity and harmonise with the work itself . . . Yes, he must make enquiries. His thoughts were interrupted by Felix, who had been making his own reflections.

'You know, I think John Smithers' suggestion about a statue of the Queen Mother was quite enlightened. Her Majesty would look very fetching against a background of hollyhocks . . . though I am not so sure about the horse.'

Cedric raised his eyes to the heavens.

As things turned out, Cedric had been right about the speed of Monty Finglestone's appointment. With the way clear and there being no suitable alternative, the Master was quick to swallow the extra cost and succumb to Gloria's choice. Thus, the sculptor was blandished, summoned and installed. And in accordance with the bursar's stipulation, he was temporarily assigned to C staircase in the spare room next to

Cedric's, and his tools and materials shipped from London to one of the lettings in the Northampton road.

Cedric's room was on the corner of the building and having nobody on the other side had suited him well. Thus, when he had learnt of Finglestone's arrival and that he had indeed been installed next door, the professor was a trifle put out. 'I trust he is not going to make a noise,' he grumbled to Felix, 'that would be too bad.'

Felix had enquired what sort of noise he had in mind.

'It could be anything,' Cedric had replied, 'banging doors, falling up the stairs blind drunk – you know what these bohemians are like – singing, sharpening his tools . . .'

'Oh, I don't think he will be sharpening his tools,' Felix assured him hastily, 'they will all be stored at his studio.'

'No, but he may sing,' Cedric snapped.

Unable to think of an answer to that, Felix just hoped the newcomer would have no such urge.

Fortunately for everyone Cedric's fears proved groundless. Finglestone's presence was barely felt: he was absent by day and mercifully quiet by night. On the rare occasions Cedric passed him in their shared passage the young man was polite but uncommunicative.

'A little affability wouldn't come amiss,' Cedric had said tartly to Felix.

'Perhaps he is in awe of you,' the latter replied. 'Being billeted next to someone of your years and distinction might make him feel inhibited.' (Privately he suspected that Finglestone cared not a jot.)

'My *years*?' was the indignant response.

Felix smiled inwardly and changed to a less delicate topic: their proposed visit to Grantchester.

This was something that had been arranged long in advance. Although often returning to the city of Cambridge itself, Cedric had never been back to the little village since his undergraduate days, and he had been intrigued to go there again, and indeed to show off its charms to Felix. An old friend had a house right in its centre, and while they could have made a day trip by walking the path across the fields, the friend had pressed them to spend a couple of nights with him – 'to escape the frenzied hurly-burly of scholarly life.' He had laughed.

The prospect was appealing, and other than the scheduled madrigal concert at Westminster, would make a fitting finale to their sojourn in the area. 'There's so much to see,' Cedric enthused. 'The ancient church with its "Rupert Brooke" clock and the old vicarage, historic water meadows, the Orchard Tea Garden – and, of course, Lord Byron's celebrated bathing pool. You might even fancy a dip.'

'Oh, can one swim in the buff like the Fellows used to in that pool of Emmanuel's?' Felix asked in sudden interest.

'I very much doubt it,' Cedric said hastily.

CHAPTER SIXTEEN

Despite not testing Grantchester's waters, clothed or otherwise, the two friends returned to Cambridge refreshed by their rural retreat and having much enjoyed the jolly hospitality of their host. Rosy Gilchrist had left a note at the porter's lodge reminding them of Westminster's madrigal event the following evening.

Rosy had been right in her assurance that it would be a pleasure and worth their going for it turned out to be an excellent occasion. The speaker was well up to his eloquent best, the singing merry and masterly, and, contrary to earlier fears, the audience substantial. The champagne, while not quite of the lavish excess Rosy had described, was nevertheless plentiful and good. Already Felix was revising his ideas about such music, and during the interval was heard to enquire of the conductor where in London he might be able to hear more.

When it was over, they hovered in the hallway congratulating the choir and chatting to Basil Leason and one or two others. During the lecture Rosy had spotted Geoffrey Hinchcliffe sitting attentively in the front row. She had meant to say hello to him during the interval, but had been waylaid by a Newnham chum. Thus, when it was over she looked for him again, eager to find out if he had enjoyed the programme, but there was no sign. She asked Cedric if he had seen him.

'Actually, I saw him slip out much earlier, soon after the speaker finished,' Cedric told her.

'What? You mean before the singing started?' Rosy was surprised, recalling how keenly he had talked of music at their last meeting and his use of the term 'balm to the soul'.

Cedric shrugged. 'Perhaps he was taken short or wanted some fresh air. As a matter of fact I did think he looked a bit peaky; and before the thing started I had seen him taking a pill in the gents. Probably had a headache or something.'

'Hinchcliffe?' asked Basil Leason, who had been on the point of leaving. 'Yes, I don't think his health is too good, apparently the ticker plays up. He has what I believe is known as a murmur – whatever that is.'

'Well, let's just trust it stays murmuring and doesn't decide to bellow,' Felix said. 'I had an aunt once with a dicky heart and I can't tell you what appalling—'

Fond though he was of his friend, Cedric had no wish to hear about the ailments of his relatives. Muttering an excuse, he went to retrieve his jacket from the concert room.

Just then Betty Withers joined them to offer Rosy a lift back to Newnham. The latter declined, saying that such a warm evening deserved to be savoured. 'I'll walk with Cedric and Felix as far as the Market Place, and then, if I am really worn out, I'll grab a taxi.'

As they crossed Westminster's wide courtyard and passed through its regal gates, Rosy looked back.

'You know that frontage is really rather striking,' she remarked. 'I don't think I noticed it much when I was here. Like Newnham it is rather tucked away from the centre and, of course, being on the roundabout makes it less obvious. I mean, if you are driving you tend to be more interested in the traffic.'

'Yes, pure Victorian Gothic,' Cedric agreed. 'A very good specimen of the late style, I should say. And what with the ivy and that moon it does rather resemble a painting by the artist Atkinson Grimshaw. All that's needed is a hazy mist and a lamplight.'

They walked on slowly along Northampton Street before turning down towards Magdalene. Busy by day, on a late Sunday night this end of town was quiet, almost uncannily so. But suddenly the faintest noise could be heard just behind them, a sort of whispering, keening sound. The kind of sound a dying cat might make.

Rosy swung round nervously. There was nothing and nobody there except Felix.

'That wasn't you, was it?' she asked sharply.

'What?'

'That peculiar moaning sound.'

'If you mean my singing, then yes. I was merely trying to recapture the charming little refrain of that last madrigal. It was sung with such verve and sprightly brio.'

There was a roar of laughter from Cedric (not given to

139

such eruptions): 'Well if that's sprightly brio, I'll eat my arse!' he guffawed.

Coming from Cedric so crude an outburst was startling in itself, and Rosy too roared with laughter. For a few seconds Felix stared indignantly at his companions, but mirth is infectious, and with a gulp the thin features relaxed and pride gave way to spluttering giggles.

'Ssh!' Rosy gasped. 'People will think we are drunk and disorderly.'

'Aren't we?' Felix wheezed. 'Besides, there aren't any people. This isn't London, you know. They are all tucked up in bed. It's as quiet as the grave.'

'Except for your ungodly warblings,' observed Cedric, and started to laugh again.

As they approached Magdalene Bridge still chortling, a figure could be seen leaning over the balustrade, head down, apparently craning to look at something in the river or under the bridge. They continued on towards it. But, suddenly, Felix stopped, spreading his arms to hold back the other two. 'Just a moment,' he whispered, 'do we recognise that rump?'

A streetlight faintly illuminated the blue floral dirndl copiously spread beneath a lilac jacket. It looked distinctly familiar.

'It's not Gloria, is it?' Rosy whispered. 'What on earth is she doing – fishing?'

'Better not to enquire,' Cedric said hastily. 'Let's cross over before she sees us.'

They started to cross the road, but paused to allow a car to pass, its headlamps briefly picking out the form – now clearly not craning, but inertly slumped.

'It *is* Gloria,' Rosy exclaimed as the car trundled on its way up the slope, 'and it looks as if she might be ill or something.' She stared anxiously.

'Oh hell, she's not being sick, is she?' Felix groaned.

Cedric gripped his arm. 'Worse!' he hissed. 'There's something sticking out of her back and it looks like a—' He broke off, and then gasped: 'Oh dear God, yes, it is . . . it's a knife. She's been stabbed! It's there right in the middle, can't you see?'

For a few seconds the three stood paralysed, gazing in appalled disbelief. And then with a convulsive start they rushed towards the bridge and to what was now quite clearly the corpse of Gloria Biggs-Brookby.

CHAPTER SEVENTEEN

As can be imagined, the ensuing uproar was tremendous. Cambridge was agog and aghast, and speculation stalked the streets imbuing all with fervid excitement.

The local paper, having only managed a brief stop-press announcement on the morning following the event, compensated fully the day after: DAUGHTER OF EMINENT SCHOLAR FOUND STABBED TO DEATH ON MAGDALENE BRIDGE, its headlines ran.

Gloria Biggs-Brookby, chairman of the Watch Committee, president of the Townswomen's Guild and a well-known figure in Cambridge's cultural circles, was discovered shortly after eleven o'clock last night draped over Magdalene Bridge with a dagger protruding from her back.

Strolling back from a musical evening at Westminster College, a visiting professor and his two companions were horrified to be faced with the grisly scene. 'It's not quite what one expects in Cambridge,' observed Mr Felix Smythe, one of the appalled witnesses, 'and even Mayfair doesn't run to such a thing, or certainly not at that early hour.'

'You didn't say that, did you?' Rosy asked Felix accusingly as they sat in the college's rose arbour, a copy of the newspaper spread on its rickety table. 'It sounds a bit fatuous to me.'

'I have no idea what I said,' Felix retorted. 'Given the circumstances it could have been anything – but I can assure you, Rosy Gilchrist, it would not have been fatuous.' He glared.

Cedric cleared his throat: 'Hmm. I don't think it is our words that matter, rather our actions, I should say. It's the latter that is of significance – or so the police will think.'

It was Rosy's turn to be annoyed. 'Oh, honestly, Cedric,' she snorted, 'you are not suggesting that the police suspect *us* of being involved – that's ridiculous.'

'Well, it wouldn't be the first time that the person reporting a crime has been its perpetrator. The police know that well enough . . . and it's not as if we had never set eyes on her before. After all, we have all been associated with the deceased, however briefly. She wasn't exactly a total stranger. Mark my words, judging from yesterday's grilling they'll be taking this further.' Cedric spoke with gloomy assurance.

'But that's nonsense!' exclaimed Felix. 'Just because we are key witnesses certainly doesn't mean we should be key

143

suspects. Our connection is totally tenuous. And frankly, from what little I saw, I couldn't stand the woman!'

'I should keep that under your hat if I were you,' Rosy said slyly, and grinned. And then becoming serious, she exclaimed, 'But who on *earth* would have done it? I mean, she may have been a pain, but to do that to the poor woman seems a bit excessive.'

'Probably a strolling lunatic,' Felix said dismissively. 'It's these cloistered academics, they get funny ideas. Wouldn't you say so, Cedric?'

Cedric affected not to hear – or perhaps genuinely hadn't, for he appeared deep in thought. 'I wonder if anyone else saw her,' he mused, 'but is hesitant to come forward, or perhaps simply hadn't been close enough to see the knife? Such revelations can take a time to emerge. With luck there may be other witnesses.'

'Yes, and if you remember we did see Aldous Phipps walking his fat Popsie,' Rosy said.

'Doing *what*?' Felix was mildly scandalised.

'Exercising his dog. That's its name: Popsie. I saw him on our way to Westminster.'

'But that was much earlier on,' Cedric said dismissively.

'Ah, but who knows, he may have been doing a stake-out,' said Felix darkly, 'assessing the lie of the land for his dastardly attack.'

Potent though her imagination was, even Rosy could not envisage the diminutive Phipps launching such an assault and plunging a dagger into Gloria's beefy form. She would have swatted him like a blowfly.

They were about to leave, when slightly to their surprise they were joined by John Smithers, who without being invited sat down at the table. 'Ah, the vital three,' he observed sardonically, 'concocting your defence, presumably.'

'Oh really!' Cedric snorted.

'A joke, Professor, a joke,' Smithers assured him, and as a mollifying gesture proffered his cigarette case and then passed it to the others. Felix accepted, but Rosy declined, eager to return to the Fitzwilliam and pursue her fact-finding for Dr Stanley . . . a prosaic antidote to the current drama.

Cedric addressed Smithers: 'You knew the lady better than we did, so what's your view on the matter – a random attack from a passing thug, or something more sinister?'

Smithers sat back on his chair and blew a smoke ring. 'Your guess is as good as mine. She wasn't exactly popular – though had Winston Reid still been alive, I'd have pinned it on him. Since she was doing her level best to block his appointment and substitute the blue-eyed boy, the green-eyed boy wasn't too enamoured. Reid didn't like being thwarted and I suspect would have had no qualms in dispatching her, given half a chance. A peculiar blighter altogether.' He paused and added acidly, 'As it is, the stairs got in the way.'

'It must be awful for Sir Richard,' Rosy remarked, 'finding Reid's body like that and now being confronted with this nightmare. He is bound to be dragged into it all. Harrowing at any time, but especially in his first year as Master.'

'Ah, it's very likely to be some fiendish plot devised by Maycock in revenge for pipping him at the post. The Senior Tutor can be very obstructive when he chooses . . . Although, as a matter of fact I shouldn't bother too much about old Dick being harrowed; once the dust settles and he recovers from his initial palpitations he'll cope in his usual way: blinkered and impervious.' Smithers flicked ash on

145

to the grass sprinkling Cedric's turn-up (something that fortunately the latter failed to notice), and then added, 'And after all, he has the stalwart Anthea at his side. She's bound to buoy him up.'

The sardonic tone was caught by Felix, but not by Rosy, who had thought of something else: 'Oh, talking of palpitations, has anyone seen Mr Hinchcliffe? He left early before the concert finished. Wasn't it Basil Leason who said he had a heart problem? I hope he is all right.'

'Praying, probably. I saw him in King's Parade earlier this morning meandering towards Great St Mary. I seem to remember chapel being his first port of call after Reid's demise, so doubtless he is now valiantly battling to assist Gloria's soul in the preferred direction.'

Rosy winced at the flippancy, but kept quiet.

Smithers smiled, and then standing up said, 'Oh, and getting back to Gloria – for everyone's immediate concern the essential thing is being able to produce an alibi. Something that I have and you haven't – unless you count loitering by the corpse being one.' He winked, and with a nonchalant wave sauntered off.

'That young man is too pleased with himself,' Cedric remarked peevishly when he had gone. 'And what's more I just hope he won't start going around making tasteless jests at our expense. Most people know that we found the corpse – the papers have seen to that – nevertheless, one hardly wants it constantly referred to.'

Some of that morning's al fresco discussion was being echoed in the stuffy office shared by Detective Inspector Tilson and Detective Sergeant Hopkins.

The question of motive had been temporarily shelved.

Both were agreed that the deceased had not been the easiest of people and was likely to have made enemies – but not, on the face of things, with sufficient cause to have prompted actual murder. Certainly face value was hardly reliable, but for the time being they were focusing on something more tangible: the victim's reason for being in Magdalene Street in the first place and at that hour in the evening.

'She lived this end of Madingley Road, so she was probably on her way home,' Tilson said. 'Getting there doesn't take too long from the centre. I gather she didn't have a car and would stride all over the place. Of course, she may have been attending some function in Magdalene College or visiting someone there. Have you checked that?'

'I haven't needed to,' Hopkins replied with a hint of smugness.

'Oh really, Sergeant? And why is that?' Tilson frowned.

'It so happens that my aunt attends sewing classes run by the Townswomen's Guild.' Hopkins fumbled for his handkerchief and sneezed violently. And then, red-eyed, he did it again. And again. 'Hay fever,' he gasped, blowing his nose vigorously.

Impatiently, Tilson waited for the trumpetings to subside, and then for fear of another eruption, said quickly: 'So what exactly have your aunt's sewing classes to do with Miss Biggs-Brookby being stabbed in the back? Forgive me if I am being a trifle dense, but the connection somehow escapes me.'

'She ran them,' the other explained, 'every Wednesday and Sunday evening in the Guildhall. Regular as clockwork. So I think you were right about her being on the way home. And I bet you the murderer knew her movements, bided his time and pounced at the opportune moment. According to my aunt she was quite a tartar and played merry hell if anyone was late or had left their cotton reels behind. Sunday was the late night because she used to play dominoes with the vicar of Holy Sepulchre after evensong. The class would pack up at about ten, tidy the room and do a bit of chatting, and then go off . . . So, I bet you that's what she had been doing, plying her needle before walking home and getting stabbed en route.'

Tilson cogitated. And then he said sourly, 'I see. At least it was done with a dagger and not with a bare bodkin. That would have been too ironic.'

'What?'

'A bare bodkin, Hopkins, don't you know your *Hamlet*?'

Hopkins did not know his *Hamlet* and Tilson was pleased.

'And so what about that dagger?' Hopkins asked. 'Bill Wilton in forensics says it was foreign.'

'Yes it's a Bursa, one of those Turkish ones copied from the Albanian original. The older ones have horn handles, which this one's got, and a long, curved blade. Most are made in Bursa, as you would expect, but quite a few are still around in Albania and the Balkans. Apparently they are favoured by the peasants for hacking off sheep's heads and pursuing local feuds.'

'So what's one of them doing hacking into the back of Gloria Biggs-Brookby on Magdalene Bridge?'

Tilson spread his hands. 'Your guess is as good as mine. 'It looks quite an old style – intricate carvings on the hilt – so it could have come from Albania: perhaps some British soldier picked it up when we were booting out the Germans and brought it home as a keepsake.' He paused and grinned: 'On the other hand, maybe some Turkish pasha came to Cambridge for fun and games, and finding none decided to vent his spleen.'

'Still it's quite a clue, I suppose . . . and I bet you that if it's old, as you say, the thing could be quite valuable. Whoever it belongs to is probably kicking themselves for having left it in the body. Lost a pretty penny there, I daresay.'

Tilson sighed. 'You have a commercial mind, Sergeant.' They turned to mull over other aspects, specifically the reliability of the three finders.

'I rather liked her,' Hopkins said.

'Immaterial,' Tilson replied curtly. 'They say Ruth Ellis was a charmer. When you've been in this game as long as I have you will learn that women are just as lethal as men. Worse, really. The trouble with you, Hopkins, is that you are susceptible to the fairer sex.'

Hopkins sneezed again and felt vaguely pleased. He wondered if the fairer sex was susceptible to him. One would have to practise! Out loud he said, 'And what about the florist?'

'The limp-fisted one? I shouldn't worry about him. It's that professor we need to watch. I know the type – crafty buggers. Cambridge is full of 'em.'

Later that afternoon the 'limp-fisted one' was sprawled (as far as he could be) on his narrow bed. He gazed at the ceiling and considered what John Smithers had said in the rose garden – his allusion to Winston Reid and his plunge down the staircase. Smithers had spoken coolly, jocularly, with no suggestion of 'inside' knowledge regarding the circumstances of the sculptor's death. And yet according to Anthea Dick, Smithers had been apprised of every detail of the truth and knew full well that Sir Richard (and himself) were not the first ones to have encountered the body that afternoon: that Lady Dick had been there previously, witnessed the fall and made certain adjustments to the result.

Felix's eye wandered to a newly purchased silk shirt draped elegantly on the back of a chair, and mentally preened. An inspired choice! But the distraction was brief and his thoughts quickly returned to the wretched Reid business . . . Yes, despite Smithers' biting comment about Anthea giving loyal support to her husband, there had been nothing to suggest he was not being entirely discreet on the matter. A good thing too: at least it showed the chap had some decency. But supposing Lady Dick lost her nerve and confessed to her lover that he, Felix, was also party to the truth and knew of their affair. That could be embarrassing. Damned uncomfortable, in fact. Yes, obviously Smithers should be avoided – or if they did meet, one would need to be blandly charming and lull the chap into a sense of security. A false sense? Certainly not – it was hardly his business to blow the gaffe. As he had gallantly assured the troubled Anthea, he would remain as quiet as the grave.

At the onset of pins and needles, Felix shifted his position slightly and turned his thoughts from one lover to the other, and wondered about Anthea Dick. So how was she coping with the situation? Obviously, the coroner's verdict of accidental death would have been a relief – but enough to allay all fears? Cedric had warned him she would be bound to regret her intemperate confession and see him as a potential blackmailer. What nonsense! . . . But was it? In her place he would be thinking the worst of everyone, would be as windy as a scalded cat. He pondered what to do: whether to seek her out and stress that her secret was safe with him (and with Cedric, of course, though he needn't mention that) or, as with Smithers, keep well away and say nothing.

He studied the ceiling morosely. Really, the whole thing was exceedingly wearing – and now there was this ghastly Gloria business. It was too bad: Cambridge was supposed to have been a joyride! He closed his eyes and began to think longingly of Cap Ferrat and Mr S. M.'s delightful ménage. With luck the invitation was still open. Ah, the balm of the Riviera with its waving palm trees, rambling bougainvillea, emerald swimming pools, the movie stars and white tuxedos . . . and who knew, perchance dear Cocteau . . .

Worn out by agitation, and despite the rigours of the bed, Felix drifted into blissful slumber.

CHAPTER EIGHTEEN

That evening in the Fellows' Garden the principal topic of conversation was inevitably the murder. Apart from a glancing sympathy for the victim, the subject generated a range of responses: largely revulsion and avid curiosity, but also expressions of black humour (mainly from Smithers), and from some quarters, indignation.

This last was most keenly shown by Dr Maycock, who, after a taxing day soothing Sir Richard, was resting briefly before escaping home to supper. 'It really is the most shocking thing,' he grumbled, 'and not at all what one expects in Cambridge. And it is the sort of publicity the college can well do without. Mind you, bad enough for us, but I shouldn't like to be in Magdalene's shoes. Mark my words, they will have nothing but gawping tourists for months on end – hanging over the bridge, taking photographs, yelling on the river, pounding at the porter's lodge demanding information. Frightful!'

'Ah well, the price of fame, I fear,' somebody observed. 'But at least it will divert them from our corner for a while . . . Oh, and incidentally, talking of fame, what of the sculptor Finglestone? How is he taking it? After all, it was the good lady herself who landed him the job, so I don't imagine it can be easy hearing that your benefactor has gone for a burton.'

'Actually,' Vernon Carter said, 'I did happen to see him this morning in The Eagle, wilting over a gin. He didn't look particularly perky. I was in a rush, otherwise I would have gone over to speak to him.'

'What has Finglestone got to wilt about?' the bursar said dismissively. 'He has the commission, a fat advance and plenty more when the job's done – plus presumably the additional kudos of having his creation displayed in the grounds of a Cambridge college. You'll see, it will feature in all the guidebooks and he'll get the kickback.'

Listening to this exchange, Cedric was mildly shocked. How cynical one's fellow academics could be! He glanced over to Felix, but the other did not notice, being too busy making eyes at a Pekinese belonging to the gardener.

'What, even if it is listed as "Finglestone's Folly"?' Smithers asked.

'Folly? Whatever do you mean?' Dr Maycock exclaimed.

'Oh, I can guess what he means.' Carter laughed. 'We don't really *know* what it will be like. After all, the Master may take one look at the finished product and then gently expire. The whole thing could be a hideous fiasco. Finglestone would collect his fee and then the statue be discreetly shoved into some darkened recess: there's a spare corner in the porter's lodge – I am sure Jenkins could make room for it. An alternative, of course, would be to secrete it among those rhododendrons Professor Turner keeps harping on about. At least that would give them a function.'

'Don't be ridiculous,' the bursar said irritably, 'we have already been shown his preliminary sketches. Admittedly, they are a bit odd, but nothing outlandish. You really are a doom merchant, Carter – and so are you, Smithers.' The younger dons exchanged amused glances, feeling rather like admonished schoolboys.

At this point Felix, abandoned by the Pekinese and hearing part of the conversation, observed that preliminary sketches did not always match the end product. 'You can start with a concept, but the whole thing can go utterly awry in the production and the result bear little resemblance to the original plan. Sometimes, of course, this can be quite a good thing. But I remember once when I was designing a floral pillar for Her Majesty, and she was most put out when—'

'Ah yes,' Cedric said hastily, 'but I think this can be true of all artists: plans are not sacrosanct and deviation is inevitable.'

'Well, let's hope the chap keeps his deviations to a minimum,' the bursar growled, 'otherwise I might be very slow in writing the cheque. Might even break my arm!'

They laughed. And then someone else said: 'But in terms of Gloria, I know that in all the best crime fiction the victim is supposed to know their assailant, but that's just a popular convention. For all one knows, this chap chose her randomly and is still around waiting to pounce again . . . on any of us.'

'In which case he will have to purchase a new knife,' Carter pointed out.

'Ah, but perhaps he has an arsenal,' observed Smithers darkly. 'One dagger down and several to go.'

Listening to these suggestions, Felix began to feel worried. The image of a skulking assassin biding his time for further attack had entered his own mind, and hearing the idea mooted by somebody else was not exactly reassuring. Clearly he would need to take a sleeping pill that night, two in fact. Meanwhile he wished they would change the subject. Covertly he looked at his watch. Thank goodness it was nearly time for dinner. He could do with some grub; it would calm his nerves.

Fortunately the dining hour soon struck, and with the exception of Maycock, John Smithers and a couple of others, the group left the garden to take their places in Hall.

As ill luck would have it, Felix again found himself sitting next to Aldous Phipps. Ill luck not because he disliked his neighbour, rather because the latter's presence could unsettle all but the most stout-hearted, and Felix was not of that ilk.

'Ah, we meet again.' The old man beamed. 'Mr Smith, the florist from Camberwell! And how are you weathering this Gothic horror, may I ask? Not the most fragrant business, I fear. I gather you were one of the unfortunate finders. You must tell me all about it! Here, let me poor you a drop of this excellent claret,' he added winsomely.

Felix was glad of the claret, but less glad about the proposed topic of conversation . . . and distinctly needled by the insistent allusion to Camberwell and the mishandling of his name (the long vowel being so important). Really, he

155

must try to put the old boy straight about such matters – it was too bad!

But before he could correct the errors – or fortunately supply any of the requested data – Phipps said, 'To my mind it is obviously an inside job. Oh yes, you can be sure of that. I know some people are suggesting otherwise, but I think that is poppycock – merely a way of making them feel more comfortable. And when I say "inside", I do not mean from within the *Town*, Mr Smith, but from within the *Gown*, if you get my meaning. How about that then, eh? How about that?' The old man fixed Felix with a look of sly relish.

Though smarting from the mode of address, Felix was nevertheless relieved that Phipps should be so sure the killer was from within the circle of scholars. At least that reduced his own chances of getting slaughtered! He took a sustaining sip of claret and was about to turn to his neighbour, when Phipps plucked him by the sleeve. 'I have it on good authority that a *foreign* weapon was used; oh yes, a dagger from the Balkans, it is rumoured. Would that have been your observation, Mr Smith?'

'Er, I hadn't really noticed,' Felix murmured vaguely.

Phipps looked disappointed. 'Ah well, I don't suppose we can all be detectives, can we.'

Not all detectives? Huh! Try looking for clues when you are being sick all over the pavement! Felix inwardly fumed and eyed the claret jug, hoping Phipps might take the hint and pour him some more. But his neighbour's mind was elsewhere: fixed on the Senior Tutor, in fact. 'An odd coincidence,' he chuckled, 'I expect you know that the Balkan peninsula is Dr Maycock's particular province. He used to go there quite often. An interesting field of

156

study, I should say, but not for the likes of me – too many hoary brigands!'

Felix didn't care a fig about Maycock's field of study or hoary brigands, but he could certainly do with some more wine. 'Terribly good claret, Professor. I would suggest a 1952?' he said ingratiatingly.

'Ah, there you would be wrong: Chateau Talbot 1955, but a good try. I daresay I could interest you in a little more . . .'

At last. And his lucky break: Phipps had collared a waiter and was busy muttering about the vegetables. In relief, Felix turned to the person on his right and began to talk fulsomely about the plants in the Fellows' Garden. The man listened attentively and then eventually said, 'Afraid I am allergic to flowers, bad for my hay fever. I give them a wide berth. It's cacti I like.'

'Ah,' the other said. They returned to their respective cutlets.

Over the port and Stilton, Felix was once more appropriated by his neighbour on the left. 'I have much enjoyed our conversation, Mr Smith. A grisly subject, admittedly, but not without interest. And I will tell you another thing: it is my considered opinion that Winston Reid's fall down that staircase is also not without interest. In fact, I would go so far as to suggest it is *fishy*. I smell a rat and suspect that the two deaths could be complementary . . . However, that is not the view shared by our stalwart police officers, so who am I to stir things up? Not my place at all. As they say, one doesn't keep a dog and bark as well. My little terrier would be most disapproving!' He smiled benignly (or with a fair imitation) and returned to his port.

Later that evening Felix complained bitterly to Cedric about Aldous Phipps and his beastly fishy rat. 'And what's more,' he stormed, 'it would be helpful if you could remind him that I live in Sloane Street and that my name is *Smythe*.'

'Oh, absolutely, dear boy. Have no fear.' Cedric patted his shoulder.

CHAPTER NINETEEN

As she retraced her steps to the museum, Rosy brooded. Being with Cedric and Felix that morning she had felt fine: shaken certainly, and yet at the same time oddly detached. The aftermath of the ordeal – the interrogation by the police, the quick-fire questioning from the press and the floods of alarmed sympathy from Newnham colleagues – had somehow helped to blur that dreadful image: the image of the knife's shocking hilt dark against the lilac jacket. The ensuing furore had bludgeoned her senses, had almost anaesthetised her feelings. So much had been going on that there had been little time to dwell on the thing itself, to register its full reality. As in the proverbial dream, she had been drifting vaguely.

But now, being alone, talking to no one and walking slowly in the warm sunshine, she had both the space and time to think and to *feel*. How alive the woman had been, how tirelessly (and tiresomely) assertive, tough and spirited. Gloria Biggs-Brookby may have been maddening – wrong-headed, perhaps – but she had certainly got life by the teeth. And now she was dead, and in horrible circumstances. A force had been fatally incised. Soberly, Rosy confronted that strange reality, and like the police officers Tilson and Hopkins, asked herself the teasing question: why?

The woman had certainly antagonised people, that was quite obvious – and she hadn't been overenamoured herself – but were those antipathies enough to prompt murder? It seemed curious. But, of course, as Felix had observed, there did not have to be a motive at all – merely the impulsive action of a passing lunatic looking for fun, and Gloria had got in the way.

Hmm. *Got in the way*. Yes, the deceased had been in the way, all right: pitting her intrusive will against the Plot and Monument Committee, thwarting their plans and intentions; and then with Reid dead, chivvying the sponsors and triumphantly pushing her man for all she was worth against diehards like Phipps, Williams and Maycock. They hadn't liked it; they hadn't liked it at all!

Rosy's mind swung back to the overheard conversation between Maycock and Lord Bantry in The Eagle. Yes, feelings had clearly been running high. It was quite apparent from what she had gleaned that both men were deeply agitated by Gloria's interference – and indeed her capacity for further meddling. Equally they were determined to put a stop to it. Maycock had implied that the Master would eventually yield to her pressure. And how had Bantry replied? She could hear the words now, dry and steely: *Then we must ensure that it doesn't reach that point, mustn't we* . . . And what about

Maycock's cryptic reference to 'ways and means' and his caustic allusion to an accident. At the time she had taken it to be a rather crude joke, but given the later event could it just possibly have held some sinister implication? Oh, surely not! But then she recalled how concerned Bantry had been about the acoustics in their corner of The Eagle – his quizzical hints that she had been eavesdropping, or at least aware of what they had been saying. Why the interest? Had it been casual, or deliberate probing?

She thought too of the Master's party and Bantry's biting allusion to Gloria's mental state. It hadn't been lightly said. Despite the mocking smile his voice had been harsh, bitter. Rosy winced as she also recalled Gloria's own crushing portrayal of Dr Maycock, painting the ageing scholar as a washed-up dinosaur, and saw again the angry flush colouring the man's cheeks as he obviously caught the scathing words.

Oh yes, the air had been full of anger, all right, but enough to induce the ultimate expedient? Dear God, she hoped not . . . And yet somebody had done it, had urged themselves to plunge and twist the knife. Someone had been on that bridge, waiting, skulking, gauging the right moment. She wondered if words had been spoken, noises made – and shuddered. For an instant the sun disappeared (literally), and in that moment Rosy felt a cloud of bleakness descend. It wasn't fear exactly, but a heavy, clawing anxiety.

Fortunately the cloud was quickly dispelled – partly by the sun's reappearance and largely by a child dancing up and presenting her with a bunch of limp dandelions. Rosy grinned and, taking the flowers from its sticky hand, walked briskly up the museum steps ready for business.

* * *

As Stanley had directed, under the pretext of being earnestly engrossed in the exhibits themselves, Rosy wandered from room to room scrutinising their positions, labels and layout. She stood at different angles, assessing the backdrops and lighting effects, the type of picture frames, the glass of the display cabinets. Dutifully she would make an occasional note, but was embarrassed lest she should be thought some crank or government bureaucrat. It all struck her as being perfectly normal and conventional: what you would expect from a distinguished and well-run museum, and, contrary to Stanley's suspicions, with nothing especially radical or 'groundbreaking'. Good. So that was fixed. Now for Purblow's lecture programme, which would be displayed somewhere.

She looked around, and in an anteroom found a collection of notices announcing forthcoming talks and events. A poster for 'Art and the Modern Public' had been given prime position, but it had a label attached expressing deep regret that the scheduled second talk had been cancelled owing to the speaker's 'vital' engagement at the Washington Smithsonian. Rosy smiled in relief: a mercy for her . . . and presumably a perk for Purblow (first-class travel and all expenses? Dr Stanley would be green with envy; she would mention it). Making a note of the lecture's date and time, she moved on.

One more task: to find the curator's office and chat up its occupier about the rumoured *Lady Chatterley* exhibition. She had glimpsed Mrs Maycock at the benefactors' reception, but they hadn't spoken. From what Rosy recalled she was somewhat younger than her husband and had looked jolly and approachable. Well, she would approach her now – and if by chance she was not available, then too bad. At least she had tried.

* * *

Fortunately the lady was available; and when Rosy introduced herself as working at the British Museum, she seemed happy to talk. She spoke vividly about the pleasures and problems of the Fitzwilliam's curatorship, and Rosy regaled her with a few anecdotes of life with Dr Stanley. And then rather tentatively she introduced the question of the museum's project concerning the Chatterley trial.

Mrs Maycock stared at her blankly. 'I am afraid I have no idea what you are talking about. I can't say I am mad about Lawrence . . . and besides, it's hardly the sort of thing the Fitzwilliam would be interested in organising. Still, perhaps the trustees know something that I don't! But whoever told you?'

Rosy felt slightly embarrassed; and not wishing to rat on her boss, was about to mumble something about the grapevine, when the other glanced at her watch and gave a sigh of impatience.

'Oh, I'm so sorry,' Rosy exclaimed, 'I hadn't realised you were busy. I come blundering in and—'

'No, no.' Mrs Maycock laughed. 'I'm not at all busy, merely waiting for my errant husband. It's my birthday and he's meant to be taking me out to lunch, but he is fifteen minutes late already. He will be dawdling somewhere – although more likely with Sir Richard discussing this dreadful business about the Biggs-Brookby lady.' She stopped abruptly. 'Oh goodness, weren't you one of the finders?' Rosy nodded. 'My dear, my sympathies. It must have been simply dreadful. Too horrible for words!'

She looked genuinely concerned. And then after checking her watch again, she said, 'Look, if by chance you should bump into my old man, could you please tell him that his starving wife is awaiting him with much impatience, and that she has a vital meeting this afternoon that can't be missed. In other words, tell him to jolly well hurry up!'

After wishing her happy returns, Rosy made her way back to the entrance hall where she did indeed bump into the tardy Dr Maycock. Or at least, she did not so much bump as observe from a distance. He was standing with his back to her talking to someone half-hidden by a pillar. He seemed very engrossed, and fractionally Rosy hesitated, reluctant to intrude. But thinking of the ravenous 'birthday girl' eager for her lunch, she went forward. And then suddenly recognising his companion, she stayed her steps. Did she really want to meet the two of them together again and so soon after that last encounter? Not necessarily.

But it was too late. They had already seen her and abruptly broken off their conversation. Rosy approached Maycock and smilingly delivered his wife's message. He thanked her affably and she half expected some sly greeting from Bantry (a reference to red shoes again?), but slightly to her surprise he said nothing, merely giving her a distant nod. She sensed a slight awkwardness which she couldn't define and, not being invited to linger, turned to go.

Crossing the then empty hall, Rosy experienced a pang of disquiet and had the uncomfortable feeling of their eyes being upon her as if she was being watched . . . being watched and assessed. She felt unnerved. And then she felt a fool. What absurdity: one was getting paranoid! The dreadful spectacle of Gloria's knifed and lifeless corpse was clearly affecting her imagination and she was investing the most neutral words and actions with sinister meaning – what Betty Withers would doubtless call 'heightened morbidity'. Yes, that's what she was suffering from, a heightened morbidity!

Putting two fingers up at such nonsense and with head in air, she marched firmly down the museum steps, slipped and almost took a header.

Idiot! she thought and, regaining her balance, turned left, intending to go down to look at the river. But just as she was passing Peterhouse she heard footsteps behind her, and a voice said, 'Ah, Miss Gilchrist – I thought it was you. Nice to see you again!' Rosy looked up into the smiling face of Dame Margery Collis. 'I'm dying for some coffee,' she said, 'and there's a new place just opened off Bene't Street; it's Italian and rather fun. Will you join me?'

Rosy was perfectly happy to do so, having enjoyed the older woman's company at Newnham on her first evening in Cambridge.

Over rather more than coffee (some novel Roman pastries) they briefly touched on the dreadful Gloria tragedy, but by tacit agreement moved quickly on to less disturbing topics: Rosy giving a glowing report of the recent madrigal concert, and the other extolling the comforts of her borrowed flat.

'It couldn't be better,' she enthused, 'and not only right in the centre, but with every mod con you can think of. And one can park right outside, so getting over to Girton couldn't be simpler.'

Rosy enquired how the lecturing was going.

'Quite well, actually, and the girls have even managed to weather the statistics that I've forced upon them.'

'Statistics? But I thought your thing was education.'

Dame Margery laughed. 'It is these days, but I was an economist originally and statistical analysis was my speciality. It's a bit of an indulgence, really, and I slip it in whenever possible . . . Doubtless your psychologist friend

Betty Withers would say it betrayed an arid mind!'

Rosy suspected Margery's mind was far from arid, and envied the woman her natural ease, self-possession and professional achievements . . . Cool and disciplined, perhaps, but you didn't become a Dame by having an arid mind.

They succumbed to another pastry and continued chatting easily. And then Dame Margery exclaimed, 'Oh, I nearly forgot: you couldn't possibly do me a big favour, could you?'

'It depends how big.' Rosy laughed.

She explained that earlier on she had been in Great St Mary talking to the verger, an old friend. He had produced a couple of notebooks left behind by Geoffrey Hinchcliffe who had also been there that morning, and wondered if she could manage to pass them on to him.

'Without thinking, I said that of course I would – but in fact it won't be possible, as I shall be at Girton for the rest of the day and out all evening. You couldn't possibly slip them into his digs, could you? There is a scribbled address on one of them – the place is very near to Newnham. Richard said the fellow had been looking rather pale and abstracted, so presumably the loss of vital notes might turn abstraction into *dis*traction! So, if you would do that I should be terribly grateful.'

Aware of how worrying (disastrous?) such a loss could be, Rosy readily agreed and put the books in her bag.

They left the cafe, and with smiles and good wishes Dame Margery said goodbye. For a few moments Rosy watched the tall, confident figure walking briskly away among the pavement strollers. *Nice to be elegant*, she thought, *especially at that age . . . still, at least I have neat ankles*. She grinned and hitched up her shoulder bag, now heavy with Hinchcliffe's books.

* * *

That evening it had come on to rain, but only lightly and not enough to deter Rosy from her task of returning the books to their owner. Of course, there was no guarantee he would be there, perhaps being still absorbed in his researches at one of the libraries. But with luck there might be a landlady she could leave them with.

She found the house easily enough, a high stuccoed semi wedged into a corner off Sidgwick Avenue. A light was on downstairs, which suggested that at least somebody was at home. Rosy rang the bell and waited.

The door was opened by a grey-haired woman clad in a mackintosh and who was vainly trying to restrain a wayward cat. The cat dived past Rosy and down the front path.

'Oh, I'm so sorry,' she began, 'I am afraid I've—'

'Let the cat out of the bag?' The woman laughed. 'Oh, don't worry about Boris. He's a Burmese – little buggers, they are, but he'll come back all right – *when* it suits him. So what can I do for you, my dear? Not canvassing, I hope?'

Rosy assured her that wasn't the case and explained what she wanted: '. . . and so if Mr Hinchcliffe isn't here, perhaps I can just leave these with you?'

'Oh, he's here all right, came in about half an hour ago. As a matter of fact he looked a bit tired to me, so I've just taken him a cup of hot cocoa. That should put the colour in his cheeks. Mind you, I did suggest a nice sweet sherry, but he didn't seem too keen – he's a mite picky, is Mr Hinchcliffe. Can you find your own way, my dear? Number 3, second floor along the passage. I'm off now – bingo night. Wish me luck!' The woman buckled her mac, grasped a brolly from the stand and disappeared into the drizzle.

* * *

Left alone, Rosy mounted the stairs feeling slightly embarrassed. If Hinchcliffe was feeling tired would he really welcome an unexpected visitor, even one bearing his mislaid notebooks? Well, she thought, the main thing was that he should get them; she needn't stay long. Tentatively, she knocked on the door.

It was opened almost immediately. 'Oh my goodness,' Geoffrey Hinchcliffe exclaimed, 'Miss Gilchrist! To what do I owe this pleasure?' He looked slightly flustered, but ushered her in and gestured vaguely to an armchair next to which stood a small table supporting a large cup of mantling cocoa.

Rather breathlessly, Rosy explained her visit and passed him the books.

'Too kind, too kind,' he murmured. 'Yes, I knew I had left them somewhere, but couldn't think where. I fear this ghastly incident on Magdalene Bridge has rather knocked the stuffing out of me. My apologies. One has rather lost one's bearings.' He gave a rueful smile.

Looking at him, dishevelled and wan, Rosy could believe that. The man seemed somehow vaguely adrift. 'Yes, I think we all feel a bit like that,' she said quickly. 'A frightful business. But you must lose yourself in that essay you were telling me about, it sounds most intriguing.' (It didn't particularly, but being used to Dr Stanley's frets Rosy was practised in tactful comment.)

Hinchcliffe gave a thin laugh and, pointing to the cocoa, said, 'You are right, and certainly preferable to losing myself in that cocoa. Not my stuff at all, and that is particularly frightful; almost as bad as the terrifying tea! But, oh dear, I really shouldn't complain. She is a charming landlady, so kind, so kind . . .' His voice trailed off and he stared pensively at the empty fireplace.

Rosy felt slightly awkward and began to get up to leave. He looked strained and the sooner she left him in peace the better.

'Oh, but please don't go,' he said insistently as she picked up her bag, 'you make me feel so ungracious. After all, by bringing my notes here you have done me a great service and the least I can do is to be the genial host!' He gave a wry smile, gesturing at the somewhat cramped and sparsely furnished room. 'Besides, we have much to talk about.'

Have we? Rosy thought, slightly puzzled. *Oh, well, if he thinks so . . .* She waited. But the silence continued as he stared blankly into space. She cleared her throat and tried to think of words that might generate some utterance. None came.

And then just as she was about to produce some banality about the weather or the landlady's cat, he looked at her and in a faraway voice, said, 'I am glad you are here. You see, it has all been rather trying and I need to unburden myself.'

Rosy felt uneasy: did she wish to have a burden lobbed into her lap by a virtual stranger? Preferably not. 'What has been trying?' she asked warily.

'Death. It sort of sticks in the mind, doesn't it?'

He was right of course. But currently the emotional trauma of death was not something she was keen to probe; after all, she had only dropped in to deliver some books.

'I do understand,' she replied tactfully, 'but try not to take it too much to heart. One gathers the attack was very deft and very quick and she would have hardly registered anything. I know it was horrible, but dwelling on it really doesn't help.' The words were inadequate, but at that moment they were the best she could muster.

The pale face regarded her vaguely. 'What?'

'I do not think Gloria suffered all that much,' Rosy declared firmly.

'Miss Biggs-Brookby?' he exclaimed, suddenly animated. 'I am not talking about *her* – I mean Winston Reid, of course – he whom I dispatched!'

CHAPTER TWENTY

So stunned was Rosy that for a split second his words meant nothing. When they did she felt she must have misheard or that they were some tasteless joke. She gazed at him astounded, but could detect no humour in the unwavering eyes.

'You look shocked,' he observed quietly. 'In your place so might I, but be assured, Miss Gilchrist, he died by my hand.'

'No, he didn't.' Rosy gasped. 'He had been drinking and fell down the stairs. Everybody knows that; it was the coroner's verdict!'

'Then everybody is wrong.' He folded his hands in his lap.

She grasped at a straw, something to lessen the horror: 'Ah, I suppose it was a mistake – you had gone there and quarrelled and somehow it just happened.'

'Oh no, I fear there was nothing accidental about it. I came up to Cambridge with the express purpose of killing him, and as things turned out the matter couldn't have gone more smoothly. So often one's intentions are thwarted – don't you find?' He raised an enquiring eyebrow, while Rosy gaped. 'What did Burns say,' he continued, '. . . something about the best laid plans of somebody or other?'

'Of mice and men,' Rosy replied mechanically, 'and, er, it was "schemes", actually.' She stared in dazed disbelief, wondering if the man was mad.

'Oh yes, that's it – "schemes", of course. Really, my memory these days! Still, at least I can complete the line: "Gang aft agley", if I'm not mistaken.' He smiled, and then with a nod of satisfaction added, 'But in this case things did not go agley: he was already half-dead when I found him – moribund, one might say. It only needed a slight adjustment to complete the process.'

God in heaven, Rosy thought, *he is either lethal or lunatic!* If the latter and living a fantasy, a show of indulgence might be the best ploy . . . But equally, if he was telling the truth and thus indeed lethal, the same too might be wise. Thus, she gave a kindly smile and, trying to match his conversational tone, enquired the reason for the 'scheme'.

'A bit of a long story, I'm afraid, but I can tell you the man had only himself to blame: he had done dire things and had to bear the consequences. "As you sow, so shall you reap" – a sound precept, in my judgement. Wouldn't you agree?'

Briefly, Rosy felt she was back in the examination hall or her tutor's study, faced by a proposition with its peremptory command: 'Discuss'. But this was hardly a Cambridge tutorial they were engaged in. It might be simpler (and safer) to steer him away from the moral aspect to the more practical. Best to keep on neutral ground!

With this in mind she said, 'I don't quite understand. It was reported that he died as a result of a fall down the stairs – broke his neck and banged his head. Sir Richard Dick and Felix Smythe found him. There was blood and he was drenched in whisky.'

'Oh yes, plenty of whisky,' Hinchcliff replied casually, 'but that had nothing to do with me, though I *was* responsible for the blood, I fear. Fortunately there wasn't too much of that, and naturally as a precaution I had taken rubber gloves and an overall with me. One can never be too prepared – always the Boy Scout, that's me! Tell me, Miss Gilchrist, were you ever in the Girl Guides?'

Rosy shook her head. 'They wouldn't let me in,' she said faintly.

'Oh, that's a pity. You would have learnt so much; an admirable organisation and full of all manner of useful little tips – at least the Scouts were, and I imagine it was the same for the ladies.'

Despite her fear, Rosy heard herself asking dryly if those useful tips included how to dispatch an injured man lying at the foot of a staircase. 'For example, I assume you bashed his head against the banister,' she remarked coldly . . . and instantly bit her lip. Fool! He must surely have sensed the sarcasm: it was hardly the tone to soothe a raving lunatic.

But to her surprise Hinchcliffe took no offence. On the contrary, he seemed eager to explain further. 'Oh no, a banister is relatively blunt – painful, no doubt, but not necessarily lethal; and besides, it would probably have needed a number of knocks. No, as luck would have it, Reid had placed some sort of bronze bust just next to the last step;

a small head on a square marble plinth with a sharp corner. It only took one biff and I knew the job was done. Couldn't have been better – though why he had to put the thing there, I don't know. Most ill-placed in my opinion: the light was poor. And highly dangerous, I should have thought, but perhaps it was just temporary . . .' He broke off, evidently pondering the vagaries of sculptors. Not caring to dwell on the details of the deed, Rosy hastily turned her mind to the postponed question: *why* had he done it? This time she was careful to make her tone suitably meek.

She cleared her throat. 'Uhm, if you don't mind my asking, what prompted you to do it? I mean to say, it's not something one—'

'Undertakes lightly? You are quite right. I thought long and hard about the problem, but came to the conclusion that in the circumstances it was all for the best.'

But not for Reid! she felt like saying, but didn't dare. Instead, assuming an expression of docile interest, she said mildly: 'I am not quite clear – so what exactly was the problem?'

'He was blighting my life: destroying my anchor and casting me into the depths. Something had to be done.' The response held a biblical ring, but it was far from mimicry and Rosy listened gravely.

'You see, when I left Cambridge and went to live in London I happened to encounter Reid, who was just starting out on his sculpting career. We became mild friends, but then things changed and he embarked on what I can only describe as a feast of harassment and calumny. He besmirched my name and caused much harm.'

'In what way?'

'It so happened that all those years ago – a good thirty – I pinched his girlfriend and he didn't like it; not one little bit.'

'Er, well, no, I don't suppose he would,' Rosy ventured. 'On the whole people do take offence when that sort of thing happens.'

'Yes, but it was a bit more complex than that and the results were unfortunate. She became pregnant.'

'Ah . . . well in that case, if you had made her pregnant I suppose he would be rather annoyed. I mean—'

'No, no! *I* didn't make her pregnant, someone else did. That's just it: she refused to name the father, and Reid put it about that I was responsible.' Hinchcliffe flushed, and then hesitated before muttering, 'If you want to know, I wasn't too good at that sort of thing – one of the reasons we broke up – so I knew it couldn't be me . . . Ironic, really: I was torn between being secretly pleased that I was evidently deemed sexually stalwart, and horrified that I should be traduced in that way. For a period, one was the recipient of righteous censure and knowing jibes. It was particularly humiliating as my uncle was a bishop and I was fearful the rumours might reach him.' Hinchcliffe closed his eyes. 'It was a ghastly time.'

Rosy nodded. 'So what happened?'

'Fortunately it eventually blew over. She went away and married, I believe. Reid lost interest and became engrossed in his sculpting, and I decamped to Africa to instruct the natives in bee-keeping.'

'Crikey,' Rosy exclaimed. 'Did it work?'

He shook his head. 'Not noticeably. They got stung and seemed to think it was my fault. After that I came home and continued my rather uninspiring life in a solicitor's office in Neasden where I remained until the miracle.'

'What miracle?'

'Well, one day, when I was feeling particularly bleak, I was tapped on the shoulder.'

'Oh yes, by whom?'

Hinchcliffe paused, and then lowering his voice, said quietly, 'Well, it was God, you see – it was his hand.' Rosy raised a polite eyebrow.

'Indeed it was,' he continued. 'You may well look surprised, and so was I. But do you know, from that very moment my life was utterly transformed. My days took on miraculous meaning as at last I had found purpose and direction. Some would term that experience an epiphany – *I* see it as my moment of deliverance!'

Rosy looked at him sharply, assuming he was having her on; but the wide eyes and earnest tone suggested otherwise, and despite a natural scepticism and his earlier revelation, she felt a brief surge of sympathy. The man's normally placid face had lit up with a radiant beam and he appeared genuinely moved by what he was telling her.

'So you found a new direction,' she murmured. 'And where did that lead you?'

'Kensington,' was the calm response.

'*Where?*' Rosy's flicker of sympathy vanished. *Huh*, she thought grimly, *who would have thought that the staid pavements of W8 might form the silken ladder to heavenly bliss.* Clearly the chap was barking, after all ... However, she enquired patiently what was so special about Kensington.

'Number 16, Erdleigh Place,' he declared, 'it's our headquarters.'

'Headquarters of what?'

'Of the Lord's work. It's the hub of our little society – where we prepare our strategies, compose our pamphlets and interview prospective candidates.'

'Candidates?'

'Candidates for spreading the Word and helping the Fallen. We're quite a thriving little community. Non-denominational, you understand – in fact, I rather suspect that one or two members may not be believers at all, or at least not in the full sense – but we all muck in and do our bit. I can't tell you what uplift it has given me knowing that I have been involved in something productive and spiritually useful.' Hinchcliffe's face fell as he added bitterly: 'It was all going swimmingly until all over again Reid started his evil nonsense. If it hadn't been for him, my life would have continued in joy and confidence. As it is, I have been wracked with anxiety – sleepless nights and desperate days.'

His eyes took on an expression of bleak hopelessness; and despite herself Rosy felt another twinge of pity.

'Yes, life had been proceeding most amiably until a year ago when the accusations started up again and with renewed force.' He gave a wan smile: 'The perverted energy of age, no doubt, the final putsch before the end. It was a sort of campaign of malice and mischief, a persecution complex in reverse. Reid kept dropping beastly hints that he would tell these lies about me to the fraternity. I couldn't have borne it . . . Dear Christ, those bloody letters and phone calls were intolerable!' His face contorted in a spasm of pain.

Rosy was startled by the sudden burst of ferocity; it punctured his usual restraint. And for a second she saw Hinchcliffe crouched by the sculptor's body as he dashed the balding head against the 'ill-placed' plinth. Yes, the capacity could well be there . . .

However, the next moment Hinchcliffe had apologised for his 'unseemly' language and in milder voice continued his narrative.

'It was sickening, and as I have said, seemed without reason. Boredom, perhaps, or a festering grudge about my taking his girlfriend? Who knows. But it was horrible; and the curious thing was I couldn't make out what he *wanted*. No demands were made, no money mentioned; so it wasn't blackmail. He seemed merely intent on filling me with the greatest discomfort and fear. Somehow, he had got wind of my activities in Kensington with the fraternity, and guessing that to be my vulnerable spot threatened to apprise them of my "past". Not only did he threaten to tell them the old lie of my getting a girl into trouble and having a secret son, but he even said he might hint at my having interfered with small boys.' Hinchcliffe flushed again and blew his nose.

'And had you?' Rosy asked.

'Certainly not,' he exclaimed indignantly, 'I do not *like* small boys!' Rosy considered the man sitting opposite her with the troubled eyes and drumming fingers, and reminded herself that he was a murderer.

'You could have told the police,' she said sternly. 'They would have done something.'

'Oh really?' he replied with some asperity. 'What exactly? I had no hard evidence. The nastiest things were said by telephone, only the more ambiguous by letter . . . although I do recall one letter more explicit than the others, but it so sickened me I threw it away. I can see the passage now: "My dear good fellow, we both know that mud sticks: a nod here, a wink there, and your pious colleagues would drop you like the proverbial hot coal – or do I mean potato? Either way, you wouldn't last."'

Rosy's distaste must have shown, for Hinchcliffe nodded. 'I see you get the picture: a despicable type and dangerous with it. He had to be stopped. He deserved to go.'

'Who said so – God?'

There was a long pause while he studied the ceiling. Finally, he said, 'Yes, I believe so: God speaking via my heart. I was his emissary doing good works. Reid tried to prevent that. Thus I smited him.'

'Smited'? Rosy wondered. Shouldn't it have been 'smote'? She pulled herself together. Really, this was hardly the moment to ponder grammatical niceties, but to work out what the hell to do next! She shot a covert glance at his briefcase. If he had 'smited' Winston Reid, who knew what might be concealed there – a meat cleaver? One false move and she could end up like the sculptor!

Would she be able to reach the door before he did? Perhaps she could throw her chair at him. Would screams be heard? Certainly not by the landlady, far off playing her bingo. Rosy's mind whirled feverishly. But then seeing the man's eyes fixed hard upon her, his fingers gripping the marble ashtray on his desk, such thoughts of escape suddenly vanished and her limbs felt riveted. She gave a faltering smile, and with pumping heart enquired what he proposed to do next.

Hinchcliffe regarded her for a long time without expression, while she felt her stomach clench and her mouth go dry like a stone. Eventually he stood up and took a step towards her.

There flashed before Rosy an image of Johnnie, shot to smithereens over Dresden. Their ends would be the same: smash and horror . . . She shut her eyes, paralysed by the man's closeness. *Oh dear God*, she thought, *this is it*, and waited for the blow.

The blow when it came was that of his voice saying: 'What I *propose*, Miss Gilchrist, is to bear my cross. My course is obvious: I must confess all to the police and take the consequences. Perhaps you will be so kind as to come with me; a companion on such an occasion would be most fortifying. Will you do that? I should be greatly obliged.'

Looking back on events, Rosy wondered why she hadn't gone out like a light there and then. The mixture of relief and incredulity had been so engulfing that she could scarcely breathe, and for a few seconds all she had done was to gaze witlessly at the man before her, his brow creased in earnest enquiry.

'Of course,' she answered mechanically with mind utterly numbed, 'if that's what you would like.'

He gave a formal little bow. 'Most kind,' he said. 'A veritable act of charity. I shall pray for you on the gallows.'

The raw term seared and, recovering herself, she said briskly, 'Oh, I am sure it won't come to that . . . besides, these days it's not a public scaffold they use, but a sort of trapdoor in the cell.'

'A great improvement,' he murmured.

On reflection, Rosy felt her response had been a bit tactless and wondered if he was being sarcastic. She heard her mother's voice from long ago: '*Think*, dear, before you speak. Otherwise the bogeyman will bite your tongue off.' Well, it was too late now – there was a matter of much greater concern to confront: a visit to the Cambridge constabulary.

But had he really meant it? Surely not. Yet presumably he must have, for already he was buttoning his coat and fiddling with his briefcase. He glanced around for his umbrella, picked it up and walked to the door, where he turned. 'Ready?' he asked.

She nodded silently.

'Then off we go.'

She may have imagined it, but he seemed to brace himself; and then opening the door he ushered her through. Flustered, she dropped her open handbag but without waiting he went ahead while she hastily picked it up and replaced the fallen debris.

CHAPTER TWENTY-ONE

The passage to the staircase was only a few yards, but in that short space Rosy felt she was moving in the proverbial dream. Nothing seemed real except Hinchcliffe's slightly stooped figure in front of her and the sound of her heels clicking on the bare boards. How bizarre to think she was accompanying a killer to meet his fate in this manner: almost as though they were setting off to the cinema!

At the top of the stairs Hinchcliffe hesitated as if to stand aside to let her pass. And it was then that Rosy's 'dream' vanished and was replaced by sudden nightmare. She looked at the narrow wooden staircase, and in a flash fancied she saw the sculptor's lifeless body sprawled at its foot . . . *Oh my God*, she thought, *he wants me to move in front so he can attack from behind and hurl me to the bottom. We're not going anywhere: it's all a trick.*

Instinctively she shrank back against the wall.

'Ah, it's probably best if I lead the way,' Hinchcliffe said, 'this thing is so ancient and rickety that one can easily trip. Besides, it would be awful if you fell – I shouldn't have a witness for my statement.' He gave a light laugh and, grasping the banister, placed his foot on the stair.

They walked in silence across the hallway and down the path, circumventing the cat, which, as predicted, had returned and sat grooming itself with studied nonchalance. Rosy felt ashamed of her earlier panic. She recalled herself as a girl manning the searchlights at Dover during the war. Had she known such fears then? Not really, or certainly not like this. Perhaps at the advanced old age of thirty-seven she was beginning to lose her grip. She sighed, and then glanced at Hinchcliffe. Perhaps in her late fifties she too would turn homicidal!

Emerging into Sidgwick Avenue, Rosy was reassured when her companion turned towards Queen's Road. At least they appeared to be going in the right direction and not into some ill-lit hinterland.

'It's quite a walk,' she said tentatively, 'should we take a taxi?'

He paused and glanced at the nearby rank. 'We *could*,' he replied, 'but there is a shortcut into Silver Street and it doesn't take long from there. And, actually, Miss Gilchrist, since this is likely to be my last hour of freedom, I should quite enjoy the evening air. I hope you don't mind?'

'Oh no,' Rosy said hastily, 'not at all. How thoughtless of me.' Inwardly she felt distinctly apprehensive. The rain had darkened the evening sky and the roads were relatively deserted. There flashed before her the memory of Gloria's fate and she bit her lip. To stem unease and introduce a note of mild normality, she said, 'I think it is awfully brave of you to do this. I mean, most people simply wouldn't have the nerve. When did you decide?'

Hinchcliffe consulted his watch. 'Oh, I should say about forty minutes ago – when you asked what I proposed to do. Up until then I was exceedingly confused. But hearing the question voiced by another person somehow clarified my mind and I realised there was only one option: the *moral* one.' He spoke with firm determination, but after a slight pause added, 'Nevertheless, although I know I must take my punishment for having wilfully mistaken God's purpose in the matter, I cannot say that I have any regrets as to the outcome. Reid was a beastly blackguard whom I still consider better dead than alive.' He spoke with a quiet vehemence which revived Rosy's fears. But the next moment he sighed, and said, 'Still, I disobeyed his precept and thus must pay the rightful due. He would expect it.' Hinchcliffe turned and regarded her intently: 'Don't you agree, Miss Gilchrist?'

This was more than Rosy had bargained for. It was one thing to go with him to the police station, but did she really want to be drawn into theological speculation about God's purpose and expectations?

She was just trying to formulate a suitable answer, when her eye was caught by a slight movement to her left. There was a shape – the figure of a man crouched in the shadows. Alarmed, Rosy gave an involuntary jump backwards, and then let out a gasp of shocked relief. 'Felix,' she cried, 'how nice to see you!'

* * *

Unused to being greeted so effusively by Rosy, Felix too was a trifle shocked. He straightened up from tying his shoelace. 'Ah,' he said, rather flustered, 'I wasn't sure if it was you and . . . well, I didn't like to intrude in case—' He broke off, recognising Hinchcliffe.

'Mr Smythe, if I am not mistaken,' the latter observed, 'what a coincidence. We were just on our way to the police station; you can come too, if you like. You would be more than welcome.' He spoke as if issuing a gracious invitation to a party.

Felix was flummoxed, as well he might be. Why should Rosy Gilchrist be strolling along with the Hinchcliffe chap at this hour of the evening (not a date, surely?), and why on earth to the police station? Had they lost something? As to joining them . . . well he had better things to do. Dragooned by Cedric into attending a particularly dreary talk on Cappadocian cave formations, he had managed to slip away pleading a headache; and now with escape accomplished he had been relishing the prospect of an early night and another peck at his article 'Playful Blooms' displayed in the current *Tatler*. Police, Hinchcliffe and Rosy did not feature in the plan.

He was about to make his excuses, but was forestalled by Rosy. 'Oh *yes*, that would be such a help, Felix,' she cried eagerly. 'It's all rather delicate and we could just do with you!' Smiling and nodding, she gripped his arm firmly, and the next moment he found himself walking with the pair of them in the direction of St Andrew's Street. He was none too pleased.

'I expect you want to know why we are going to the police,' Hinchcliffe said to him, conversationally.

'Er, well it had crossed my mind,' Felix replied politely. 'Is there some problem?' Rosy's grip on his arm tightened. *Really*, he thought, *did one wish to be quite so roughly manhandled?* He shot her a sharp look and was met with an anxious grimace.

The next moment Hinchcliffe had answered his question: 'Not just now there isn't, but I suspect there soon will be. You see, I doubt very much whether the police will believe what I have to tell them. A cynical bunch, so one hears . . . I fear there could be an argument.'

Felix was just about to say that in his experience the forces of law were always inclined to argument, when Rosy stopped abruptly and pointed: 'Oh look, we're here already. There's the blue lamp,' she announced rather nervously.

'Ah yes, the blue lamp,' Hinchcliffe echoed soberly, 'I see it beckoning.' For a few moments he stood staring fixedly at the imposing building in front of them, and then turning to Rosy said quietly: 'I think I have changed my mind.'

'*What*?' She gasped, thinking he was about to flee into the night.

'Yes, I am afraid so,' Hinchcliffe murmured apologetically, 'and you may feel I have brought you both here under false pretences. But the fact is that I have been thinking things over and have decided that it would be best if I faced the ordeal alone. This is a crucial moment in my life and my only support must be the hand of God . . . I, and only I, should confront the custodian of the front desk.' The tone was resolute, but Rosy could see a film of damp on his forehead – traces of rain or something else?

'What on earth is he talking—' began Felix.

'Be quiet!' Rosy snapped, gripped by relief and wonder. She turned back to Hinchcliffe and asked if he was really sure. 'We are only too happy to come if you want,' she said stoutly.

The latter shook his head and with a pensive smile said, 'You are most kind – but no thank you. As my father used to say, this is my party.'

They watched, as slowly but with head erect Hinchcliffe approached the stern Victorian portals. At the threshold he paused fractionally between the heavy columns, the ray from the blue light illuminating his hollow profile; and then, without looking back, he disappeared inside.

'What in heaven's name was all that about!' Felix exploded. 'Surely he can speak to the duty sergeant without divine assistance, can't he? What's the chap done – failed to pay a parking fine?'

'No,' Rosy replied shortly, 'assuming he was telling the truth it is a bit more serious than that.' She reached into her coat pocket and fished out a packet of cigarettes, and with unsteady hand tried to light a match. At the third attempt it flickered and went out. She shrugged, threw it away and replaced the cigarettes in her pocket.

Felix watched these fumblings with some curiosity, and then, producing his lighter, offered her one of his. She took it gratefully. 'If you don't mind my saying,' he observed gallantly, 'you look frightful.'

She gave a rueful nod. 'I daresay. Actually, if you want to know, I've had rather a trying time: Hinchcliffe has been telling me how he murdered Winston Reid.'

For a few seconds Felix was speechless. And then

without thinking he burst out, 'Utterly absurd – I know for a fact he couldn't have!'

Rosy was taken aback: Felix did not usually speak with such conviction. 'What fact?' she asked.

He hesitated, recalling his vow of silence to Anthea Dick. 'Well,' he muttered rather lamely, 'it does seem unlikely. What has he been saying?' And so as they walked back to the Market Place, Rosy gave him a graphic account of her time with Geoffrey Hinchcliffe and the man's startling confession. As the details emerged things began to make sense; and Felix saw that although clearly barking, Hinchcliffe could have been telling the truth. After all, the two versions, his and Anthea's, did rather complement each other.

His initial instinct was to tell Rosy of the part played by the Master's wife in the event, but a twinging conscience dictated otherwise. Besides, he would first have to chew the cud with Cedric. With luck, his friend should be back from the Cappadocian talk by now, and so the whole thing could be aired over strong nightcaps. The prospect was appealing. And thus on reaching the city centre he hastily found Rosy a taxi to take her back to Newnham. As he held the cab door open, he said, 'I wonder what the poor chap is doing now.'

'Still arguing, I expect,' Rosy replied.

She was right. When Hinchcliffe presented himself at the reception desk, the duty sergeant – tired from dealing with drunks, professional complainers and those seeking errant pets – was in no mood to listen to some half-baked rigmarole from one claiming to have battered an evil man to death with the hand of God on his shoulder. Whether the hand was on the shoulder of the victim or of the assailant was not entirely clear. But certainly God featured somewhere. On being asked the identity of the victim he was told tartly that such details were for the ears of the interviewing officer alone and not for minor functionaries.

The minor functionary knew his place, and wearily enquired whether the man could do with a mug of cocoa. 'Very soothing is cocoa,' he assured Hinchcliffe. 'In fact, I was about to have one myself. You'll soon feel better. Take a pew and I'll get Charlie to bring it.' He gestured to the young constable.

Hinchcliffe regarded the policeman indignantly. 'I am not a fool, you know – and one is a killer not a cocoa addict! And as to taking a *pew*, the only pews I am familiar with are those in God's House. This is no such building, but an establishment operating the law of the land. That being the case it is incumbent upon you to arrest me.' Hinchcliffe glared defiantly and folded his arms.

The sergeant yielded, took down his name and address and switched through to the inspector's office. 'We've got a right one here,' he muttered, 'you had better come down.'

Back at the college Felix was too excited to stop off at his own room, but scrambled up the staircase and knocked loudly on Cedric's door.

Cedric, who had been listening to the Bruch violin concerto on his rather tinny transistor, was startled. He was also annoyed, for his favourite section was imminent and despite the poor tone he resented the intrusion. Thus, his face as he opened the door was not exactly welcoming.

Felix was undeterred, knowing that his news would soon change that. 'You will never guess!' he began.

'The Queen Mother has sent you a telegram,' Cedric said coldly.

'Oh no, something *far* less likely,' Felix exclaimed, and embarked on his tale.

Cedric sat impassively throughout. But when it was finished (and rather as predicted) he reached for the whisky and poured two large glasses. 'Well,' he observed, 'that does put a different complexion on things. Who would have thought that fusty little Hinchcliffe had it in him . . . extraordinary really, the things people do. Just as well I didn't see more of him when we were undergraduates. Who knows, I might not have been here today!'

'Praise be the Lord,' Felix tittered. He took a sip of whisky, and then looked suddenly sober. 'But what are we going to do?'

'Do? We?' Cedric asked, looking surprised. 'Nothing at all – that is to say, keep quiet, of course. *We* have no connection with anything.'

'But supposing he wants me to corroborate his story, to tell the police what I know?'

'But dear boy, you know nothing. It's Rosy Gilchrist who got the brunt of his confession; she's the one they may want to interview. He hardly said a word to you – in fact,' Cedric added mischievously, 'he probably doesn't remember you at all, a mere shadow on the way to the scaffold.'

Felix was both peeved and relieved – but also unsettled. He took another sip of whisky and brooded . . . 'Uhm, do you really think he will swing? After all, one can't help seeing his point about Winston Reid. The chap sounded most unsavoury; a thoroughly nasty piece, in fact. He tried

190

the same sort of thing on Anthea Dick, pursuing her for no obvious reason, but just for the hell of it.'

'Oh, I agree. But if one bumped off everyone not to one's taste I don't suppose there would be many of us left . . . And as to Hinchcliffe's fate, I doubt very much if he'll swing. The fact that he has given himself up is likely to be a mitigating factor; although I also suspect he could be found of unsound mind. It's the religious aspect – the authorities get flustered and don't know what to make of it.'

Back in her bedroom at Newnham, Rosy was also flustered . . . well not so much flustered, perhaps, as deeply perturbed. Her evening with Geoffrey Hinchcliffe had been unsettling to say the least and she wondered how he was coping. But she now had another problem to confront, a decision to make: should she tell the police of her involvement? Shocked though she had been by his revelation, she had to admit to feeling sorry for the chap. Despite the awful deed, he had shown a curious vulnerability and a sort of meek mannerly stoicism. Dastardly acts should be enacted by dastardly people, and somehow she didn't feel Hinchcliffe fitted the type. It was perplexing.

And yet by giving her that explicit and graphic account of the murder he had made her his confidante, and were she to withhold that knowledge she would become an accessory after the fact. It was surely her bounden duty to report to the police station and tell them what she knew. The prospect was sombre and she instinctively recoiled from the task. Besides, she had had quite enough of 'helping the police with their enquiries' over the Gloria case. It would be embarrassing to confront them again on a completely different issue . . . a far from happy déjà vu.

It also struck her that the following morning was Purblow's lecture at the Fitzwilliam. To miss that would be to deny Dr Stanley his 'vital' information. She switched out the light and brooded further, but ruefully conceded that her own distaste and Stanley's needs were small in comparison with the needs of justice. Yes, quite patently she would have to be the good citizen . . . Thus Rosy drifted off to sleep in a haze of reluctant duty.

Waking three hours later she started to visualise herself being yet again at the police station: introducing herself to the desk sergeant, stating her business, narrating her account to some grave official who wondered how it was that this earnest young woman seemed so drawn to the strange and unsavoury. She lay pondering the irony . . . and then, with a start, sat up and stared into the darkness. *Wait a minute, wait a minute*: there was a let out, of course there was! Why on earth hadn't she realised? Not only had Hinchcliffe confessed of his own free will, but more to the point he had voluntarily given himself up. It certainly hadn't been her idea that he should march off to the police station and spill the beans. He had chosen to pay his due freely and openly, had deliberately placed himself in the hands of the law. There had been no coercion. What on earth had Rosy Gilchrist to do with the matter? Nothing. The murderer had taken his own responsibility and was prepared to pay the price. What more could be done? For her to make an unsolicited visit to the police station and give a 'corroborating' statement would be irrelevant and officious. By now the truth was already known (presumably) and thus any intervention on her part nosy and gratuitous.

Rosy relaxed on her pillows; and sedated with the prospect of Purblow's lecture, slept soundly for a further three hours. When she awoke the sun was shining. She thought of Geoffrey Hinchcliffe in his cell and hoped they were treating him kindly.

CHAPTER TWENTY-TWO

Sir Richard Dick had also slept soundly on the night of Hinchcliffe's confession, having spent a most congenial evening playing bridge with the bursar and Dr and Mrs Maycock. The matter of Finglestone's appointment had not been mentioned; and while at first the recent appalling outrage had been the subject of comment, it had been eclipsed by the pressing matter of tricks and trumps.

Anthea had been pleased for her husband to be so occupied: it was a brief respite from the strain of Gloria's tragedy and the insistent attentions of police and journalists. Things had been bad enough with the Reid affair (she shuddered), but this latter event was even more irksome and already taking a toll on his digestion and temper.

She had thought of giving him breakfast in bed, but was diverted by the telephone. Glancing at the clock she saw it was only eight-thirty. A bit early for a call, wasn't it? Perhaps it was the police again wanting more details about Gloria, e.g. could the Master say whether the victim had had any special cronies? No, Anthea thought acidly as she picked up the receiver, only browbeaten lackeys.

Five minutes later she replaced the receiver on its cradle and gazed disconsolately at a butterfly crawling across the windowpane. As she had guessed, the call had come from the police . . . but this time it was nothing to do with Gloria. Something else.

For a few moments she stood pondering the news. Oh, how awful, the poor chap! But at least it had been quick – a sudden seizure, a heart attack they had said: 'Came over all queer and just collapsed. Sipped his cocoa and that was it.' Coma, ambulance, death . . .

Anthea turned to the window and released the butterfly, which fluttered gaily into the sky. She wondered vaguely what he had been doing at the police station at that time of night. (Being Hinchcliffe, it seemed unlikely he had been hauled in for gross misconduct or dislodging a policeman's helmet.) But still, she supposed it was as good a place as any to face death. Quite convenient, really – safe hands and all that. She sighed and went to take a cup of tea up to her husband and report the bleak tidings.

Understandably, the Master was not bolstered by the news. 'Poor old fellow,' he murmured, both genuinely saddened, but also annoyed. Why now, for God's sake, just after everything else! He sipped his tea and closed his eyes.

'I think we could invite the sister here for a couple of days,' Anthea suggested. 'They said she was coming up to identify the body and deal with things.'

'What?' he said vaguely.

'The sister. The police have asked her to come. I mean, doubtless she could stay at his lodgings or a hotel, but in the circumstances it would be pleasanter for her here, don't you think?'

'Of course, of course,' he agreed, sipping his tea and gazing glumly out of the window.

News of Geoffrey Hinchcliffe's sad demise filtered through to the college members and to those few sponsors extending their stay in Cambridge. These, of course, included Cedric plus Felix and Rosy as important witnesses in the Gloria knifing.

The latter was stunned to hear the news on her return to Newnham from the Purblow lecture (long and self-promoting) and was once more undecided what to do. Betty Withers, always a reliable bloodhound, had ascertained the main details.

She told Rosy that apparently Hinchcliffe had presented himself at the police station in a heightened state, not of inebriation but of considerable confusion, and looking pretty ropey. (Yes, he had certainly looked ropey, Rosy recalled. But confused?) He had rambled something about sin and being a killer, but had declined to elaborate and instead demanded to see the inspector. Asked to wait, he had taken one sip of the cocoa they had brought him, made a face and keeled over. And that was that. He hadn't responded to resuscitation and died in the ambulance.

'And he didn't say anything?' Rosy asked.

Betty shook her head. 'Nothing that made any sense.'

She also told Rosy authoritatively that in her professional experience it was often the case that those leading up to acute heart failure frequently suffered delusions and mental muddle.

Rosy noted the information, but was firmly convinced that Hinchcliffe had been far from deluded. She also recalled his detestation of cocoa. Had that been the final straw?

Any residual doubts about what she should do were banished the next day. It had dawned bright and fresh, and that afternoon she had taken the chance to wander along the bank of the Cam and admire the houseboats moored by Jesus Lock. She had often done that as an undergraduate and doing it again stirred happy memories.

Strolling back across the Green she noticed three people sitting on a bench at the side of the avenue, and rather to her surprise saw that two of them were Lady Dick and Dame Margery Collis. They began to get up and were clearly about to leave, but seeing Rosy the latter waved and beckoned her over. Their companion was a small whey-faced woman whom they introduced as Hortense Hinchcliffe, evidently Geoffrey's sister. The lady smiled brightly, but there were tears in her eyes and the thin fingers trembled slightly as she shook Rosy's hand.

Lady Dick explained that Hortense had travelled up from London and was staying at the Lodge while she coped with the sad task of sorting her brother's belongings. 'It's such a lovely day and we thought a stroll in the sunshine would do us all good,' she said brightly.

Rosy nodded, and uttered words of kindly sympathy to the guest, feeling sorry for the woman but also rather awkward.

'He was such a sweet boy,' the sister murmured. 'I don't know what I'll do without him. He was so kind . . . He would do anything for me, you know.' She smiled wanly. 'So kind,' she repeated. '"Hortense," he used to say, "you must always be happy. I insist!"' She bit her lip and looked pensive, and Rosy feared she might give way. But then with a little toss of her head and a squaring of the frail shoulders, she declared, 'And with his dear help, so I will!' She had the look of a battered but resolute robin.

The group continued on their way, and Rosy was left knowing she would never shop the ghost of Geoffrey Hinchcliffe.

Firm in that knowledge she watched them go, and then walked on slowly down the main avenue, savouring the blessing of the blue sky, the dappling canopy of plane trees and distant sound of children's laughter. No longer hemmed by buildings and traffic, she felt the weight of the last forty-eight hours gradually subside, the tension stealthily relax. What a bizarre business it had all been, surreal almost, and so sad . . . But at least it was over now, a thing of the past. Laid to rest. Buried. Normality could be resumed.

Normality? What on earth was that? A bit of an illusory concept, surely. The Hinchcliffe episode might fade, become unreal – but what about the very real and unfaded matter of Gloria Biggs-Brookby? That most certainly remained and made things far from normal!

As she walked, Rosy pondered the affair, wondering if any progress had been made. The newspapers didn't seem to think so, announcing that the local police were foxed and it was high time Scotland Yard was summoned. A large amount of print was taken up with the journalists' own speculations, empty but lucrative.

As with the other two witnesses, she had been recalled for additional questioning. They had been interviewed separately (something that had made Felix nervous), but whether their accounts had yielded anything further Rosy rather doubted. Neither officer had looked especially jubilant. They had been quizzed not just about the murder scene itself, but also about their impressions of Gloria when seen at the Master's reception. Comparing notes afterwards, it emerged that their accounts had been identical in describing her mood as being robustly assertive, and that far from seeming worried or tense the victim had been alarmingly confident.

Hmm, Rosy brooded, *too confident for her own good?* She had certainly got her own way over the appointment of the sculptor (so presumably had died happy!). But others had been less happy, had been infuriated by those plans and confidence, had been determined to block further intrusion . . . *Always ways and means – and accidents, of course . . .* Once more Dr Maycock's words came echoing back to her. Oh, but he had been joking; of course he had been joking.

Yet even as she dismissed such nonsense the more recent image of him and Lord Bantry at the Fitzwilliam hung before her. At the time she had scolded herself for being a paranoid fool for thinking they might be watching her. And she had probably been right: a couple of chaps conversing in low tones and stopping abruptly at her approach – one could hardly call that sinister. A little plotting, perhaps, but surely not about murder. They were respectable elderly gents with positions to protect, not knife-wielding thugs. She almost laughed out loud – and then remembered that Geoffrey Hinchcliffe had also been someone of sober gentility. More so, really: there had been a meekness there that couldn't be said of the other two!

Such were Rosy's twirling thoughts that by the time she

had arrived back in the city centre the benevolent effects of Jesus Green had somewhat waned. In fact, she felt quite worn out. To restore equilibrium she marched into Robert Sayle's and bought two lipsticks, a mascara wand and some luridly pink nail varnish. Armed with these trophies she then treated herself to a large pot of coffee and a doughnut in the Italian cafe introduced to her by Dame Margery. No more mulling over murder, she decided. She would buy a glossy magazine and return to Newnham for a good chinwag.

In her room experimenting with one of the lipsticks she heard a knock at the door and, on opening it, was faced by the nice girl from the office.

'There's a telephone call for you,' the girl said, 'but you'll have to come down to the hall, I'm afraid we don't have anything on the landing.'

'That's quite all right,' Rosy said, wondering who on earth it might be. 'I'll be there in a second. Please tell her to wait.'

'It's a him, actually.' The girl smiled and went off down the passage.

A him . . . who? Rosy wondered, fearing it might be the police again. Down in the hall she picked up the receiver, relieved that it was not the police, but equally unnerved to hear the voice of her boss, Dr Stanley.

'Everything all right?' he demanded. The question had a peremptory ring.

'Er, yes,' she said guardedly, 'shouldn't it be?'

'Oh, just checking,' he replied airily. 'A funny place Cambridge; Oxford's far safer – though if you must go gadding off to the eastern wilds, I suppose you know what you're doing.'

'Er yes, I suppose I do,' she said vaguely, wondering what he wanted. There was bound to be something, there always was. And then of course she knew: obviously the espionage.

It was. 'So, what's the progress on the Fitzwilliam front? I trust you have been keeping your ear to the ground. What are they up to?'

'Nothing. And the curator was dismissive of the Lawrence idea, said it wasn't in keeping with the museum's image.'

'*Nothing*? Are you sure?' Stanley sounded almost disappointed. 'And what about Purblow's lectures – you did attend, I assume?' The voice had sharpened.

She explained that one of them had been cancelled and the other was of such nebulous waffle that she doubted if the Fitzwilliam would take note of his views.

That seemed to please Stanley, who gave a derisive snort: 'Running true to form, I see.' There followed a pregnant pause. And then he said: 'I gather you've had a spot of trouble – someone bumped off, some woman to do with that Biggs-Brookby cove.'

'Well, yes,' Rosy said, 'she was his daughter – but I didn't do it. It's not the sort of thing that is expected of visitors.' She gave a weak laugh to cover the lie of being one of Gloria's finders on Magdalene Bridge. It was not something she had any desire to publicise.

'Glad to hear it. Make sure you take care.'

Rosy was startled. Solicitude for the welfare of others was not one of Stanley's noticeable traits. Had he been over the road in the Museum Tavern?

He then asked when they could expect her back. 'It's in your diary,' she reminded him, 'first thing on the eighteenth.'

'Good. Just as well. Nothing seems to work without you here. It's most tiresome.' The normally abrasive tone sounded not so much petulant as pensive. The last time she had heard that note was when his spaniel had died. But then with a brisk laugh, he told her to watch her back and that on her return they would celebrate. She heard him mutter something about a table at Wiltons, and the line went dead.

Rosy contemplated the kiosk's blank wall in some puzzlement. Celebrate? What did he mean? How curious . . .

CHAPTER TWENTY-THREE

The matter of Reid and the Master's wife continued to trouble Felix. He was nagged by the urge to assure her more strongly of his utmost discretion. She had told him her story impulsively and in a state of great agitation, and, as Cedric had so helpfully pointed out, despite the enquiry being closed she was bound to be feeling vulnerable. And what if, as Cedric had also slyly suggested, she really did fear him as a likely blackmailer? Preposterous! To be cast in such a role was demeaning, to say the least, and besmirched his dignity. Things must definitely be clarified. But how? Since their encounter in the Botanic Garden he had been assiduously avoiding her (and possibly she him) so how now to approach her alone? What pretext could he use?

Such were his thoughts as he strolled across the Market Place to inspect some flowers displayed on one of the stalls.

And then just as he reached it he suddenly caught sight of a familiar figure on the corner of Trinity Street. Good Lord – it was the woman herself! He stopped and dithered. Certainly she was alone, but so public a place was hardly suitable for a serious talk. What should he do? He continued to dither.

And then as she started to walk briskly up Trinity Street he was suddenly galvanised. He opened his wallet, withdrew a note and, without waiting for change, bought three lavish bouquets of Regale lilies. Then almost smothered in these he hastened onwards in anxious pursuit of his disappearing quarry.

At last he caught up with her and triumphantly thrust the blooms into her arms, while at the same time embarking on a breathless explanation.

'Lady Dick, I fear you may have been harbouring anxiety,' he began (sensing he sounded peculiarly like Cedric), 'but I can categorically assure you that you have nothing to fear. As I told you earlier, my lips are sealed – sealed and riveted. The thing was an accident entirely beyond your control. You were blameless and that's an end of it. And as to related matters, they are not remotely any business of mine. As far as I am concerned the whole issue is dead as a doornail. As a *doornail.*'

Delivered of his spiel, Felix stepped back still panting slightly, but looking very stern – or he would have done had it not been for the large smudge of lily pollen streaking his cheek and nose. Somehow it lessened the effect.

Anthea was flustered by the sudden overture and, clasping the enormous bunch of flowers to her chest, regarded him in wonder torn between relief and mirth. What an odd little fellow! But how remarkably decent. She felt quite moved.

She thanked him profusely for his gift and they parted on terms of mutual comfort . . . Lady Dick because she could now finally put the damn thing to rest, and Mr Smythe because he knew he had acted with style and gallantry.

Returning to the Market Place, Felix bumped into Rosy who had also been shopping (not for flowers, but chocolates to anaesthetise Stanley).

'Goodness, what have you been up to, Felix?' she asked, eyeing him intently.

'I have just been chatting to Lady Dick,' he replied airily. 'We were saying that—'

'Yes, yes, but what's that orange splotch in the middle of your face? It looks suspiciously like the onset of jaundice to me.'

With face averted Felix hurried back to the college eager to expunge the embarrassing stain. Really it was too bad – you pay a lady a compliment and get that in your face!

Halfway up the staircase he almost collided with Monty Finglestone coming down. The young man mumbled an apology, and then stopped and smirked. 'I say,' he observed, 'is that a touch of jaundice or just a smear of marmalade?' Without waiting for an answer he clattered on down the stairs.

Felix was incensed. 'Insolent sod,' he seethed. He was about to continue when his eye was caught by a small pocketbook lying on one of the steps. It hadn't been there a moment ago and had obviously been dropped by the sculptor. It flashed through his mind to run back and return it to its owner, but the impulse was instantly dismissed. Why the hell should he? Hulking barbarian!

Finglestone could wait for it. In fact, he was in two minds to leave it where it was. But Felix's better nature (which he certainly had) dictated that he retrieve the thing. Once in his room he shoved it aside and returned his attention to a more pressing concern: erasing the mark of Cain.

Meanwhile, Cedric was feeling put out. Much as he enjoyed being back in his old stamping ground, the unsavoury events of Gloria's killing and the Reid imbroglio were considerably more than he had bargained for. Such crude melodrama was ill-fitted to such a civilised city and had cast a long shadow on the trip. He felt guilty too about Felix. He had persuaded his friend to accompany him to Cambridge in the expectation they would share a jolly time and that Felix would be charmed by so special a place. And yet far from being a merry idyll away from the hurly-burly of London's social life, their stay had been engulfed with the tiresome and grisly. It was too bad!

That afternoon he expressed these feelings to Felix and ruefully apologised for embroiling his friend in such dark events. Felix had been touched by Cedric's concern and had brushed aside his fears, effusively insisting that things could not have been lovelier – a claim that made Cedric smile and filled him with gratitude.

'I tell you what,' Felix had said gaily, 'let us dine out tonight, somewhere plush and expensive where we can have fun and drown our sorrows. I heard somebody talking about a smart new place in Green Street – we could try that. How about it?'

Cedric polished his glasses and gave the idea sober consideration. It was, he pronounced, a most sane proposal.

So that is what they did: took themselves off to the restaurant and spent a time of genteel frivolity and bibulous pleasure.

They returned to the college in good spirits; and eager to sustain the mood decided to have a final nightcap in Felix's room. Thus, on opening the door they were surprised to find the room already lit, with both lamps full on. They were even more surprised to be confronted by the figure of a man, tall and broad-shouldered. Slung on the bed was a raincoat and large rucksack.

With his back towards them Monty Finglestone was reaching up and running his hands across the top of the wardrobe.

Initially they were too startled to say anything and it was the intruder who broke the silence. 'That's torn it,' he said sullenly.

'I should think it has, Mr Finglestone,' Cedric snapped, recovering himself. 'What on earth do you think you are doing? This is Mr Smythe's room and Mr Smythe's belongings you have thrown all over the floor!' He gestured to the mess of toiletries and shirts littering the carpet.

'Yes, it is a bit of a mess,' the other conceded truculently 'but if Mr Smythe had returned my diary in the first place, I shouldn't need to be here. I realised I had dropped it, but when I went back there was no reply to my knock and I assumed he would give it to me later. But I haven't got time to waste while he sits on it. I want it *now*.' He glared at Felix. 'So where is it, bright arse?'

Never before having been addressed as 'bright arse', Felix was enraged. The cultivated Knightsbridge vowels slipped somewhat and were replaced by a Lambeth twang.

'If you hadn't been so damned rude, I might have,' he rasped with feeling.

'Oh yes? Like hell,' Finglestone retorted. 'I know your sort, creepy little faggots. I bet you've inspected the whole thing, haven't you!'

Felix stamped his foot. 'I am not a bleeding fa—'

'Be quiet!' Cedric ordered. He looked at Finglestone: 'If my friend has anything of yours, then he will be only too ready to return it. And why he should want to read anything you have written I cannot imagine – it is unlikely to be edifying.' With studied disdain he surveyed the young man over the rim of his spectacles, and Felix couldn't help thinking that age was giving him the look of a cadaverous owl.

Finglestone scowled, but ignored the jibe. 'Say what you like, I bet he's got it and I want it.' He stepped towards Felix, who backed hastily.

'Felix, dear boy,' said Cedric gently, noting the signs of mounting fury in Finglestone's face, 'if you do have anything belonging to this gentleman, I suggest you give it to him. The sooner he is gone the better.' He turned and glared at the intruder: 'Naturally, we shall report this matter to the authorities in the morning. I suspect you have had too much to drink, but that is hardly an excuse to ransack Mr Smythe's bedroom. You may be a *sensitive* artist, but your behaviour is gross.'

There was a fraught silence during which the sculptor looked increasingly fierce – but also increasingly taut, his face pale and beads of sweat showing on his forehead. For a second Felix was reminded of poor Hinchcliffe, except that the latter had been strangely controlled whereas this one was simmering with rage . . . Oh well, anything for a safe life. He cleared his throat.

'As it happens, I do have it,' he said. 'I didn't want to muddle it up with my other things, so I popped it into the po cupboard for safe-keeping.' Felix pointed towards the small wooden chest. 'After you dropped the thing I was naturally going to return it – but you know how it is, one is so often overtaken by more congenial events and it completely escaped my mind. Silly me!'

Felix's last words betrayed more edge than he had intended. Had he meekly retrieved the diary from the po cupboard and said nothing things might have been different. As it was, with a grunt of rage Finglestone wrenched the little door open, snatched the book and brandished it in Felix's face. 'You've looked at this, haven't you, you little shit,' he snarled. 'I can see it in your prying eyes!'

'Of course he hasn't,' Cedric said angrily, 'and kindly watch your language. Your behaviour is disgraceful.' He stared furiously at the young man. But his words were lost on Finglestone, who was busy leafing through the pages; until coming to a particular one he stopped, and clutching Felix's arm thrust the book in front of his face. 'That's what you've seen, isn't it! Safe-keeping? Huh, you were hiding it away. Going to give it to me later? Like hell. You were going to take it to the police. Well, not now, you aren't – but, in any case, I've got more than the police to fucking worry about!'

Dazed by the onslaught, Felix gazed unseeingly at the diary and its open page. And then gathering his senses he looked harder. There was no writing – or virtually none. But there was a drawing. A pen-and-ink cartoon of a fat female sprawled over a bridge with a knife stuck in her back. Underneath was the caption 'Gloria done', followed by a tick in red ink. The entry was dated the day the deceased was found.

'Christ,' Felix muttered. And mechanically taking the book from the other silently passed it to Cedric.

Cedric adjusted his glasses and scrutinised the drawing. 'Hmm. Not a bad likeness,' he remarked, 'but her skirt was longer than that and her hair a bit shorter. But you've got the dagger all right – unmistakeable really.' He nodded and returned it to its owner.

The mildness of Cedric's response seemed to flummox the young man and he fixed the other with a challenging stare, clearly poised for something more violent. But the professor stared back impassively saying nothing. Astounded by the drawing, Felix also remained speechless, but out of shock more than anything else. He looked anxiously at Cedric, wondering what the hell was going to happen next.

In fact, what happened was that, sobered by Cedric's silence, Finglestone stuffed the book into his raincoat pocket and sat down on the bed. He glanced at his watch; and then in a rather lordly manner gestured to the chairs opposite. Tactfully, they obeyed. 'I've got a few minutes,' he said calmly. 'I suppose you want to know why I did it.'

'Can't wait to hear, dear boy,' Felix said brightly, his voice at a slightly higher pitch than usual.

Cedric gave him a warning frown.

CHAPTER TWENTY-FOUR

'She was in my way,' the sculptor said simply.

'She was in a lot of people's way, but that hardly justifies your action,' Cedric said severely.

Finglestone pulled a face. 'Yes, I agree it was rather tasteless – but an act of expedience rather than malice. And the point is it had to be done quickly. I couldn't afford to mess around.'

Felix gasped: '"Mess around"? But that's exactly what you were doing! The whole thing was perfectly gross – I couldn't sleep a wink for at least three days. And in any case, why use an Albanian knife, whatever that is? I mean to say—'

He broke off, interrupted by Finglestone's laugh. 'Ah,' the young man said, 'I suppose you wonder what was wrong with a decent British knife, one I could have purchased

from a Cambridge ironmonger and sharpened up a bit.'
He paused, frowning, and then said, 'As it happens I rather
wish I had. That knife was an heirloom, and I didn't really
want to leave it *in situ* – but needs must when one is in a
hurry. I had to scarper quickly.' He gave a rueful smile.

'The knife is an irrelevance,' Cedric snapped. 'More to
the point is your motive. Why do it, for God's sake?'

Finglestone sighed and spread his hands. 'I am a victim,'
he said simply, 'a victim of circumstance and misplaced
honour.'

They gazed at him in astonishment. '*You're* a victim!
What about Gloria on that bridge?' Felix exclaimed.

Finglestone shrugged. 'There are categories of
victimhood,' he replied dismissively, 'and if she hadn't been
so damned interfering she would be alive now. She brought
it on herself.' He spoke with finality and seemed to think
that was the end of the matter.

But Cedric wasn't having that and, adopting a tone of
ingratiating interest, murmured: 'Fascinating. But I'm not
quite clear about that misplaced honour you mention . . . I
don't suppose you would care to enlighten?' He gave a
polite smile.

The other glanced at his watch, and then evidently
reassured both by the time and Cedric's emollient tone,
nodded. 'Well, you see I am originally from Albania, and—'

'I don't care where you come from,' Felix cried
impatiently. 'I can't see what that has to do with you
murdering that woman . . . and besides, where *is* Albania?'
he asked, looking at Cedric.

The latter frowned, irritated by the interruption. 'Oh,
it's a most *charming* country,' he said hastily, 'by the Ionian
Sea and a little north of Greece. Glorious landscape and

fiercely independent people . . . Isn't that so?' he asked blandly, turning to Finglestone.

The other shrugged. 'So they tell me,' he said indifferently, 'but I don't remember much. I was a small child up in the mountains; and then mercifully, in 1939 when the Eyeties came in, my family was able to escape to England. Since then I have never been back; don't want to. Safer here – or at least it was until I met the fragrant Gloria again.'

'Ah, so your family were keen to escape the Italian fascists at the outbreak of war. They were lucky to get out, I imagine,' Cedric remarked, but wondering what Gloria had to do with it all.

'Oh, there were worse forces to escape than the fascists,' the other said bitterly, 'still are, in fact.'

Felix gave a derisive snort: 'Oh you mean like marauding mountain bears, I suppose. Tribes of grizzlies eager for their breakfast.'

Finglestone regarded him coldly. 'No, Mr Smythe. I mean creatures more dedicated, more dangerous: marauding locals out for vengeance.'

There was a bemused silence while they digested his words. Cedric cleared his throat: 'Er, I see – so what exactly were they trying to avenge?'

'A death. One I happen to have caused and which triggered a manic blood feud. It's what they like doing there: feuding. It's part of the culture,' he added carelessly. 'And now I am a marked man.'

A marked man? Cedric thought quizzically. The phrase had the ring of a John Buchan novel or one of those derring-do thrillers, Bulldog Drummond or some such. Was the young man a fantasist? Still, he recalled with a shudder, there had been nothing fantastic about Gloria's murder; that had been real enough! Could there really be truth in what he was saying about the blood feud? The Balkans, of course, had always been notorious for its vendettas, but surely that sort of thing had long died out – hadn't it?

'But if you were such a small child, how could you have caused a death, and whose was it?' Felix demanded accusingly, echoing Cedric's scepticism. He sniffed. 'Anyway, you don't sound at all foreign to me. Sloane Square, I should say.'

The young man gave him a pitying look. 'Not all barbarians speak with a guttural accent, Mr Smythe. I was educated at Winchester, followed by the Chelsea School of Art – not within your province, I imagine.'

Felix tossed his head. 'Well really!' he exclaimed indignantly.

'Ssh!' Cedric said curtly and, turning away from Felix, asked if Finglestone would care to enlarge. 'So who was the victim?'

'An uncle's child, my first cousin. I was six, he was four. A nasty little brat, always grabbing my food. I couldn't stand him. One day he went too far: he had discovered my cache of goats' cheese and raki, and—'

'*Raki*? But that's surely not a child's drink?' Cedric was mildly shocked.

Finglestone grimaced and shook his head. 'You're right, it wasn't very nice: bravado, I suppose – anything to put one over the grown-ups. I had a secret store in an old hut my grandfather used to keep his pigs in. And then one day when I was sitting there quietly, fat Fico came crawling up and tried to nab the cheese. So I biffed him one. Two or three times actually. It was rather fun . . .' A faraway look came into Finglestone's eyes as if recalling the scene. 'Or at least it was fun until the little blighter

214

failed to get off the ground, and then, of course, all hell was let loose. The cousins never forgave my family and swore undying vengeance. Fortunately their plans were stymied by Mussolini's invasion, and amidst the ensuing havoc my father was able to smuggle us out to England to live with an exiled aunt in Islington.'

'Exciting days,' Cedric remarked with veiled sarcasm, still not convinced. 'But I can't for the life of me see where Gloria Biggs-Brookby fits in, let alone why you had to kill her. You said something about meeting her for a second time. So when was the first?'

'In the war, when I was an evacuee. It may not have been central, but Islington was getting the fallout from the Blitz and thus my sister and I were packed off to the country. Our worthy hosts were the Biggs-Brookbys – mummy, daddy and the darling daughter. Gloria was a bit too old to be in the ATS but, as you may imagine, she was tireless in organising the civilian war effort: local fire-watching rotas and all that sort of thing.'

Finglestone paused reflectively, before adding, 'On the whole, I suppose she had her uses.' And then he laughed: 'As a matter of fact, despite all that activity, she had quite a bit of time for me – must have been the curly hair. She used to give me her sugar ration; and I once overheard her telling my sister I was her refugee cherub.'

'Some cherub!' Felix muttered, but was silenced by a look from Cedric.

'All right, so you were once the spoilt blue-eyed boy, but that hardly explains why you had to—'

'Dispatch her? It certainly does. The woman was like a minefield: you could negotiate her so far, but you knew that one day, if you put a foot wrong, she could unleash an explosion. I simply couldn't take the risk. The knifing was necessary, a pre-emptive action.'

'Pre-empting what?' Felix expostulated. 'I really don't understand *what* you are talking about!'

'Pre-empting her opening her fat trap and announcing to everybody that I had killed bloody Fico. Becoming a known fratricide, or whatever its cousinly equivalent is, would hardly get me my next commission. Such biographical titbits may be useful once you are safely dead, but not while you are alive and trying to make your name. But far worse than that was the chance of my Albanian pursuers getting wind of my whereabouts. Frankly, I didn't fancy the idea of being assassinated in the middle of Trinity's Great Court . . . Although if I don't get out quick they might try that anyway,' he added grimly. 'I've had a tip-off.'

'Oh, they wouldn't do it *there*,' said Felix scornfully, 'far too public. Some sinister side alley is much more likely. I know just the place: how about down by—'

The other regarded him narrowly. 'You think I am making this up, don't you? Well, I can tell you that—'

The thought had also crossed Cedric's mind, but noting the man's steely tone and bitter eyes he began to wonder. 'Oh, Felix never believes anything,' he said lightly. 'In fact, the only person he really trusts is the Queen Mother; and if one of those corgis nips him again she too may lose that accolade . . . But tell me, I still can't see why Gloria was such a threat. I mean, how would she know about Fico?'

'Because like a fool I told her. It was when I was their evacuee. I didn't normally think about the incident, but one night I had a terrifying dream and woke up yelling the house down. Gloria and her father came rushing into the bedroom and I blabbed it all out. At that age you don't think of consequences; and besides, three months later with the Blitz more or less over we returned to London and I got on with my new life. I forgot all about the Biggs-Brookbys, and the Albanian business became a vague and irrelevant memory.'

The narrator paused to light a cigarette, and then gave a grim laugh. 'Ironic, really. When years later I bumped into Gloria at a small gallery displaying some of my work it seemed a happy coincidence. She was delighted to see me, went into raptures about my exhibits and then told me about her father having been an eminent scholar (something I hadn't realised as a kid), and that his old Cambridge college was about to commission a sculptor for his memorial bronze. "Yippee," I thought, "this might be handy!" . . . And so it was. She took me under her wing, pushed my chances like hell – and then, lo and behold, with the death of old Reid the job was virtually mine for the taking.'

'So why on earth kill the woman?' Felix exploded. 'Talk about biting the hand that fed you!'

'Have you ever been sickened by someone's fawning attentions, and then feared and hated them for what they might disclose, Mr Smythe?'

Felix thought hard for a few seconds, and then with a modest smile replied that all attentions were most gratefully received; and as for disclosures – well his life was pure as the driven snow: 'An open book,' he smirked, winking at Cedric.

The latter remained grim-faced and, ignoring his friend, asked why Gloria had seemed likely to disclose anything. 'She was irritating, perhaps, but not vindictive – or at least I shouldn't have thought so.'

'No, not vindictive, merely garrulous and with an elephant's memory. I was horrified when recently she suddenly brought up the whole subject, described the details (which I could barely remember myself), and then graciously assured me that she would never say a word to anyone and that it would be "our little secret". Personally, I didn't want to share any secret with Gloria, least of all one like that – it would bind me to her for life.' Finglestone paused, and then muttered quietly almost to himself, 'There was something else, too, although she never brought it up, but I suspect she may have guessed.'

'Guessed what?' Felix interrupted. But other than an impatient sigh there was no response.

'And so to prevent that life allegiance you killed her?' Cedric asked. 'Rather an extreme measure, I should say. And after all, *had* she said anything surely you could have brazened it out and said she was merely a frustrated middle-aged lady seeking attention.'

Finglestone shrugged. 'Perhaps. But it would have been a tedious inconvenience and a waste of valuable time. And in any case, mud sticks as they say. I couldn't risk it.'

He stared at them with cold defiance, and then said slowly, 'But you see it wasn't just a question of professional safeguard. Certainly, she was a threat to my reputation – but as I have just told you, there are those who want my *life* and who will not rest until they have dealt with me as I dealt with the kid Fico . . . They call it family honour,' he added bitterly. 'The merest hint from Gloria, however unwitting, and they would be on my trail immediately.'

'With guns blazing?' enquired Felix.

'Shut *up*, Mr Smythe! I've had enough of your damn fool remarks!' Finglestone glowered.

And Felix, with the unsettling image of Gloria's spreadeagled corpse, was duly silent.

Astonished though Cedric was by Finglestone's revelations, he was also puzzled. 'Tell me, Monty,' he said affably, 'if you killed Gloria to keep her quiet and to preserve your life and reputation, why are you now in such a scramble to leave Cambridge? In theory, you should feel safe. Has there been a development since you, er – dealt with her? I mean, what is this tip-off you mentioned?'

Finglestone put a hand in his pocket and drew out a crumpled postcard. 'Read that,' he said curtly. 'It came this afternoon.'

The message bore a Belgian postmark and was scrawled and ill-spelt. *Get out quik. They are cuming. We meet you Brussels. Vite! Toni.*

'Who is Toni?'

'My sister's husband, a reliable source. If he says they are coming then they will be. But I'm not staying to find out.' Finglestone stood up and began to put on his raincoat.

Cedric was momentarily nonplussed, but then as calmly as he could, pointed out that in view of what they had just been told it was their duty to hand him over to the police. 'If what you say is true, then clearly the authorities will need to be informed,' he murmured in his most professorial voice.

This clearly amused Finglestone, who with a caustic laugh enquired how exactly that would be achieved.

Cedric hesitated, and then declared firmly that if he wasn't prepared to cooperate, he feared they would have to take him prisoner. (Felix felt a bit uneasy about this, but tried to look appropriately tough.)

Finglestone regarded the pair: the one thin and elderly, the other thin and weedy. They were not exactly the most daunting adversaries: pathetic, really. He gave a superior smile. 'On the whole, gentlemen, I don't *think* you are

219

going to stop me. I am expecting a car any minute and you are in my way.' He had taken Felix's room key from the mantelpiece and swung it in front of them. 'I fear it will be you who are detained, not me. There's nobody on this staircase tonight, they've gone racing at Newmarket. Your bawling won't be heard.'

He stepped forward to pick up the rucksack, but was impeded by Cedric, who, suddenly lunging towards him, delivered a swift uppercut followed by a deft left jab to the solar plexus. Finglestone staggered back, tripped over Felix's new shoes neatly placed by the bedside, and collapsed to the floor – felled less by force than by astonishment.

'Oh my flaming aunt,' Felix squeaked, 'what *have* you done!'

'I'm not quite sure,' Cedric replied breathlessly, 'but grab that paperweight and when he gets up clock him one.'

Thus, when Sir Richard Dick and the bursar opened the door their eyes were met by a curious spectacle: a broad-shouldered young man sprawled on his back staring up wildly at two slimline bruisers poised for business – or at least their attitude suggested bruisers, age and physique hinted otherwise.

'What *are* you doing?' the bursar cried.

'Good Lord, why is Finglestone like that?' chimed the Master.

Cedric and Felix lowered fists and paperweight. 'Ah, well you see—' Cedric began.

But before he could get any further his victim had leapt up and, thrusting the two visitors aside, rushed through the door and down the staircase. In the silence of the night, his feet could be heard pounding across the gravel path of the inner court.

Steadying himself and adjusting his glasses, Sir Richard

rounded on Cedric. 'What on earth's going on here? Really, Professor, I should have thought that—'

But his thought was never uttered, for at that moment two clear gunshots rang out from the direction of the porter's lodge.

'Oh my God, he's shooting someone!' the bursar cried.

'Absurd,' the Master snapped, 'that's Jenkins potting rabbits; they come up from the Backs. It's his evening sport.'

'Rabbits or not, we've got to catch that man. He's highly dangerous and thinks he is being pursued by avenging fiends,' Cedric panted, still not recovered from his fisticuffs. 'I'll explain later. Come on!'

They clattered down the stairs, Felix warily lagging behind . . . *Really, one was not cut out for such rampage!*

Once through the archway, the rampage came to a sudden halt and they stared at a recumbent shape on the grass by the porter's lodge. One thing was certain: the shape was no rabbit. Instead they were confronted by the body of a man – broad-shouldered and curly haired. Another sculptor lay before them: very dead. He had been shot in the back.

The Master closed his eyes. 'That's all I need!' he groaned silently.

CHAPTER TWENTY-FIVE

Roughly at the same time as this drama was being enacted, Aldous Phipps was comfortably settled by his fireside, book and pencil in hand. Suddenly, the dog pricked its ears, scampered into the hall and gave an irritable bark. It had been dreaming happily about bones and rabbit holes, or whatever it is that engages small terriers, and was none too pleased to be woken from its slumber.

'Oh, do be quiet, Popsie,' snapped its master, also irritably, 'you know it's only the evening paper.' The dog knew better and continued to emit testy yaps.

With a sigh Aldous Phipps cast aside his pencil and reading matter (a rather clumsy translation of a Plato work he was caustically annotating), and went into the hall to quell the dog and pick up the newspaper.

Letter box and mat were bare, but what the elderly don

did see was a face peering in at the side window. The next moment the doorbell rang.

The noise set the dog off again. 'Ssh!' commanded its master. 'Friend or foe we'll let neither in, I am far too busy.' He slid back the bolt, keeping the chain in place (with the number of scoundrels invading Cambridge these days one couldn't be too careful!) and cautiously squinted into the evening gloom.

A man stood there: not very tall, thickset and wearing a raincoat with turned-up collar. Aldous Phipps had never seen him before in his life. 'Yes?' he said tentatively through the narrow gap. (He had no intention of releasing the chain.)

The man took a step forward, stooping slightly to get a clearer view of the doorkeeper. 'Is this where Monty lives?' he asked.

Phipps frowned. 'Who?'

'Monty Finglestone. He is staying at this college I am told: number 6.'

'Oh, you mean the sculptor person,' Phipps replied indifferently. 'Well, you may be right about the number, but this is hardly the college. Where you are now is the private mews opposite, and number 6 is my residence. The *college* is that rather large edifice directly behind you – normally rather difficult to miss, I should think. If you enquire at the porter's lodge around the corner I daresay you will be directed – unless they have already closed the gates: their schedule is a trifle whimsical. Now, if you don't mind, I have important matters to attend to . . .'

Phipps gave a wintry smile and firmly shut the door. 'Really, Popsie,' he muttered on their way back to the sitting room, 'what an absurd mistake. Foreign, I daresay – I detected a guttural note.'

The dog said nothing. Its silence was rewarded with a biscuit; while to compensate for the disturbance its master poured a dry sherry.

Twenty minutes later, and once more immersed in the pleasurable task of damning the latest Plato translation, Professor Phipps did not hear the two gunshots that rang out behind the high wall opposite.

However, when later apprising the investigating authorities of his own experience on that disturbing night, he was able to tell them categorically that the visitor looking for Finglestone's lodging had been a foreigner – having a very thick accent and a distinctly swarthy countenance. (Phipps was not quite sure about the latter, but was warming to the idea.)

'Naturally, Chief Inspector, had I *realised* what his intention was I should have withheld my guidance. As it is, I fear I may have unwittingly paved the way to his unfortunate victim.' Phipps spoke in a tone of ostensible regret.

Later, regaling his colleagues at High Table, he was emphatic in saying he had glimpsed a distinct bulge in one of the stranger's coat pockets. 'And,' he added with a glint of triumph, 'I don't imagine it was a bag of toffees!'

CHAPTER TWENTY-SIX

Being unquestionably a murder, and one following so soon after the Magdalene Bridge knifing, it was Chief Inspector Wait who accompanied Tilson to the crime scene.

After the removal of the body to the pathology lab, the four witnesses were asked for their statements. These were taken separately in the porter's lodge in the hope that being so close to the shooting its custodian could supply some revealing detail. But Jenkins reported he had heard nothing, being engrossed in a book. (He had been asleep.) Sir Richard and the bursar gave a brief account of the scene they had witnessed when entering Felix's room, plus the hectic chase across the court. Asked why they had happened to be in that quarter of the court, they explained they had gone to call on one of the guests there, but receiving no reply assumed he was out. Passing Mr Smythe's room they had heard a loud commotion and felt they should check to see if all was well – the last occupant having complained bitterly about marauding moths. They had been distinctly put out to find not moths but mayhem.

Their statements completed they were permitted to go, and the officers then turned to Cedric and Felix. The two friends corroborated the others' account, but added much more: namely the murdered man's confession to killing Gloria, his motives and his fear that he was being pursued by avenging Albanians. Cedric also made the helpful suggestion that prior to the corpse being examined by the forensics they might like to retrieve the damning evidence he had stuffed into his raincoat pocket.

'And what damning evidence would that be?' Wait asked suspiciously.

'A small pocket diary with an entry virtually admitting his guilt. It's in the June section; you can't miss it.'

'Hmm, we'll see about that,' Wait grunted, and told a constable to alert the lab.

He resumed the questioning.

'You don't think he was having you on, do you? I mean it sounds a bit far-fetched to me – this tale of foreign hoodlums haring across Europe intent on doing him in because of some peasant kid he had allegedly killed for eating his cheese ration.'

'Yes, and that was all of twenty years ago,' Tilson chimed. And then he added thoughtfully, 'It would make quite a good film, really. Hitchcock could handle it, though I don't know who the master villain could be – Sidney Greenstreet, perhaps.' He grinned, and Wait frowned.

Cedric shrugged and in his most haughty tone, said, 'We can only report what we were told. It is hardly for us to make judgements as to the young man's veracity. I rather think that is your job, Officer.'

Felix nodded vigorously, but said nothing.

This was just as well, for in response to Cedric's snub Wait said woodenly, 'A coincidence, really, you two being the same gentlemen who found the unfortunate Miss Biggs-Brookby . . . and she, according to you, happening to have been the victim of Mr Finglestone. You must find your time in Cambridge a mite repetitive. Odd the way things work out, isn't it?'

'Oh yes, Chief Inspector,' Cedric agreed blandly, 'very odd. But then that's life – a long, disjointed trail of chance and coincidence. In fact, a great friend of mine has just made a study of it. It's a fascinating book and if you like I can give you its reference.' He took a pen and notebook from his pocket.

'That will not be necessary,' Wait said curtly.

After more probings the interview was concluded, but the witnesses told to keep themselves available for further questioning. They were also warned sternly that since the Biggs-Brookby case was still under investigation that on no account should they divulge what they had been told by Finglestone, neither to Sir Richard and the bursar, nor to anyone else.

'His tale may be all hogwash,' Wait said, 'but we can't be sure and at this stage any leaks would prejudice that enquiry. People will ask questions, of course, but you must say that the man was drunk, broke into the room for no coherent reason and attacked you. You need go no further than that.'

Cedric and Felix nodded obediently.

* * *

'A pompous little smart-arse, that professor,' the chief inspector observed sourly as he got into the car. 'Mind you, you didn't help much – making that damn fool comment about a film. This is a serious investigation; facetious humour is not part of it.'

Po-faced bugger, thought Tilson.

Back at the station Wait found the requested notebook already on his desk. It contained a few entries, mainly appointments and the occasional sketch of an anatomical feature presumably of some sculpting value. He leafed quickly to the June section and stared down at Gloria's posterior propped on Magdalene Bridge. He gave a low whistle and summoned Tilson.

Tilson was excited, but was told curtly to hold his horses. 'This doesn't *admit* anything,' Wait pointed out. 'It merely suggests the chap was pleased to learn the woman was dead. I expect a lot of people did something similar when they heard Hitler had died: drew a pretty picture and added, 'Hooray, the bastard's gone!'

Tilson nodded. 'Still,' he said, 'as circumstantial evidence goes, it's not bad, is it? Not something to be discounted, exactly.'

'Not exactly.' They grinned.

The victim's tale of being hounded to Cambridge by would-be assassins was in some degree supported by Aldous Phipps, who, later learning of the matter and recalling the stranger at his door that evening, toddled along to St Andrew's Street to give his version of events. Such action had less to do with civic duty than with a desire to add his pennyworth and thus stir the pot.

Rather reluctantly Tilson accepted his statement. A foreign-sounding stranger seeking Finglestone a little before the man was shot did rather fit the story as reported by the witnesses Dillworthy and Smythe. Clearly an alert would have to be put out for thickset swarthy-looking thugs with guttural accents. He sighed. A pointless task, surely. The man was bound to have slipped away; these professional assassins were good at making themselves scarce. But on principle a search should be made . . . Meanwhile, he would have to get Hopkins on to checking the alleged link between Finglestone and the Biggs-Brookby woman. If it could be proved that he had indeed been her killer that would save a lot of messing about, and with luck provide some kudos. It was about time they had a really good coup!

Much to the disappointment of Aldous Phipps (and to Tilson's annoyance) the professor's version of the night's events had taken them down a blind alley. After a search for the sinister fellow of foreign mien, it transpired that Phipps' visitor had been a taxi driver from a small firm on the Cambridge outskirts. Apparently Finglestone had called the company earlier in the day booking a cab to take him to London Airport that evening. The request had been at short notice, something that the fare duly reflected. Thus, the job was marked top priority with the boss himself in the driving seat. But as luck would have it he had fallen ill and been replaced by an underling new to the area. The man had spent a fruitless time getting spectacularly lost and knocking on doors opened by the seductive likes of Professor Phipps. Finally cheesed off by the whole thing he had given up in frustration, gone to the pub and thrown in the job.

Inspector Tilson recognised the inclination and felt some sympathy. Still, he reflected, even if the sculptor's Albanian pursuers were elusive (or mythical), at least something concrete might emerge from the searches Hopkins was making about the alleged link between the dead man and the murdered woman. A slender hope, but not beyond the realms of possibility – what might be termed a decent outside chance. One couldn't be sceptical all the time.

Shelving Gloria, he returned his thoughts to the sculptor's own death. Unlikely though the assassination theory was (and old Phipps' report of a mysterious visitor being a non-starter) it would be rash to discount it. After all, there was that postcard that Finglestone had shown to Smythe and Dillworthy. Though terse and semi-literate, its warning could not have been clearer: *Get out quik. They are cuming* . . . Tilson studied the thing again. It was genuine, all right – Belgian stamp and postmark. The latter was too indistinct to fix its exact source, but the date was clear enough and would fit the man's claim that he had received it on the afternoon before his murder. Had the helpful Toni's advice to scarper come too late? Had 'they' indeed found their quarry, done the job and then quickly and slickly removed themselves . . . ? Improbable, but not impossible. Tilson frowned. Apart from the fact that the weapon was likely to have been a Webley (an old service revolver) they had nothing to go on. A search of the immediate area had yielded nothing. He smiled ruefully: a return plane ticket to Albania would have been handy.

There was a knock and a constable entered. 'Got a present for you, sir,' he announced. 'Jenkins, the porter from that college sent it over. He found it caught up on a rose trellis by the side gate and said he thought you might find it useful.' He placed a crumpled green handkerchief on Tilson's desk.

The latter gazed at it. 'So what am I supposed to do with this – blow my nose?'

Disregarding the question, the constable explained that Jenkins had found it the day after the shooting and put it in his Lost Property box. It had been lying there for a couple of days when it recently occurred to him it might be of some relevance.

'Recently? So why didn't he bring it straightaway?' Tilson growled.

'Apparently he is a very busy man and such incidentals have to take their turn in his demanding schedule.' The constable grinned.

'I see,' the inspector said grimly. 'So, if Mr Jenkins has so many pressing duties to fulfil, perhaps he had overlooked its presence in the rose bush, perhaps the handkerchief had been stuck in the thing long before the murder.'

'He says not.'

'Why not?'

'Because one of those duties is to fertilise the roses. He says it's a job he takes very seriously and applies the stuff as regular as clockwork. The most recent application was in the late afternoon of the day Finglestone was shot. He swears blind it wasn't there then.'

Tilson sighed. 'Thank you, Constable. Send in Sergeant Hopkins, will you.'

'Have a look at this,' the inspector directed when Hopkins arrived.

The sergeant made an examination. 'It's a man's

handkerchief,' he said brightly, 'you can tell that from the size: a woman's hooter is smaller.'

Tilson groaned. 'Obviously it's a perishing handkerchief, but what about the material and those fancy initials – what does that tell us?'

'Silk, rolled edge, hand embroidered. It's expensive, sir, not any old thing like you'd buy at Woolworth's,' Hopkins declared smartly. (He had deliberately inserted the last bit knowing that the inspector's own supply came from that source.)

'Good. Glad you noticed, Sergeant,' his boss said dryly. 'Should this have belonged to the murderer then we are in luck: most clues do not come with initials attached. Now my reading of them is V. Z. C. Might that possibly accord with yours?'

Hopkins agreed that it did.

Suddenly, Tilson laughed. 'Do you think the names Vladimir and Zeus have a Balkan ring?'

'What about the C?' Hopkins replied soberly.

Tilson shrugged. 'Ceauçescu might fit.'

'Hmm. So what shall we do with it?'

'Well, Sergeant, we'll keep it up our *sleeve*, naturally. How about that? . . . Now go and file it, would you, I've got a report to do for the chief inspector. We can't keep Mr Wait waiting!'

Hopkins flinched. *His wit will slay me*, he thought gloomily as he departed for the filing cabinets.

CHAPTER TWENTY-SEVEN

'It's a plot,' the Master declared, 'that's what it is, a confounded plot! Quite clearly a plot to foil our monument proposals. A sponsor dead, two sculptors down and none in the offing – and the daughter murdered in a public place. Mark my words, some fiendish bastard has it in for this college!'

He glared round at his colleagues hastily summoned for an Emergency Consultative Meeting to discuss the latest developments.

'Cuff?' someone vaguely suggested.

Sir Richard waved his hand impatiently: 'Hasn't got the gumption. Besides, when he's not droning away in the Council House he's much too absorbed with that obnoxious brood of his . . . No, it's obviously someone far more astute and wily, someone utterly tenacious and unencumbered by domestic claims.'

'In that case,' Aldous Phipps ventured slyly, 'were it not for your charming wife it might be you yourself, Master. Tenacious, astute . . . the conditions are undoubtedly there.' He flashed a mocking smile at the rest of the table.

'This is no joke,' the other snapped, 'it is a serious matter. And I would thank you, Aldous, to keep your *witty* pleasantries to yourself.'

Phipps gave the merest shrug and murmured something to the effect that one should never discount the impossible.

The Master affected not to hear, wishing with all his heart that someone would do away with the elderly don. After all, why should fate stop at four? he wondered.

Dr Maycock cleared his throat, before remarking that actually two of the fatalities were purely accidental and therefore could hardly be a factor in any hypothetical plot. 'If I may say so, Master, I think you are being a trifle hasty in your assumption,' he remarked blandly.

Sir Richard regarded him with undisguised irritation. Trust Maycock to be so damned literal! 'As it happens, I am not so sure about that, Dr Maycock,' he retorted. 'I suspect there may have been more to the Reid business than meets the eye. However, since the police seem entirely satisfied with that particular demise, naturally I shall say no more. And as for Hinchcliffe, well, yes, he was always frail . . .' He drummed his fingers. 'Now, gentlemen, to our purpose: given the unfortunate circumstances, what is to be our next move?'

'Scrap it,' a voice said.

There was silence as all eyes turned towards John Smithers.

Sir Richard fixed him with a steely gaze. 'Really? And on what do you base that helpful suggestion?' he said coldly.

The younger man flushed slightly, but held his ground.

'Look,' he said slowly, 'as you have rather implied, this statue project seems to have been unaccountably doomed. Don't let's chance our arm and invite further trouble or dig ourselves deeper into an already uncomfortable hole. Acquiring that bit of ground has cost us considerable time and money. Are we now to spend more of both by seeking yet another sculptor for the job? It has become pretty obvious that artists of the right calibre are thin on the ground, and thus the task of finding someone suitable – or willing – may be tediously protracted. Do we really want to start the whole thing all over again?' Smithers cast a challenging eye around the table, but not waiting for an answer continued.

'Now those are the practical considerations – but it also strikes me that because of the violent nature of three of the deaths, a statue of Sir Percival may become a focus not of respect but of crude curiosity. Any guide worth his salt would be bound to spice up his spiel by emphasising the events surrounding the thing. It would be those events, not the man, which would grab the public's attention. "The college with the jinxed statue: a sinister tale!" Is that what you want?'

'But why not?' interrupted Aldous Phipps. 'If it would increase our revenue, then by all means. We could advertise the monument as a special feature and make the visitors *pay* for the privilege of viewing it. Just think, we might make quite a financial killing. Never pass up an opportunity, that's my motto.'

The bursar gave a snort of mirth. 'Ah, and doubtless you would volunteer to stand at the garden gate with collecting bag in hand, all poised to shovel in their coins!'

'I might be persuaded,' Phipps replied.

'*Advertise?*' the Master thundered. 'This is not a fairground we have inherited but an ancient college of noble distinction. Our aim is to elevate its name, not grind it into the dust of Mammon! I should have thought that you of all people would recognise that, Professor.'

Phipps shrugged, quite unscathed. 'Just trying to be helpful,' he murmured.

The Master sighed silently and shuffled his papers. When had Aldous Phipps ever been remotely helpful? he wondered.

Dr Maycock, seated at the opposite end of the table from Sir Richard, also sighed, but in his case the sound was audible and followed by a loud clearing of throat: obviously the prelude to speech.

Instinctively, John Smithers closed his eyes, expecting some lugubrious pronouncement. But on hearing the mention of his own name immediately opened them, surprised to hear the Senior Tutor applauding his proposal to abandon the project.

'I think that Dr Smithers has made fair comment,' Maycock declared. 'This whole business has gone on long enough and the matter is already attracting unwanted attention from the press. There was even an article about us in yesterday's *Times*. The essential thing is that we now have ownership of that piece of land. It has become part of the college's curtilage and as such we can do with it exactly as we choose. It is not as if the presence of a statue was a condition of its sale.'

'No, not a condition as such,' somebody observed, 'but nevertheless the City Council was given to understand that that was why we wanted it – to honour Sir Percival, a distinguished Cambridge scholar who has done much for the university. And other than Alderman Cuff, I think all were persuaded that our case was a worthy one. If we were now to change its purpose they might take a dim view.'

'With all due respect to the council,' Maycock remarked dryly, 'I cannot see that their dim views are of much account. The point is the plot is *our* property; and if in our wisdom we decide to use it for something other than first intended, then so be it. After all, it is only fools who never change their minds.' This last statement was delivered with smug assurance and his eye swept the room defying a fool to object.

There was a silence followed by a burble of voices. Eventually the Master rapped the table. 'Gentlemen, if we accept Dr Maycock's view that the college cannot be expected to kowtow to the council's preferences, then I should like to hear some concrete proposals as to how it might be used. Come on now, specific examples!'

'What about a canine playground?' suggested Aldous Phipps. 'I gather a number of the kitchen and maintenance staff are dog owners. I am sure they would be most appreciative of the gesture – and I know that my Popsie would love the occasional frolic. We could call it "Hortus Canum", although I think "The Dogs' Paradise" has a friendlier ring, don't you?' He beamed, while the Master glared.

'Why not just "The Dog Plot"?' someone said brightly. His neighbour agreed, adding that he liked the snappy title – a comment eliciting good-humoured groans, except from Sir Richard, who quietly seethed.

'In all seriousness,' Maycock said, 'I think we should retain its commemorative theme. For example, it could be dedicated to the memory of the college's past Masters and there could be a plaque listing their names and perhaps fields of study. Speaking for myself, I find the sound of

"The Masters' Walk" rather appealing. It lends an air of quiet *gravitas* befitting our function.'

'Hmm. But it's not a very large plot,' Sir Richard observed doubtfully, 'so where exactly is one going to walk?'

'Round in circles, presumably,' Professor Turner replied. 'It is said that such circular perambulation feeds the brain.'

'Is that so? How *very* helpful. And now, if you don't mind I should like to—'

'And you see,' cut in Aldous Phipps quickly, 'we could plant tufts of aromatic spurge, rosemary for remembrance and tendrils of charming forget-me-nots to spiral around the base of the plaque. Highly appropriate.' His eyes held a malicious glint.

'Oh yes, and how about a gigantic clump of rue at the entrance,' added Turner grinning, 'easier to contain than perishing rhododendrons and just as picturesque.'

'Rue? I trust there would be nothing to *regret*,' the Master said tightly. 'If this is indeed to be a viable venture we need suggestions that are practical and sober. Personally, I—'

'If you want my opinion,' John Smithers suddenly said, 'I think it's a lousy idea.'

'What – rue at the gate?' Turner asked.

Smithers shook his head. 'The whole idea. There's already a list of previous Masters up in the Combination Room. We hardly need any more of them. If anything needs to be commemorated it's the college's martyrs – those who laid down their lives in the two wars. Admittedly, there is a Roll of Honour in the chapel, but it's not in a very conspicuous place and I think we can do better than that. I suggest we make the plot a Garden of Remembrance, a place for quiet reflection on the horrors of war and the sacrifice of our fellow scholars.'

He sat back in his chair and folded his arms.

There was a long silence. And then Turner cried: 'First class! And we can fill the whole area with scarlet poppies and white lilies. It would look and smell delightful! Unless anyone else wants the job, I should be most honoured to take on the design. A good idea, Smithers.' He smiled broadly, clearly pleased with the prospect of himself as head gardener.

There were one or two grunts of approval from others around the table. And somewhat to his own disappointment, Aldous Phipps also thought it a good idea. 'Most thoughtful, if I may so,' he murmured, 'the best suggestion yet.' And rather reluctantly he mustered a gracious nod in Smithers' direction.

Dr Maycock was a little more fulsome in his congratulation, pleased that his protégé had evidently absorbed his advice on the value of 'soundness'. Perhaps he could be persuaded to replace him on the confounded Town and Gown Committee; he had been trying to resign for ages. He leant across and warmly shook Smithers' hand. Such gestures never came amiss.

Sir Richard, who had been silently debating which would look better, i.e. his full name and title carved into the plaque or just modest initials and surname, hastily cancelled such deliberations and composed his features into an expression of sage acceptance. Already he could see the newspaper's report:

College Executive Pays Tribute to the Fallen: Sir Richard Dick announces that his college's latest acquisition, a plot of derelict land once owned by the council, will be a memorial to those gallant scholars who in WWs I & II made noble sacrifice for their country. 'It will be,' he said pensively, 'a place of rest and grateful contemplation; a place where dons and undergraduates may sit and muse upon the sadness of war and the heroism it engenders. We shall call it,' he declared, 'the Hortus Pacis *– the Garden of Peace.'*

Yes, undoubtedly the public would approve of that – considerably more than they would of a statue to an academic of whom most had never heard. With luck, too, it would help deflect their interest away from the appalling outrage of recent events.

Out loud he said, 'I consider that most fitting. An extremely sound suggestion, Dr Smithers, and I trust that all here will support it.' Challengingly his eye swept the table, and the room resonated with murmured endorsements.

'Excellent. So we are all agreed, then,' he declared firmly (and with concealed relief). 'We shall start preparations immediately.' He took a covert look at his watch. With luck, Anthea would have replenished the whisky; he had need.

There was the sound of a chair being pushed back. The bursar stood up and, resting his hands squarely on the table said, 'Ah, but haven't we forgotten something, Master?'

'I don't think so,' Sir Richard replied evenly. (Typical of Williams, always had to have the last word!)

'But if you don't mind my asking, what about the *sponsors*? After all, they do have a certain role in all of this. It is just conceivable that they may not *like* the change of plan and thus be reluctant to contribute. Admittedly, swathes of poppies and lilies may be less costly than any sculptor's fee, but there is still the purchase price of the plot itself to be recouped. It would be unfortunate should the college have to pick up the tab for the whole project without additional aid. Wouldn't you say?'

The Master regarded him steadily. The bastard was right, of course, but he could deal with it. 'My dear, Bursar,' he replied coolly, 'I commend your concern for our vital resources and applaud your vigilance in the matter, but I can assure you that neither the plot's contents nor its purpose are likely to affect our benefactors' generosity. Given the nobility of Dr Smithers' proposal, I really cannot imagine anyone wishing to oppose it.' He paused, before adding, 'Besides, I think you will find that provided a suitable notice is displayed with their names writ large, the sponsors will be only too keen to dig into their pockets and support the cause . . . whatever that cause may be.' He flashed a sardonic smile, which was rewarded with appreciative chuckles.

The bursar gave a peremptory nod and sat down. 'Let us hope you are right,' he said.

CHAPTER TWENTY-EIGHT

Of course one was right, Sir Richard Dick told himself as he made his way back to the Master's Lodge. Smithers' idea was first class; and as Maycock had implied, if the City Council didn't like it they could take a running jump! He had had enough of outsiders questioning his decisions – though at least now he was spared the awfulness of the Biggs-Brookby onslaught. That was a mercy – though naturally one would have preferred a less brutal resolution . . . as presumably would the lady herself. Ironic, really, what crude forms fate's benignity could take.

But then, he mused, much the same could be said about that extraordinary Finglestone business. Most certainly an outrageous end, but at least a stroke of financial luck for the college: his suggested fee had been enormous. Besides, one had never really taken to the chap – too self-satisfied and clearly keen on calling the shots. (Sir Richard stopped abruptly, his eye fixed on a clump of peonies. No, *not* the most suitable of idioms. He flinched, recalling the sight of the body gunned down on the grass.)

Continuing on and temporarily shelving the strange drama of Finglestone's fate, his mind returned to John Smithers and his plot proposal. Coming from that young man the idea was remarkably sage. It had been a good contribution. So perhaps he should show his personal approval by inviting him to tea at the Lodge – privately, without the overbearing presence of Maycock or Mostyn Williams. Anthea could make one of her excellent chocolate cakes and perhaps rustle up some choux buns, her speciality. She would enjoy doing that, and besides it would be good for her: take her mind off recent events. She had been looking a little drawn of late – in fact, although he couldn't be certain, she seemed to have lost some weight. Yes, quite clearly what she needed was a diversion and some rousing compliments about her cooking. And meanwhile he could do with a damn good whisky. It had been an arduous afternoon.

He opened the front door of the Lodge and entered the hall (fragrant with Felix's lilies). 'I say, Anthea,' he called, 'I think we might ask John Smithers to tea. What do you think?'

Lady Dick thought it was a rotten idea, but was hardly in a position to explain why. Since experiencing her paramour's patent lack of gallantry regarding the Winston Reid debacle, Smithers had fallen distinctly low in her estimation. In fact, she had been berating herself for being so foolish as to have become involved in the first place. Oh yes, handsome enough and superficially amusing, but clearly not up to supporting a lady in distress. No knight in shining armour there, that was for sure. She must have been mad! Even Richard would have been more stalwart – though given the situation, he was the last person she could have turned to.

But what bothered her more than her lover's lack of spine was the fact that unlike the police he *knew* the truth of what had happened that dreadful afternoon. In her naiveté she had told him . . . as too she had told that Felix Smythe. *Really*, she thought, *I may be approaching fifty, but I have behaved like a half-witted schoolgirl!* Still, the one sure thing (or so it would appear) was that the florist was going to remain mum. Those flowers were lovely and he had been so insistent in assuring her of his silence, touchingly so. Yes, on the whole she felt she was safe with Mr Felix Smythe. Indeed, when she was next in London she might even make a complimentary call at his shop . . . Anthea pulled herself up sharply. No! Leave well alone. Certainly the man had been kind, but luck should not be pushed. As Nanny had always counselled, the less said and seen the better. Let it all just fade into the dust and the past.

Anthea gazed at the lilies and brooded. Smythe's words had indeed lightened her mind, but what of her other confidant? Would John Smithers be so gallant? Perhaps not gallant, but he might be prudent. With luck, his fear of being seen as remotely linked with the event would prevent him from saying anything to anybody.

But then what about Richard? Supposing that in the fullness of time he should ever sniff a rat about the affair, let alone suspect she had been at Reid's house. What then, for God's sake? Could she handle him, smooth him over? Admittedly, his finding out was unlikely, but not impossible. After all, that snide little fox Phipps was still wheezing on about Reid's taste in whisky; suppose they should reopen the case? She had overheard him only the other day muttering about it to Professor Dillworthy. Fortunately the other seemed to be paying only perfunctory attention. And knowing Phipps, with any luck his interest would have been diverted by some fresh theme – namely, the conviction that but for the grace of God he had almost opened his door to Finglestone's killer.

Though somewhat comforted, Anthea still gave a heavy sigh. Really, life was fraught with so many sneaky hazards . . . And now she was expected to bake a cake for sodding Smithers!

Back at his flat sodding Smithers was feeling rather pleased with the way things had gone. His argument regarding the land usage had been absolutely genuine and he was gratified that the committee had seen his point. But quite apart from the principle of the matter, it was also nice to think that tactically, too, he had made a good move, which could well be to his future advantage. Old Maycock had counselled winning the approval of his peers, and judging from the afternoon's discussion that is exactly what had happened. His proposal had certainly not been made with that in mind, but it was what one might call a handy spin-off. The Master, in particular – who had always regarded him with a slightly distant eye – had been clearly impressed.

Smithers frowned. That was the plus side, but then there was the minus. It was all very well winning Dick's approval, but would he be so approving if he ever learnt of the wife business? Pretty short odds, he guessed. Not even short: a forgone result with no bets taken. He winced. If Anthea

Dick cared to open her charming mouth, something that out of pique or weakness she might decide to do, he would be in the can – Hortus Pacis or not!

How far could her discretion be trusted? Anyone's guess. Since apprising him of the Reid event and his failure to respond with the sympathy evidently required, her attitude to him had cooled – which in the circumstances was no bad thing. But equally it could suggest a mounting resentment that she might pursue. You could never be sure with women; they were contrary creatures and hard to assess: devoted to you one minute and ditched you the next. Take Myrtle Miller, for example! (Smithers bristled with annoyance, recalling the scene of his recent overthrow.) Could it be that his jovial hint about her expanding girth had been a tactical error? He briefly pondered the question, and then returned his mind to the more pressing matter of Anthea.

Her role in Reid's demise was mild dynamite – far from mild, in fact, the personal repercussions could be considerable; and with that hanging over her she was unlikely to confide the liaison to anyone, let alone her husband. Yes, *unlikely*, but one couldn't be sure. Or perhaps one could. After all, in compliance with the coroner's verdict the case had been closed. Thus, on the face of it she was safe . . . but *only* on the face of it. For he, John Smithers, held the one key to the truth (she would hardly have been fool enough to tell anyone else): he was the scaffolding to her whole deception. Mess with him at her peril!

Just for an instant he felt a satisfying sense of power. But it swiftly vanished, punctured by a stab of shame and the knowledge that such power was ignobly won and fragile, anyway. Nothing was certain. They each held a card, and if she were rash enough she might just decide to play hers and damage the pair of them. Smithers closed his eyes, unsettled by such thoughts.

He was even more unsettled when a minute later the telephone rang and he heard the Master's voice inviting him to tea. 'I thought we might discuss your proposal a little further and in more comfortable surroundings,' Sir Richard said affably. 'My wife would much enjoy your company. She's a very good cook, you know, so you won't starve.'

Pulling a face of spectacular contortion in the mirror, Smithers made the requisite response. In return he was directed to be at the Lodge by four o'clock sharp two days hence.

He returned to his chair and reclosed his eyes. Charming: a tea party threesome with scones and buttered toast. What more could a chap want? He swore gently.

In fact, contrary to the expectations of guest and hostess, the proposed tea party went surprisingly well. This was not simply because Anthea had baked a superb cake, which both men had obviously relished, but because John Smithers delivered some news likely to free both himself and his erstwhile mistress from their mutual suspicion.

At first he and Anthea had behaved with guarded courtesy: she only thinly welcoming, he stiffly polite. However, the tension was undetected by Sir Richard. Although still reeling from the disgraceful Finglestone palaver, he was much cheered by the committee's enlightened decision re the usage of the plot. A moderate triumph, perhaps, in the recent ghastly scheme of things, but a triumph nevertheless. This and the fact that it was largely Smithers' doing, made him treat his guest with uncritical warmth and any signs of awkward reserve went entirely unnoticed.

Thus such was his host's genial manner, that in a pause between scoffing a scone and accepting a second slice of cake, Smithers saw fit to make his announcement. This was to the effect that on that very morning he had received an invitation from Yale to become their resident exponent on his specialist subject, the writer Henry James, with exclusive access to some recently unearthed manuscripts (sources untapped even by the eminent authority Leon Edel). Diffidently, he enquired whether Sir Richard would endorse his absence. Yale had offered a year's initial appointment with minimum teaching and maximum research. 'It would enhance my current study enormously,' he said eagerly, 'and naturally the college's name would appear in the book's dedication. Indeed, you might be so kind as to write a brief foreword yourself – that would really be its crowning distinction!' This last remark was delivered with jocular ease, but it was not without purpose and Anthea could see that Smithers had clearly profited from the Senior Tutor's influence.

She glanced at her husband, hoping he would take the bait and approve the transfer.

Sir Richard was acquiescent. 'Well, you have certainly earned your Fellowship here, Dr Smithers, and Yale will be lucky to have you. Spend your time wisely, as I know you will. Meanwhile, I will make a note to myself about that foreword. It will be a pleasure – though you may need to tell me what to put!'

'Oh, and who knows,' Anthea said gaily, 'you may even return with an American wife. You had better watch your step!'

'I must indeed, Lady Dick,' he had replied with mock gravity.

There was general laughter and the guest was prevailed upon to have another scone.

When it was time to leave, Anthea accompanied Smithers into the porch where he gladly accepted the remains of the cake which she had wrapped for him to take home. He thanked her for the delicious tea and its accompanying gift and started to walk away, but then stopped. He turned and winked. It was a valedictory wink and she knew she was safe.

At about the same time as Sir Richard had been considering inviting Dr Smithers to tea, i.e. soon after the Emergency Consultative Meeting, Maycock had telephoned Bantry with news of the committee's decision and urged him to dine later that week. 'There are one or two things we might mull over,' he had chuckled.

Thus a few hours after John Smithers had left the Master's Lodge, Lord Bantry was being entertained by the Senior Tutor in the latter's large and cheerful sitting room. On the table between them stood a polished whisky decanter and two glasses. (Sally Maycock was slurping Asti in the kitchen, cooking up a feast of coq au vin, her new recipe gleaned from Elizabeth David.) Although summer, a small fire was flickering brightly and the two men were on good form, verging on the gleeful even. The smells from the kitchen enhanced their spirits and the whisky was being liberally shared.

'One has to admit,' Maycock observed, 'that just occasionally things turn out with astonishing good luck.'

'Astounding,' Lord Bantry agreed. 'What you might call a left and a right. I've never achieved that on a grouse moor, birds are too damn fast, but here in Cambridge . . . well, things are different, aren't they.' He grinned and raised his glass.

His host reciprocated. 'We owe someone a debt, that's for sure, but who I cannot imagine. But as you say, two birds at one go . . .' He raised his glass again.

'I see the crabbed hand of Aldous Phipps in this,' Bantry said darkly. 'You must admit he puts the knife into most people and he disliked both Gloria and Finglestone. My God, when I think of how he hounded me when he was my tutor!'

'Doubtless deserved.' Maycock laughed. 'But I don't see Phipps in quite so active a role. I should think poison would be more his style. But, of course, we don't *know* that the murders were done by the same person. There might have been two of 'em. In which case a second toast is needed.' He reached for the decanter.

At that moment his wife appeared announcing supper.

'Join us, my dear,' Dr Maycock said, extending a fond arm, 'we were just pouring libations to the gods for granting our prayers. You must admit things have resolved themselves most satisfactorily – no more interference, the college saved a heap of money, and a plot of land destined to be a noble garden of which we can be justly proud.'

'Some may be proud, but you may not get the chance,' Sally Maycock replied crisply.

'What *can* you mean?'

'I mean that the murderer has not been caught and that for all we know is still out there lurking in a side alley just waiting to pounce. I suggest you avoid Laundress Lane for the next few weeks, you could be the next target . . . Now, hurry up and come and taste the stew.'

'Your wife has the most exquisite imagination' – Bantry laughed – 'and such a good cook too!'

The evening was passed most agreeably and the following day the Senior Tutor was able to telephone the bursar to announce that Lord Bantry was now more than ready to proceed with his scholarship endowment for the Lame and Indigent.

CHAPTER TWENTY-NINE

Stay cool, whatever the circumstances. That is what their father had always counselled. *Rush and you will stumble, panic and you are lost. Instead speak slowly, think quickly and above all retain your poise and dignity. By acting thus you will always be in control . . .*

Since their father had been the most impetuous of people and often the victim of his own quick temper, Dame Margery Collis and her twin brother had found such advice amusing. And yet as they had quickly learnt it was very much a question of 'do as I say, not as I do'. For while being quizzical of the parental practice, their own lives had proved his precepts sound. Both children had developed a shell of austere self-discipline, which together with natural talents had brought to each considerable professional success: the girl as a respected educationalist and government advisor, the boy as an eminent heart surgeon.

But ten years ago Victor had died, mown down in his prime by 'a senseless joyrider' as the newspapers had described his killer. 'Juvenile high jinks tragically misfired,' they had reported. It had been termed a terrible accident, they declared, one of those grievous quirks of fate . . . An accident? Margery thought bitterly. Not in her view it wasn't. A gross uncaring murder, that's what it had been! But now, nurtured by parental advice (staying cool, watchful and resolute) she had avenged both the crime itself and what she deemed the disgraceful travesty of justice that had allowed the killer to thrive.

Well, not any more he doesn't, she thought triumphantly, eyeing the Webley nestled in her open suitcase. The gun had been Victor's, one of several he had used at their local pistol club in London. They had joined together, in those days an unusual choice for a woman. But she had soon demonstrated a natural skill and become a welcome member. Indeed, with their quiet confidence, steady nerve and almost impeccable aim, brother and sister had made quite a formidable team. The 'terrible twins', they had been dubbed. Margery smiled wryly. It was a term more apt for one of them now than had ever been dreamt of.

She glanced again at the gun, and thanked her lucky stars that it had been in the car when she had driven up to Cambridge. She had been competing at the pistol club prior to setting off. Her luggage was already in the boot, though she had intended to make a quick dash home to drop off the gun and cartridges. But it was Friday night, and with the traffic already thickening she had decided to press straight on. Yes, it had been a bit of luck . . . She thought of her father again and another of his constant sayings: *Some things are meant,* he would assert confidently. Fatuous! Meant by whom or by what? Yet for once the words made sense. She had certainly *meant* to kill Monty Finglestone (or Montino Fingi as his name had been at his court appearance ten years previously), so perhaps keeping the pistol in the car had indeed been oddly destined.

It was destiny too, perhaps, that the opportunity for the task had arisen on the very anniversary of his death – and ironically the same day she had completed her fortnight's lecturing at Girton. It would have been galling to have had to quit Cambridge halfway through her contract and with valuable insights left unsaid. Not at all her reliable style. (Admittedly, she *could* have stayed put, tensely riding out the storm, but it might have been dangerous; no point in taking unnecessary chances. The sooner she left and the more distance put between herself and the dispatched the better.) Thus things had worked most conveniently: her departure would go unremarked with no queries made or eyebrows raised. She could then retire discreetly for a three-month sabbatical to her cottage in France; a quiet little bolthole. There was a backlog of reviews and correspondence she had to attend to – not to mention that article for the *Times Higher Education Supplement* they had been pestering her for. Yes, plenty to do all right.

Methodically, she gathered up books and papers and began to pack her other belongings, placing the pistol securely at the bottom of the case. Seconds after the shooting her instinct had been to toss it away into the nearby hedge or the ornamental pond. But then a stronger instinct had made her hang on to it. It had belonged to her beloved twin. It had to be cherished, not chucked aside like a piece of garbage. And besides, the thing had performed stout service! And so, with task accomplished and gripping it firmly like a talisman, she had slid deep into the shadows and walked calmly away, leaving the body to face the hullabaloo of its finders. The dispatch had been as simple as that.

Yes, as simple as that . . . although, she recalled with slight irritation, there had been the mildest of glitches – a hiccup really and nothing of consequence. Despite her smooth exit into the seemingly deserted alley, she had in fact met someone, but it had been a meeting so piffling as to be of no account. As she reached the corner of the alley she had been accosted by a squat figure smelling heavily of drink and who had mumbled something in what she took to be a foreign tongue. She had the impression he was making a request (for a light?), but given the momentous thing she had just performed she had been in no mood to parley with foreigners. 'Go to hell,' she had snapped and brushed past. There had been silence, except for the faintest sound of a disgruntled belch.

She folded her clothes carefully, interlacing them with tissue paper; and put her shoes, their toes stuffed with newspaper, into drawstring bags. Margery had always been a meticulous packer, and present circumstances made little difference to her habitual routine.

As she busied herself her mind roved over the preceding events. Before getting involved with the tiresome monument business she had never heard of Finglestone, and it was only after she arrived in Cambridge and had seen the rival candidate with the Biggs-Brookby woman that it had dawned on her that she had once known the man. 'Dawned' because since her first encounter both his name and his looks had changed. At the time of the trial he had been Montino Fingi, and at sixteen – shorter and with much fairer hair – he had had the features of a youth, a boy really. Now, tall and filled out, he displayed both the physique and assurance of a man. The slight trace of a foreign accent she had detected at the trial had also disappeared. And yet as she had watched him talking to Gloria he had seemed oddly familiar. It had been something about the soft brown eyes with the long lashes, the curly though darker hair, the way he held his head and the rather supercilious grin. God, how she remembered that grin! Questioned by the prosecuting barrister at the trial he had given whingeing, tearful answers, but just fleetingly there had been that beastly little smirk. It would flash upon him suddenly for no apparent reason, and it had made her sick. It was that smile, seen again a decade later in the staid surroundings of the University Arms, that had jolted her into definite recognition and had sealed his fate. There had been no question as to identity: boy and man were the same. The shock had been tremendous, but so too had been her instinct . . . the instinct to kill.

And thus with project firmly established and mind clear as a bell, she had followed him, waited and caught him. Dame Margery Collis, respected government mandarin, had fulfilled her latest project: scuppered the sculptor.

At last the packing was finished, coat and handbag ready, and room spick and span. She consulted her watch. Good, barely eight o'clock; a few hours and she could be in Dover ready for France. She would just have time to catch the afternoon ferry. For a second she allowed herself a pang of jaunty pride:

what foresight to always carry her passport – a habit advised by her brother. 'You never know' – he had laughed – 'one day you might need to make a quick getaway!' They had laughed and she had called him an idiot, but had followed his advice all the same.

Leaving a note warmly thanking her friend for the use of the flat and regretting her early departure (pressing engagements), Margery stepped into the street, and as far as suitcase would allow walked briskly to her car.

Already the sun was out and at that peaceful hour Cambridge at its best – fresh, benign and beautiful. Being Sunday there could be heard the age-old sound of a distant bell chiming for matins (from Great St Mary?) and, as she passed the gated lawns and placid frontage of St Catharine's, Margery wondered if this was a city to which she would ever return. With a pang of regret she felt it unlikely.

But Dame Margery was not the only one awake and alert at that early hour. Felix too was up betimes. After the drama of the previous evening, let alone yet another tiresome police interrogation, he had spent a night of wakeful tedium and violent nightmare. Thus, by seven o'clock the shafts of bright daylight came as a welcome relief. He decided to do what he rarely did: leap from the bed and go for a reviving walk. (Admittedly, it might not *revive*, but it would be better than languishing sleepless in that spartan room with Finglestone's sullen ghost as a companion!)

Thus the decision made, and like the other early riser, Felix was soon dressed and ready to go. And also like Dame Margery, he too was appreciative of the morning's soothing calm unruffled by scurrying dons and clanging bicycle bells. He strolled through silent streets, the tensions of the night gradually fading. He thought of Cedric, presumably still slumbering dead to the world . . . not surprising after that astonishing display of pugilism. Goodness, he had had no idea his friend was so disposed! He really must ask him about it at breakfast.

He wandered down a deserted Bene't Street into King's Parade, pausing to take in the lofty stillness of the college opposite. How stately it was, how regally imposing – and how utterly aloof from the mean and sordid events so recently enacted. Felix gazed at it, debating. Which way to turn, left or right? On a whim he chose left in the direction of Trumpington Street and Peterhouse. He could perhaps take a look at the river; it would be especially appealing at this hour.

Occasionally he met a random dog walker, but such encounters were welcome for on the whole Felix felt attuned to dogs (except for corgis) and was always ready to murmur a kindly word. Besides, confronting such trusting, tousled faces helped to erase the image of that raving idiot's the night before. What a frightful business that had been, and how bad for one's nerves! Cambridge was all very nice and historical, but he was beginning to think fondly of the safety of Sloane Street and his own floral habitat of *Smythe's Bountiful Blooms*. For all its charm and antiquity Cambridge clearly held a sinister aspect for which, being of a sensitive nature, Felix felt he was far from suited.

He crossed the road, and preoccupied with such thoughts did not at first see the woman with the suitcase. It was only when she stopped beside a blue Hillman and started to fiddle with its boot that he both noticed and recognised her.

He was slightly surprised that Dame Margery should be about at this early hour, and not a little disappointed to see that she seemed on the point of leaving. He had been intending to compliment her upon the striking blue jacket and tactfully enquire if it was bespoke, and if so might she divulge her tailor. Besides, he had quite liked the woman: poised, elegant and unusually knowledgeable about hothouse flowers. It was a shame he hadn't had a chance to speak more with her. And who knows, with a little discreet nudging he might even have persuaded her to open an account with *Bountiful Blooms*. He recalled her saying she often visited the Knightsbridge area, so the idea was perfectly reasonable. Well, at least now he could give her his card. He quickened his pace.

About to access her vehicle Dame Margery was none too pleased to be confronted by the Smythe fellow; or indeed, given the circumstances, by anyone. All she wanted was to stow her things, jump in the car and make a quick getaway to Dover. However, seeing Felix approach with a greeting on his lips and clearly about to help her with the case, she knew she was caught.

'Why, Mr Smythe, how nice to see you, and so early on a Sunday morning!' she exclaimed and lied.

'I could say the same,' Felix responded eagerly, 'but in my case I am up because of the dreadful tragedy last night. I expect you've heard all about it – although at this hour perhaps you haven't. But anyway, it was too dreadful. I couldn't sleep a wink!' Then hastily brushing Finglestone aside in favour of matters sartorial, he swiftly broached the subject of the jacket.

'*So becoming,*' he smarmed, 'and such style. I can assure

you it turned every head in the Master's drawing room! Tell me, do you have a pet tailor?'

'No,' she said curtly, 'I bought it in a sale at Selfridge's.'

In a Selfridge's sale? Felix was shocked. Huh! And in the bargain basement no doubt! Well, that was the end of *that* subject. He tried another, and deftly withdrawing a card from his breast pocket thrust it towards her. 'Do visit my little place when you are next passing. We stock some intriguingly exotic blooms, which might be just up your street. Indeed, the Queen Mother often says that—'

But Margery wasn't interested in Her Majesty's words or indeed the man's wretched flowers. All she wanted was to be away! With a perfunctory and ill-meant smile, she snapped shut the boot and opened the driver's door. As she did so she dropped her handbag. It fell into the gutter, its clasp undone. Felix scrabbled to retrieve it, hastily stuffing a compact, nail file and fountain pen back inside.

'Oh, clumsy me,' she said, grabbing the bag from him. 'Thank you *so* much, but I simply must fly otherwise I shall get caught in the morning traffic.' She rammed the starter, yanked the choke, and with a brisk wave sped off in a cloud of exhaust.

Slightly nonplussed, Felix stared after her wondering vaguely why Cambridge should expect heavy traffic at quarter past eight on a Sunday morning. He shrugged. Oh well . . . Ruefully he looked down at the card still in his hand. At the same time his eye was caught by a couple of objects in the gutter, small things which he must have overlooked when scrabbling for the other stuff. He bent to pick them up. At first he took them to be lipsticks, but on closer inspection recognised them as something else. He slipped the items into his pocket. Really, it was amazing what women carried in their handbags!

He set off back to the college feeling put out, though why it was difficult to define. Things had been going well until he encountered Dame Margery: his night-time fears had calmed, his headache gone and he had been enjoying the unaccustomed early morning exercise. Yet after he had waved her goodbye he felt vaguely ruffled. Why?

Had she been there observing the encounter, Betty Withers, Rosy's psychologist friend, might well have had the answer: disappointment and let down. The admired Dame Margery had failed to live up to expectations. Overtly polite, she had nevertheless shown little interest in talking to Felix, was unmoved by his allusion to his patron, and her departure had been marked by haste and indifference. Not only that, but she had spurned his business card, made the dire admission of having bought her jacket in something as lowly as a department store sale, *and* (he had wincingly observed as she climbed into the car) she had been sporting a whopping double-lined ladder in one of her stockings. Thus, while shoes may have been polished, the feet were definitely showing traces of clay.

To quote Robbie Burns via Geoffrey Hinchcliffe, the best laid schemes of mice and men 'gang aft agley'. And so it was to prove for Dame Margery. Having extricated herself from Felix Smythe and sped on down to Dover to catch the ferry, she reached the port in excellent time. Pleased by her progress and in need of a coffee, she went into a small snack bar . . . and it was there that she made a prosaic but unfortunate discovery: her passport was out of date.

It was an appalling shock – not just because it stopped her flight to the Continent, but because it was the sort of absurd mistake that someone of her undoubted competence should not have made. It went against all her training and professional pride. Rarely had she felt so devastated. Her immediate reaction was to approach the officials and to try to sweet-talk them into allowing her on to the boat. A vain hope, but worth a try. Or was it? Her whole object was to keep a low profile, to melt unobtrusively into the ether; not to invite attention by creating a palaver, however mild, in public and with a line of impatient cars behind her. Highly imprudent, as her father would have said.

She drove dismally back to her flat. Here she telephoned the London passport office in Petty France, but regretfully they explained there was an unusual backlog of renewal applications and she could not expect to receive anything under three weeks. Thus, adopting her most managerial but charming voice, she had tried subtly to pull rank and persuade them it was a matter of some importance. But to no avail. They conceded that as a special favour they could reduce the waiting period, but only by one week. In this they were adamant and Dame Margery was left fuming and helpless.

However, she resigned herself to the situation. Her plan to flee to France had been precautionary rather than vital, and a similar purdah could be moderately maintained at home in London. Thus she stayed largely within the flat, pursued her writings and avoided contact with inquisitive friends (or journalists) intrigued by the curious goings-on at Cambridge. A detached reticence was the name of the game – and thus, with luck, any unscheduled knock on the door would be merely that of the meter reader!

The days went by uneventfully and Margery relaxed, became blasé almost. She was sure that there was nothing tangible to connect her with the sculptor's disposal. But what really nagged her (if anything, more than fear of being questioned by the police) was the passport blunder. How humiliating to think that she was capable of such idiocy – such sloppiness. Scrupulous attention to detail had been her great thing, her professional strength; and now she had messed things up like some bovine typist or gormless first-year. Disgraceful!

CHAPTER THIRTY

Since the convivial celebrations at the Master's Lodge and Maycock's house, Detective Sergeant Hopkins had been a busy man. Busy and productive. At Tilson's instigation he had been laboriously tracing and checking the details of Finglestone's past as disclosed to Dillworthy and Smythe. It had been a challenging, painstaking process, but it is amazing how the odd discovery here and a hint there will spur one on to renewed effort. It had been like a jigsaw, recalcitrant and frustrating but ultimately submissive, with pieces eventually fitting and images gradually cohering . . . until at last, *voilà!* a whole picture was formed.

He had tried to explain the analogy to Inspector Tilson, but his efforts had been met with a stony stare. 'Cut the cackle, Hopkins, and get to the perishing point,' his boss had said irritably. 'What have you found out?'

Hopkins hesitated, relishing his moment of power. Eventually he said, simply, 'Everything.' And then just for good measure, he added carelessly, 'Oh, and I think there is something else you might be interested in . . .'

'Oh yes, what?'

Hopkins prevaricated. 'Well, it's a bit complicated. Do you mind if I sit down, sir?'

The other sighed. 'If you must.'

Hopkins took a chair and commenced his tale. This amounted to the fact that his researches had pretty well supported what the sculptor had told the two witnesses: that he originally came from Albania, from a poor family in the mountains of the southern part; had arrived in England in the early stages of the war and as a refugee escaping the Blitz had been taken in by the Biggs-Brookbys. His later studies at Winchester and the Chelsea art college had been verified.

'Very neat, Hopkins, you've established the chap's origins, but hardly why he thought he was the target of some Mafia-like compatriots.' Tilson observed tartly.

'But you see, sir, I have managed to ascertain the name of that family. They lived above Butrint and were called Fingi. Apparently there are quite a few still there – cousins, uncles and such. According to an old newspaper article, one branch of the family with the same name sustained a loss: the death of a small child in tragic circumstances, a little boy of about four years old. The date coincides with our man having been six years old at the time – 1939, I think it was, just before he came to England . . .' Hopkins took a quick glance at his notebook and then at Tilson. 'Do you see a picture forming?' he asked eagerly.

Tilson assured him that he did see a bloody picture forming and would he please hurry up.

The other mentioned one or two more details establishing the close link between Gloria and her protégé, and then with concealed relish produced his *coup de théâtre*. 'Oh, by the way,' he said, 'I forgot to mention that other bit of his biography, quite important really. Ten years ago, under his family name of Montino Fingi, Finglestone was had up for running down and killing Sir Victor Collis, that London heart surgeon. The trial was featured in all the newspapers and there was quite a rumpus. I don't remember a lot about it, but I expect you do. Anyway, the press reports all refer to his having had a twin sister, Dame Margery Collis. She had been present at the young man's trial and kicked up quite a shindig when the judge recommended leniency on account of his age. Apparently she is here in Cambridge at this very moment . . . was here on the night of his murder, in fact, maybe still is.'

For a few moments Tilson regarded his sergeant impassively and then studied the ceiling. 'Was she now?' he murmured. 'Now there's a coincidence.'

Hopkins nodded. 'Yes, and here's another coincidence. Finglestone was shot on the same date of her brother's fatal accident – exactly ten years to the day. Sir Victor died immediately, never recovered.'

'Is that so, Hopkins, is that so . . .' Tilson looked thoughtful. 'It's a nice little motive, all right – not the first time that someone has been killed to avenge a sibling's death, and I like the anniversary touch. Gives it a sort of theatrical twist, wouldn't you say? But where's the evidence, old son?'

There was a long pause as Hopkins contemplated his boots, and Tilson assumed he was stumped.

But then, lifting his eyes from his laces, Hopkins cleared

his throat and said, 'Identical twins: they have a sort of rapport, don't they? A mutual need stronger than the usual kind – or so I've heard. It's a need that if one of them died the other might carry around a sort of souvenir, perhaps wear the deceased's watch or tie – socks, even. A way of keeping close, I suppose.'

Tilson was baffled. What was he chuntering on about now?

'It's that handkerchief, you see,' Hopkins continued. 'It's my belief it once belonged to Sir Victor Collis. I've looked him up in *Who's Who*. His second name was Zachary . . . V. Z. C.'

'Christ,' Tilson murmured. His fingers drummed the desk rhythmically, pausing between the three set of beats: VZC, VZC, VZC, he drummed. It could have been the Morse code. 'But that's still not hard proof, though not bad for a start,' he said quietly. 'Makes you think, doesn't it . . .'

Hopkins nodded. 'I suppose she could have passed through that side gate – the mains being closed at that hour – and either before or after the shooting dropped the thing. Perhaps it had slipped from her cuff or maybe a piece was sticking out of her pocket and it got caught on a twig.'

'Or maybe she had been blowing her nose, and in her haste to get out dropped it,' Tilson suggested helpfully.

Hopkins was a bit doubtful about that, and moved on: 'As you say, given her link with the victim and now this handkerchief, I suppose she ought to be questioned – if only to eliminate her from the enquiry.'

'You bet she should, Hopkins. Find her and pull her in,' Tilson said curtly.

Contrary to Hopkins' surmise, the bird of course had already flown, albeit only as far as London. After making enquiries both from Girton and from the friend who had lent the flat, Hopkins learnt that she had left Cambridge the day after the sculptor's demise, although it was unclear exactly when. He asked Tilson if they should bring her back to Cambridge.

'No, Wait will probably want us to keep things low-key. After all, these are only preliminary enquiries – or they are, as yet. If our suspicions are up the creek, things could be embarrassing and the super will get egg on his face, and we shall all be splattered. I think Wait will suggest a nice day out in the Smoke. Stand by.'

Immured in her Chelsea flat, Dame Margery was working quietly on her professional papers. It was a way of resuming normality and keeping distasteful thoughts at bay. So far there had been no ominous knock on the door and certainly no mention of her in any of the newspaper reports . . . But then why should there be? Other than the man himself blundering across the grass, the court had been empty and windows unlit; she had left no tell-tale trace and had vanished immediately. Easy-peasy!

So easy, in fact, that perhaps soon she could boldly raise her head above the parapet: the essentials were dealt with. And yet ironically, what really continued to nag was the vexing thought of that laddered stocking! She told herself sternly that murder was no excuse to slacken standards of dress. (*Murder*? What nonsense – it had been justified homicide. Of course it had.) Yes, she must definitely avoid that brand in the future, and she just hoped that no one had noticed . . .

Barely had she finished dwelling on such matters, when the telephone rang. 'This is the Cambridge Police,' a sombre voice intoned. Would she kindly make herself available for a few routine questions. Two o'clock would be a convenient time and she could expect them on the dot . . .

Oh, how *very* efficient, Dame Margery had fumed when she put down the phone. Presumably one should be grateful for such punctuality! She stalked to the bedroom, changed into her severest suit, donned high heels and applied a liberal squirt of Arpége. That should do it!

Sergeant Hopkins had liked the scent very much, but he was not so sure about its wearer. All very charming, but a bit hoity-toity in his view, a bit too pleased with herself. He looked at the high heels: a woman of her age could come a cropper in those if she wasn't careful. He remembered his Aunt Alice.

Tactfully, probingly, they had broached the matter of her brother's death and her past connection with Monty Finglestone, or Fingi as he had then been.

She had coolly confirmed the link and acknowledged she had been appalled by the trial's outcome. 'But that's fate, isn't it?' she had said. 'Life has to take its course; one can't let tragedy grind one down – or at least not in the long run. Weak as we are, we have to go on, don't we?' She had fixed them with a quizzical gaze and they had nodded, evidently impressed by such stoicism.

'You are so right, Dame Margery,' Tilson agreed soberly. 'And tell me, when exactly did you realise that Monty Finglestone and Montino Fingi were one and the same?'

'What? Oh . . . er, well, I don't think I did, really. That is to say, I only saw him a couple of times at a distance. It, uhm – it was only when I got back here and saw a photograph in the papers that I realised it could be him.

And now, from what you have been saying, it clearly was. It has all been quite a shock, Inspector.'

Tilson nodded sympathetically. 'I am sure it has. But just for the record, can you list your movements on the day you left Cambridge? A mere formality, you understand, but our masters require us to ask the same of anyone who had the remotest connection with the deceased, or those who shared his college staircase or were known to visit him at his studio.' (All lies.) 'It would help us to comply with our brief and tick a few boxes.' The inspector smiled ruefully. 'For example, what time did you set off from your lodgings?'

Margery would have liked to say she had gone in the afternoon, as it would suggest an unhurried innocent ease, but the truth might be safer. Thus she explained that she had left early, as with the Girton commitment ended she had been impatient to get home and push on with work that had been delayed for far too long. 'I hate to leave things overdue, don't you, Inspector?' she said brightly.

Tilson cleared his throat, ignoring the question. 'And did anyone see you at that time?'

Margery hesitated, weighing up the pros and cons of mentioning Felix. Ideally, she would prefer to make no reference. If asked, who knew what the man might say about her obvious haste, her impatience to get away. She recalled that her manner to him had been less than attentive, bordering on the rude, really. Might he have resented that, and if interviewed emphasise or exaggerate what he had seen of her tension? However, to say she had met no one could be even more dangerous. If the truth came out and the lie exposed, things could be tricky.

'Oh yes,' she said casually, 'I bumped into a friend

of one of the sponsors, a Mr Felix Smythe, rather a nice man – awfully keen on flowers, you know. He was taking an early morning stroll and we did exchange a few words.' She spoke lightly, trying to imply her departure had been easy and unhurried. But then she felt impelled to add: 'I have to say, Inspector, this whole thing is truly appalling; it has quite knocked me sideways!'

Tilson regarded her expressionlessly. 'I can imagine that, madam. But you have been most helpful.' He hesitated . . . 'Oh but there's just one more thing before we go.' He turned to Hopkins: 'You've got that have you, Sergeant?'

With a flourish Hopkins produced the green silk handkerchief and spread it on the back of a chair. (What the hell does he think he is, thought Tilson irritably, a blooming conjuror?)

'Ever seen that before?' the inspector asked.

Margery regarded it, her eyes widening slightly. 'No,' she said. 'No, I haven't.'

Left alone, Margery found that her hands were shaking and her breath unsteady. This was not so much because she had been horrified by the handkerchief (as she most certainly was), but by something potentially worse. Throughout the interview a thought had been stealthily boring away at the back of her mind, a growing realisation that, for all her outward poise, had been making her feel slightly sick. It was all to do with the Smythe fellow and her handbag.

Knowing what she would find, or rather not find, she rushed into the bedroom and pulled from the wardrobe her two Rayne handbags. The smaller she kept for everyday

271

use, the larger for travel. It had always been her practice to keep in each a duplicate set of essentials – pen, powder, comb etc – thus when she had returned from the abortive trip to Dover, apart from removing her purse she had put the travel one away untouched. Feverishly, she now unzipped it and rummaged inside . . . Oh Christ, just as she had feared, they had gone! She closed her eyes, recalling dropping the bag as she leapt into the car, the things spilling out and Smythe retrieving them. She had grabbed it from him and slung it on the passenger seat.

But another image also danced before her eyes: it was what she had glimpsed in the driving mirror as she sped away. The man had been stooping down . . . to tie his shoelace? Or to pick something up? Oh yes, she thought bitterly, obviously the latter: he had been picking up those two spare cartridges – the remaining Webley slugs surplus to requirements and which she had left in their open packet at the bottom of her bag. And now presumably sodding Smythe had got them!

She sat on the bed and stared into space. Well, one thing was certain, she could hardly visit his flower shop (as he had eagerly suggested) and enquire sweetly if by chance he had happened to find a couple of her bullets. So what could she do? Nothing at all. Sit tight, wait, hope and if necessary brazen it out . . . whatever 'it' might be. The image of the handkerchief fluttered sadly before her eyes. She had kept one of Victor's and without thinking had stuffed it up her sleeve before setting out that evening: a subconscious talisman, perhaps. Some talisman! It had probably destroyed her freedom . . . what you might call a sacrifice of safety to sentiment! She heaved a sigh: the gun had better go. She would chuck it in the Thames that evening.

She returned to the drawing room, lit a cigarette and poured a Scotch. Mission accomplished all right, but at what cost? She shrugged. It remained to be seen.

CHAPTER THIRTY-ONE

The two policemen agreed that their time in the Smoke had been well spent.

'I think we've got something there,' Hopkins said. 'All very cool to begin with, but you could see she was getting agitated. Something was worrying her, all right – and you noticed how she stumbled over the Finglestone/Fingi question? She seemed flustered, sort of off guard, if you ask me.'

'Yes, and by the looks of things she didn't like that handkerchief either; not one little bit, she didn't. I've never seen a blank face look less convincing.' Tilson laughed.

'But appearances aren't proof.' Hopkins sighed. 'If we are going to nail her, we shall need something stronger than our noses.'

'So let's go and talk to the little guy. You never know, he

may be able to tell us something. Patience and optimism, that's my motto,' Tilson observed airily.

Sergeant Hopkins could not recall his boss exhibiting either of the two qualities, but he thought it a good idea all the same. There was an outside chance that Smythe could be useful.

Satisfied with the witnesses' statements, and doubtful if much more could be gleaned from that quarter, Chief Inspector Wait had announced that Cedric and Felix would no longer be required and were free to leave Cambridge. Naturally, should anything further emerge pertinent to the shooting they would be contacted. The news had been received with some relief as both were becoming restless to return to their more predictable lives in London.

These lives were being discussed in Felix's room before dinner, with engagement diaries being consulted and dates noted. But although deciding to make a swift departure, there were certain issues that needed to be settled first. One of these was whether to tell Rosy Gilchrist about the part played by Lady Dick in the drama of Winston Reid's death. 'We know all about Rosy and the Hinchcliffe business and have sworn not to divulge it to anyone, so perhaps we should even things up and complete the full picture for her,' Cedric mused.

'Certainly not,' Felix protested. 'In no circumstances!' He looked very fierce.

Cedric was startled. 'Well, of course not, dear boy, not if you don't want to,' he said hastily.

'I have given Lady Dick my word to keep silent on the matter,' Felix replied with dignity. 'A gentleman does not renege.'

'But you have told me.'

'You don't count.'

Cedric heaved a sigh: 'One's role in life, I fear.' He smiled, proud of his friend's decision.

'But I tell you what,' the friend said, leaning forward and tapping him on the knee, 'I am blowed if I know what I should do about those cartridges. That sergeant said the gun used on Finglestone was a Webley – and you say these are the Webley style. It seems a bit fishy to me.'

'It would be fishier still if they were spent,' Cedric observed, 'but I do agree it is odd – very peculiar, really.'

They embarked on an interesting discussion as to whether Felix should apprise the police of his find: to what extent such information would be justified and to what extent gratuitously officious.

'After all, we didn't like Finglestone,' Cedric remarked, 'and given his murder of Gloria and that child he told us about, he was clearly an utter scoundrel. I cannot see that his death is to be lamented. Besides, she may not have done it.'

'On the other hand, she may have,' Felix retorted. 'And if so, for a woman of her position and status I consider it a bit much.' He sniffed and looked indignant. (Had Dame Margery shown a more emollient attitude in their last encounter, Felix may have been less disapproving. And as the lady was to later discover, such hasty lapses can bring unfortunate results.)

They continued to argue the pros and cons of the matter, but were interrupted by a knock on the door. It was Jenkins, the porter, who announced that there were two gentlemen to see Mr Smythe. 'Police,' he said in a darkened voice, 'they are out 'ere now.' He winked and cocked his thumb towards the passage.

'Ah, Inspector,' Cedric murmured, politely beckoning them in, 'I thought you had finished with us – or so your Chief Inspector Wait implied. We were thinking of leaving for London tomorrow, but I take it there is something else we can help you with?' The distant tone belied any particular desire to help.

'Ah yes,' Tilson explained, 'that is what we have come about. As the chief inspector said, you are of course at total liberty to leave Cambridge, but I must stress that those two cases are by no means closed. We are at a very delicate stage in our enquiries and any loose talk could be highly dangerous. I don't mind telling you in strictest confidence that we are on the trail of those assassins Mr Finglestone was telling you about. It wasn't such a tall story, after all! So for the time being I must remind you that you are required to keep silent about anything Mr Finglestone divulged about his past association with Miss Biggs-Brookby. Once the "gagging" order is lifted, we shall of course inform you immediately.' Tilson's voice was stern but affable.

He turned to Felix. 'I realise these rules are tiresome, sir; and it's easy to let something slip, especially when having undergone the kind of ordeal that you did. Don't suppose he was the easiest of chaps!'

Felix was about to reply that he most certainly was not, but wasn't given the chance for Tilson went on quickly: 'For example, Dame Margery said that she happened to bump into you when she was leaving on the morning after the shooting and had a brief conversation. You didn't by chance say anything to her about it, did you? I mean like some mention in the course of your little chat – because if you did, I shall have to include *her* in the warning too.' Tilson gave a hearty laugh, which to Hopkins, standing by the door, sounded uncomfortably fake and he hoped he wouldn't do it again.

A little chat? Felix thought sourly. There had been no such thing. She had been most curt. Out loud he said: 'I don't recall much chatting taking place, she seemed in a tearing hurry. I think her mind was elsewhere. In fact,' he said, vividly recalling his spurned overtures, 'as it happens, I think she thought I was in the way.'

'What, because she was in a hurry?'

'You can say that again,' Felix replied with sudden asperity. 'She drove off like a bat out of hell. I got smothered in exhaust and practically choked!'

The inspector smiled politely, thanked Felix for his cooperation and seemed satisfied.

But then Hopkins gave a slight cough, and said casually: 'So that was the only thing you noticed, was it – the speed factor? I take it there was nothing else that struck you as odd or unusual in her behaviour?' It was a long shot, but no harm in asking.

Felix bit his lip, hesitated and looked at Cedric. The latter remained impassive. Felix wavered and then made his decision. He marched to the po cupboard, which this time harboured not a notebook but two revolver cartridges. He took them out and passed them to Hopkins. 'These fell out of the lady's handbag,' he said.

Strong motive, lost handkerchief, found cartridges – things were looking bad for Dame Margery. All that was needed now was for someone to have seen her at the time and place of the shooting. Then they could make an arrest, or at least descend with a search warrant for the weapon and give her another grilling . . . CHANCE WOULD BE A FINE THING, Tilson doodled on his desk pad.

Sergeant Hopkins appeared, looking smug. 'There's a chap here who says he saw somebody and wonders if he can claim his reward.'

'Oh yes? Who is it?'

'Says he used to be a cab driver and lost his way.'

'Ah well, there's a lot of those about,' Tilson remarked sardonically. 'Wheel him in.'

It transpired that the gentleman who had accosted Margery on that fatal night was the same one who had disturbed Aldous Phipps and then gone to the pub. He had parked his cab, but couldn't remember where. With a number of sheets to the wind, he had been seeking his bearings when he noticed a woman emerging from a gate in the wall. The gate, he now realised, opened into part of the college he had been trying to find earlier. He had thought she might be interested in suggesting where his vehicle could be. On being told to go to hell it occurred to him that such interest was unlikely.

Flashing the inspector a matey smile, the man asked how much money was on offer.

Tilson shook his head doubtfully. 'Ah well, we shall need a bit more than that, I'm afraid. Just a couple of details, maybe – for example, what did the lady look like?' He waited tensely.

The man frowned, screwed up his eyes and scratched his head. It had been a bit dark, he muttered, he would need to think.

Tilson nodded, but said nothing, fearful of hindering the thinking. *It's not going to work*, he thought. *It's not going to bloody work.*

'Well,' the man said at last, 'tall, thin – in her fifties, I should say. Her hair was short.'

'Colour?'

'I dunno – fair, sort of whitish, I suppose. Will that do?'

'And she had come out of that side gate, had she?'

'Yeah, that's right.'

Tilson got up from his desk and opened the door. 'Come in here will you, Sergeant, and bring your notebook. I would like you to take a statement from this gentleman.'

She had known they would be back. And as planned she had reluctantly chucked the gun in the river. But it wasn't enough, of course – they had found its leather case with the initials V. Z. C. inscribed. Her last memento of Victor, she had been unable to part with it and had shoved it in an old shoebox in the loft. Pointless, the police had been like sniffer dogs and there hadn't been a chance. She had asked the officer in charge if she could have it back some day. Oh yes, he had said with a kindly smile, one day. Whether he had meant it she had no idea. Wryly, she thought of the incriminating handkerchief. Would she see that again? Probably not. What a trite little piece of evidence – but at least it had been expensively elegant!

Not being short of funds she would naturally ensure she had a first-class lawyer; and in view of Montino Fingi's appalling record the sentence might be lenient. As usual (or almost usual) she would show gracious fortitude . . . and who knew, with a bit of luck or parole she might even be available for a sixty-fifth birthday celebration at Claridge's. Meanwhile, she could enjoy the challenge of instructing the other inmates in the art of public speaking.

CHAPTER THIRTY-TWO

The Newnham reunion had been splendid; and thankfully with no negative findings, Dr Stanley's espionage mission duly accomplished. Thus in both respects Rosy's time in Cambridge could be counted a success (and indeed with Felix's 'help' she had even managed a punt on the Cam). It was just everything else that had been so disturbing. What bizarre, what fearsome events she had encountered – and those occurring in one of the country's most loved and beautiful cities. How ironic its fusion of the quaint and the sinister, the crude and civilised, grim and lovely . . . Yet in that way perhaps Cambridge was simply an emblem of life itself – disarmingly seductive, craftily dangerous. Human nature did not change, however beautiful its context.

With those rather sober thoughts, Rosy dealt with her packing; a process that, unlike Dame Margery's, was mildly shambolic. Travelling out one tried to be orderly, but going back there was little such effort. By now most things had been collected and hurriedly stowed, but her eye was caught by something on the mantelpiece – Dr Stanley's chocolates. Vital. Omit those at her peril! She stuffed them into the case and closed the lid.

Thinking of Stanley had strangely lifted her spirits. In a curious way it would be refreshing to be back in the old routine, at least you knew where you were: hectic eruptions, mordant sarcasm, fuming impatience, fuming cigarettes, fisticuffs with the trustees, wheedling apologies, the drama of lost lecture notes, fiendish scheming, gin . . . Oh yes, it would be nice to be back. Quite soothing, really, relatively speaking.

Rosy paused remembering something he had said on the telephone. What had it been – something about a celebration? Yes, how curious. Even more curious had been his reference to Wiltons restaurant. Not known for his prodigality, she thought she may have misheard. Perhaps he had been alluding to his arch-enemy, Wilson, at the Royal Academy. Still, if it *was* Wiltons it was just as well she had bought that new lipstick and mascara! She checked her watch. Plenty of time before her train. If she was quick she could nip down to Sayle's and get that snazzy top she had seen in its window. Yes, her last fling in Cambridge.

Rosy procured the blouse and was duly pleased. It really was rather smart! Hovering on the corner of Downing Street debating whether to get a taxi back to Newnham, she was startled to be confronted by Lord Bantry.

He stood full square in front of her. 'Red Shoes,' he cried, 'I have been hoping to catch you to apologise. I fear

I was rather preoccupied the other day at the Fitzwilliam. I was cooking up something with old Maycock about my scholarship endowment. Sir Richard wanted to modify its terms, but I was telling Maycock he could think again! Anyway, it's all wrapped up now and the college will get the funds all right. I gather you work at the BM. Who knows, I might zoom in one day and lunch you at Wiltons. Bye for now.' He raised his hat and limped off.

Crikey! Rosy thought. *Another one?* Wiltons was going to be busy! Somewhat dazed she made her way to the taxi rank, holding her purchase tightly. By the looks of things it would come in useful.

As they drove back to London, Cedric and Felix had much to mull over.

'I know there's an embargo on our mentioning anything except the bare bones of that Finglestone affair, but I suppose at some point Rosy Gilchrist will get to hear,' Cedric remarked. 'At the moment she only knows we were set upon by that inebriated thug and that we chased him. I trust she won't be too huffed about our not confiding the full details.'

'Well, she will just have to take her turn with everyone else,' Felix replied. 'It will all come out, eventually. 'And besides,' he added primly, 'she can't expect us to infringe police regulations; after all, we have our reputations to consider.' (He was thinking of royal corgis and related matters.) 'Incidentally,' he mused, 'I wonder what she will do.'

'Do? What do you mean? As far as I know she was planning to return to work fairly soon.'

'I meant beyond that – her future, as it were.'

Cedric laughed. 'Oh, that's easy: she will settle down and marry Dr Stanley.'

'Good God! You don't call that settling down, do you? The man is impossible!'

'Rosy Gilchrist enjoys stimulus.'

'Well, she will certainly get that all right. Most unwise, I should say. He is like a rampaging rhino.'

'Ah, but she will tame him. You forget that she was stationed at the Dover battery during the war. She will cope, she always does.'

'I suppose so, but it is amazing what bizarre choices people make.'

Cedric looked sideways at his passenger. 'Oh, amazing, dear boy. But there's no accounting for tastes: the world would be very dull if we could predict these things, don't you agree?'

On the whole Felix thought he did agree, and for a while they drove in silence, pondering the perversity of human preference.

And then the passenger reached into the glovebox and donned a pair of sunglasses. 'I say,' he said brightly, 'we shall have an awful lot to tell Mr S. M. when we get to the Riviera.'

'I rather think Mr S. M. has plenty of his own melodramas to narrate,' Cedric replied dryly. 'He has certainly done quite well so far.'

There followed a further silence, during which Felix scanned the passing scenery looking for the first signs of London. Catching a glimpse of the Marconi radio mast he relaxed and enquired casually, 'And, uhm, might you be having any engagements scheduled for Oxford?'

'Certainly not,' Cedric replied indignantly. 'A most dubious place!'

* * *

Some time after the close of both cases and the key witnesses to both events safely returned to the capital, Sergeant Hopkins had asked Inspector Tilson about the murdered man's postcard: 'Do you think that Toni chap was right and that they really did come for him?'

'Who can say? But the message had obviously put him in a muck sweat. Just think, if it hadn't been sent he might be alive now and we none the wiser about Miss Biggs-Brookby's death.' He chuckled. 'They probably came and went, and felt miffed finding they had been pipped at the post. Bit of a wasted journey, really – Tirana to Cambridge is quite a trek. Still, I suppose that's the hazard of being a hitman, you never know who's going to steal your thunder or waste your time.'

'And what about the lady?'

'Oh, she will cool her heels for a bit and then get out duly chastened – or apparently so. It's amazing what you can do with money, good looks and the gift of the gab. She'll survive – probably write a bestselling memoir, I expect.'

In the early autumn while Cedric and Felix were basking in the south of France being indulged by their eminent host, Sir Richard and Lady Dick were also planning a holiday. They had not decided where exactly, but it would be somewhere safe and sumptuous, and free of sculpture.

To put it mildly, the Master's first year had been a challenge, a veritable baptism by fire. But with Lady Dick at his side he had weathered it valiantly, and with the incendiaries largely extinguished had emerged unscathed . . . or at least, such scars as he wore were of the honourable duelling variety.

The change of plan for the plot had been an inspired

move: the Hortus Pacis as it was now officially named, being a pleasing refuge for seekers of peace, repose and the companionship of birds and flowers (but not rhododendrons). It was a haven beloved by scholars and visitors alike, and the handsome plaque displaying the names of its benefactors received close and frequent scrutiny. Near the top of the list was the name of Professor Cedric Dillworthy and about halfway down that of Geoffrey Hinchcliffe. The name of Dame Margery Collis did not feature. Her donation had been withdrawn, an unfortunate loss as the sum might have been substantial. However, this was more than offset by Lord Bantry's generous scholarship endowment, a foundation of great value to the Indigent, although less so to the Lame (there being fewer candidates).

Thus it was generally agreed among members of the erstwhile Plot and Monument Committee – Dr Maycock; Professor Turner; the bursar, Mostyn Williams; Professor Aldous Phipps et al. – that St Cecil's College had reaped considerable benefit from their deliberations. The result had conferred additional renown on that prestigious institution. In this respect – and to the private pleasure of the Master's wife – the name of the absent John Smithers was being duly applauded.

SUZETTE A. HILL was born in East Sussex, and spent much of her childhood playing spies and smugglers on Beachy Head and picnicking at the foot of the Long Man of Wilmington. Hill worked as a teacher in both public school and adult education before retiring in 1999. She now lives in Ledbury, Herefordshire. At the age of sixty-four and on a whim, she took up a pen and began writing. Hill has since published over ten novels, including the Reverend Oughterard series.

suzetteahill.co.uk